PRAISE FOR LINDSAY GIBSON

"A charming romance that's as warm and cozy as hot chocolate on a winter's day."–*Kirkus Reviews* on *The Christmas Promise*

"Lindsay writes the type of stories that will stay with you and have you reaching for your loved ones."–*USA Today* **best-selling author Jenny Hale**

"This new author is automatically a favorite."–*Page-Turners Reviews*

"…an engaging story and a sweet romance with a dollop of mystery."–*Book Banter Café* on *The Christmas Promise*

"A truly lovely story that gently unfolds…"–*Splashes into Books* on *The Christmas Promise*

Included in "That Artsy Reader Girl's 2023 Christmas Romances"–*thatartsyreadergirl.com*

Included in "Over 50 Must Read Kindle Unlimited Christmas Romance Books"—*everydayeyecandy.com*

Fly Away Summer

Fly Away Summer

LINDSAY GIBSON

HARPETH ROAD
PRESS
Nashville

HARPETH ROAD PRESS

Published by Harpeth Road Press (USA)
P.O. Box 158184
Nashville, TN 37215

Paperback: 979-8-9887744-7-1
eBook: 979-8-9887744-6-4

Fly Away Summer: A Delightful, Heartwarming Summer Romance

Cover Design by Kristen Ingebretson
Cover Images © Shutterstock

First printing: May, 2024

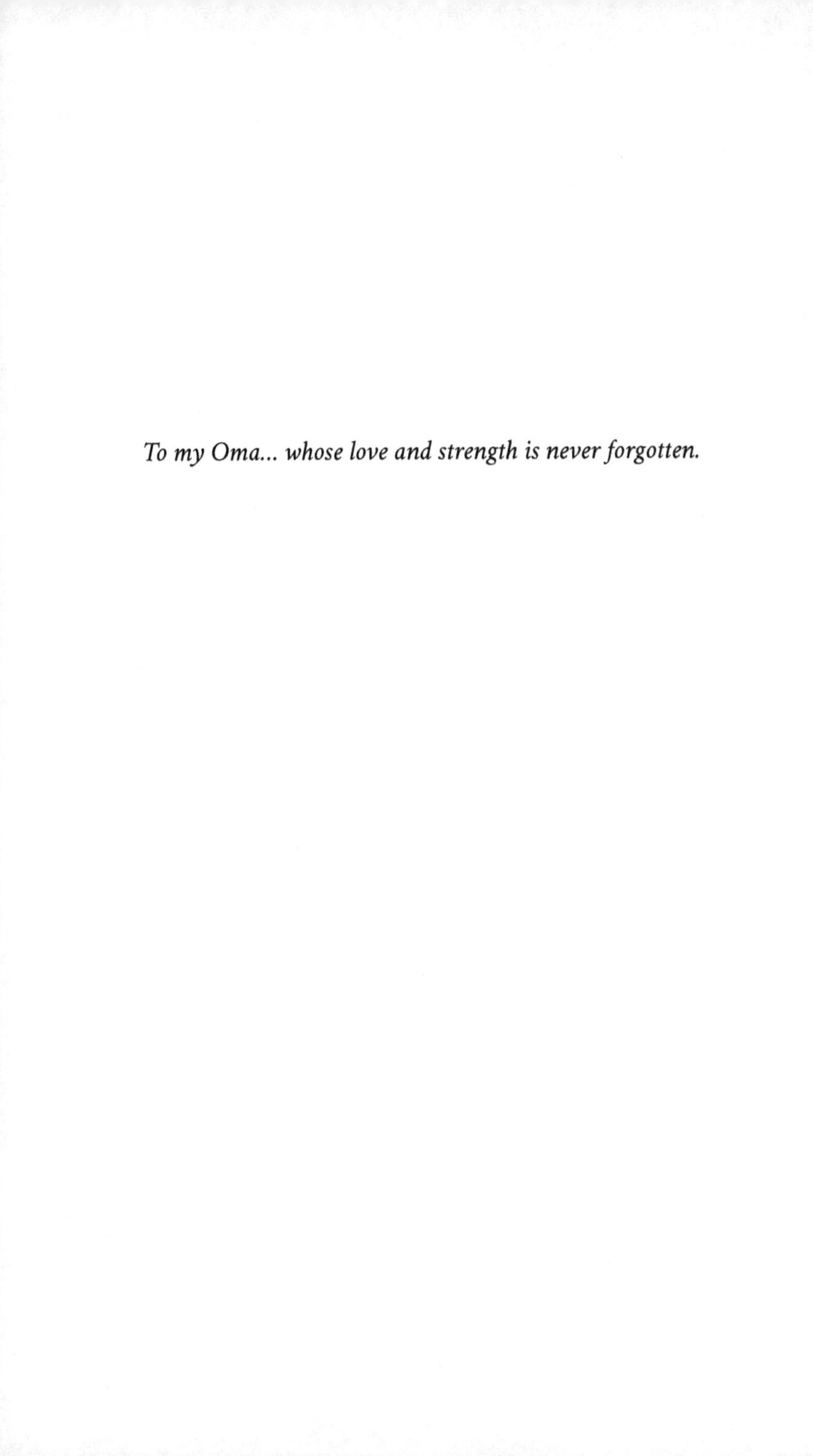

To my Oma... whose love and strength is never forgotten.

PROLOGUE

"Lana, there really isn't an easy way to say this, so I think it's best I come right out with it," the lawyer explained, leaning forward onto his desk. "The inn is in active foreclosure. And it was just sold in an auction."

A sharp gasp left Lana Kelly, and she instantly felt dizzy. She must have heard the family lawyer wrong with the heavy rain that was pounding against the windows from the storm outside. "Did you say... *foreclosure?*" She looked at her grandad, but he wouldn't meet her eyes.

Was it possible that she was just dreaming—and this was a nightmare? For the past month, she had been running on endless coffees, little sleep, and preparing for her last set of finals at Johnson & Wales's culinary arts program in Rhode Island. It was a whirlwind of a semester, and she couldn't have been more thrilled to be done. Maybe she'd been pushing herself too hard, focusing too much on the future that lay ahead of her, and this was her subconscious lashing back by manifesting her deepest fear.

But as much as she wanted to believe that to be the case,

the sinking feeling in her stomach, and the awful sympathy in the lawyer's expression, told her it was all too true.

Until this moment, her life had felt as if she were turning the page to a whole new chapter for her as a chef. The past four years of college, with her grandad cheering her on every step of the way, were now met with silence as those plans dissolved in front of her.

In a matter of weeks, she'd planned to step in and start running the inn, taking it off her grandad's hands and making sure to honor nearly forty years of his hard work since he'd opened it with her grandma.

"Yes… foreclosure," the lawyer repeated, barely able to look her in the eye, which she presumed meant, knowing the history of their inn, that he understood how important it was to her grandad.

The words were miles away against the sound of her thudding heart now raging in her ears.

"I don't understand." She shook her head. "How could this have happened?"

Her grandad finally spoke, explaining that he'd had to take out an equity loan to pay for her college tuition, and how the lack of revenue growth in recent years had made it difficult to keep up with the payments. She tried to listen, but all she could concentrate on was how frail he seemed. A foreclosure didn't feel like the only reason this meeting was taking place. Something about him seemed… off.

She remembered a week ago when he'd called her, asking her to drive home to Bluedale, Cape Cod, for this meeting. She'd thought the problem he wanted to discuss with her was something to do with his health. She'd never expected this.

As if he could hear her thoughts, her grandad continued, "And there's more."

Lana tried to brace herself—she knew how to deal with loss. Whatever the news was, she was sure she could handle it. She'd be there for her grandad, whatever he needed. He was all the family she had left. And when he said the word "dementia," it was almost a relief.

The past four years without her grandma, she'd worried about him while away at school, and now she'd come to find out, her intuition about his condition had been right all along. She'd first noticed it six months ago, when he called to say he needed to move into a nursing home. After that, it had felt like a race to get through school and take the inn off his hands, only to find out it'd been too late. Piecing together all she had witnessed—from moments of simple forgetfulness to the way he would pause and stare at her at times, like he didn't know her—it all made sense. And now that they had an official diagnosis, she could at least finally stop guessing.

"There is one piece of good news," the lawyer said.

Lana stared at him blankly. The inn had been foreclosed on and her grandad had dementia. She was losing her home, her future, and her grandad's health in one fell swoop. What good news could there possibly be?

"As stated in your father's will, his old fish market next door to the inn has moved fully to your ownership now that you are twenty-two. It's yours to do with what you wish," the lawyer informed her. In all the years since her parents passed, the fish market had sat empty. They'd tried to sell it a few times, but without success. She'd dreamed of utilizing it somehow for more space next to the inn once she took over —and now it was all she was left with.

The lawyer began to talk her through the next steps with the inn. "Your grandad has struggled to get the inn cleared out in time, but the new owners are willing to provide a grace period to allow you all to gather your personal belongings from the property. Then you'll need to close all the accounts associated with the property."

She took notes, knowing that she'd need to remember all

of this information, even if dealing with it was the last thing she wanted to do right now.

"And one more document I need you to sign for the nursing home..." the lawyer took in a breath, glancing quickly at her grandad before pushing a piece of paper across his desk. Lana reached over for her grandad's hand. "With your grandad's condition officially diagnosed, I need you to sign for power of attorney over him." Looking down at the document, Lana tried hard to keep the flood of emotions contained. A heaviness pressed on her as she signed her name, knowing she was now the soul decision maker for her grandad—a responsibility she didn't feel ready to do.

Finally, the meeting came to an end. A nurse aide arrived shortly to take her grandad back to his nursing home, where he said he'd wait for her so they could talk. Watching him walk with help jarred her, especially after many years of running the inn with such strength. She'd known he was slowing down—first hiring a temporary manager to handle most of the inn's day-to-day operations, and later passing everything off to the manager after moving into the nursing home—but this was the first time it truly struck home how much he'd deteriorated. Now that she understood what was happening with his health, guilt panged in her. She couldn't shake the feeling that she could have stopped this from happening had she not been away at school.

Making her way past the cherry trees toward her car, the spring sunshine captured her attention, softening the shock and slowing her down enough to even her breathing. Thunder rumbled in the distance from the storm that had pulled away, and Lana could still see dark clouds off in the distance. It seemed fitting considering how she felt, having just gotten news that dimmed the bright future she'd planned for so long. A falling petal caught her eye, twisting in circles in front of her, gracefully showing off, as if it knew she needed to savor this moment of stillness.

Tears suddenly stung her eyes, and she decided she was in no shape to drive. Maybe walking for a while would help clear her head. After a couple of blocks, she stopped next to some newly planted flowers, finding comfort in staring at them. The lush greenery blanketed the ground, and spring colors of pink, purple, and yellow exploded throughout the flower beds. They reminded her of the fresh blooms she'd placed against both her grandma's and parents' headstones earlier that day on her way up.

"What do I do now?" she said out loud, as if someone would answer.

Looking toward the sky, childhood memories of the inn began to flood her mind, and she knew she had to see it. It wasn't far—just a short walk toward the water where the inn sat right beside the shoreline. She arrived in a matter of minutes and decided to stand by the bay to collect herself and face the ocean, kicking off her shoes and watching the waves lap over and over against her bare feet. It was far too cold to swim, but the spring rainstorm that had passed through brought enough warmth to comfortably stick her toes in the shallow water.

The tears that had pooled in her eyes from before began pouring out of her once she got to the beach, releasing everything she'd just learned. Turning away from the water's edge, she sunk down to the sand, facing the inn.

How could it be gone now? Years of memories, family history... all of it just gone, already auctioned off to new owners. Even though she wouldn't have been able to fix the financial setbacks the lawyer had gone over in the meeting, she still wished she had known sooner how much trouble her grandad was in so he didn't have to go through it all alone.

Shielding her eyes against the sun that was peeking out of the last of the rain clouds, she looked at the windows on the second floor, specifically the last one on the right—her old bedroom. The very first night she'd slept there after losing her parents to a terrible fire on their friend's boat when she was just eleven years old flashed across her mind, her grandma holding her for hours while she cried, comforting her broken heart.

Despite the pain, the inn had felt like home after such a tragedy. And as time passed and the edges of her grief softened, she was able to appreciate the years of happy memories before the accident. When she was at the inn, she felt closer to her parents, remembering all the time she'd spent there with them right next door, working their fish market, while she was in the kitchen at the inn waiting on her grandma's delicious food or helping her grandad fix something—not to mention the endless hours playing on the beach.

Lowering her gaze to the sand, she could almost hear the laughter of her younger self through the breeze, whipping by her, and she closed her eyes, her past blanketing her thoughts and bringing her to that fateful last day... only hours before the tragedy.

"LANA!" her grandma called after her, trying to keep up, and her mother trailed behind. "Don't scare the seagulls like that!"

"I'm not scaring them! I'm flying with them!" Lana opened her arms wide, flapping them around in circles before running straight into the water.

"Look, Lana!" her father called out to her, a little farther down the shore. "Look at the broad wings on that one!" She'd followed his gaze to a seagull soaring over the blue ocean, ready to dive down. Its dark wings reflected against the bright sun while it searched the water.

"That one is so big!" she called back, running up to meet him.

"It's called a great black-backed gull," he told her. "Looks like it's diving for food. I'm sure we'll see the gull hanging around here. Its nest must be close because they never go far from home."

Lana began to imitate the bird, flapping her arms again, calling out to it. Jumping into a wave, she popped back up with her arms still straight out. Strong hands picked her up from behind, swinging her around, as giggles escaped her. Wrapping his arms around her shoulders, her father kissed her on both cheeks, before he scooped both legs under his arms, holding her out, while she spread her arms straight out to her sides. A wave crashed down all around them, but her father's steady grip held her tight against the splash.

"Lana!" he called out…

LANA'S EYES POPPED OPEN, her body trembling to will itself out of the memory. Feeling like the wind had been knocked out of her, she stood up from the sand and took in the ocean air. School had kept her so busy the last few years that she rarely found herself thinking about her parents. Here, now, in a place so tied to their memory, a heaviness welled up inside of her for the first time in a while, ripping through every barricade she'd tried to keep in her heart since that final day in the hospital when she'd said goodbye to them. Grief showed no mercy.

She began walking along the sand back to her car, passing by her father's old fish market. For a moment, it felt as though he were about to appear around the corner hauling the large wooden crates of freshly caught seafood. An image of her sitting on top of those crates flashed across her mind, laughing uncontrollably as her father would pop up and scare her from behind them. She stopped walking as something began to brew in her, ideas swirling in her mind, and she knew that, out of all the things her grandad had taught her after her tremendous loss, giving up was never an option.

The inn sat in front her now, so close yet out of reach. Its legacy lost… but never forgotten.

CHAPTER 1

FIVE YEARS LATER

s the sea retreated into low tide, the rising sun slowly lifted above the water, reflecting its rosy hue off the dock behind her. Lana pushed her curls behind her shoulders and tipped her head up to take in the perfect view of the colors before daylight. Within the last moments of twilight, her floating basket was already nearly filled with long-neck clams—enough for the forty-two-person Memorial Day party that her restaurant was expecting. Her hip waders pulled slightly against her shins as she moved through the lowing ebb of water.

It would be the first clambake party of the summer—her specialty—and one of the most sought-after events at her small seaside restaurant, On the Bay. Five years had flown by since she'd begun transforming her father's tiny fish market. The new patio that she'd designed herself provided a simple outdoor oasis with a wide variety of fine seafood dinner choices.

She also had an offering that many other restaurants on the Cape didn't—beach space for her customers to host private clambakes, which had become a fast favorite among both the regulars from Bluedale and the tourists. It was her favorite addition, but for Lana, this part of being a chef had come easily. Her father had been a master of the New England seas before he died, providing the best seafood at his market here in Bluedale for many years, and that talent certainly hadn't skipped over Lana. Digging for clams, the way he had taught her starting at the age of five, made clambakes the perfect fit for her restaurant. However, teaching her how to fillet fresh fish with practiced skill, and properly determining the quality when buying or catching her own, had made Lana's reputation what it was.

Making her way to the first soft mound of sand, she placed the full basket down next to the others, and picked up a fourth and final basket to fill. Stepping back through the water as the tide continued its retreat out to sea, she bent down to begin raking through the sand some more.

Her phone rang in her jacket's front pocket, and she yanked it out, answering before looking at the screen to see who it was. "Hello?"

"Hey there!"

"Oh," Lana said, letting out a disappointed sigh when she recognized her best friend Alicia's voice. "It's you."

Alicia laughed. "If I didn't know you so well, I'd be pretty offended right now."

Lana grimaced. "I'm sorry, it's not that I'm not happy to hear from you. I was just—"

"You were just hoping I was the bank," Alicia said. "I know. Although it would be a bit odd for them to call you this early. Not everyone starts work at sunrise like you. Are you digging?"

"Oh, right. I forgot." Lana looked down at her basket. "Yeah, I'm out here digging. I have my first clambake party this weekend."

"Still no word?"

"Not yet."

It had only been a few weeks since the inn had gone back up for sale, and without a plan or a second thought, Lana had contacted her bank for a preapproval for a loan to buy it. Everything in Bluedale moved at a slow pace, but each day felt like it was crawling by as she waited on an answer.

The vision of opening her restaurant in the inn after culinary school hadn't gone exactly as planned, but if things went well with the bank, then she would be able to move her restaurant into the inn *and* honor her family in the greatest way possible.

"They'll like the plan, won't they?" she asked.

"Girl, they're going to love the plan. How could they not? These types of things just take a while, is all. Besides, my brilliant husband and I helped you put that plan together, so how could the bank say no?"

Lana grinned. "It was pretty detailed. Maybe they're still reading through it," she joked. "But you two are amazing. Not sure what I'd do without both of you."

Alicia was an estate planning lawyer, who Lana had met one night at a party in downtown Providence during her final year at school. While she was busy in the kitchen, Alicia was in her second year of law school at Roger Williams University. They'd become fast friends, and after five years, they were inseparable. Alicia's husband, Nathan, a marketing professional, had helped Lana get On the Bay launched after she'd remodeled it from the old fish market, and they'd both given her plenty of notes on her loan proposal before she sent it to the bank.

"You're Bluedale born and raised, you run a successful business, and you're looking to take back over a local landmark that was in your family for years. What could be better?"

Lana nodded along, but none of Alicia's reassurance

could stop the anxiety she felt. "I just… I want this so badly. For me, but also for my grandad."

In the five years since his official diagnosis, dementia had been slowly making its way through his memories, yet despite the challenges of watching him battle the disease, their time at the inn was still vivid in his mind. He didn't always remember who she was as an adult when she went to see him at the nursing home, but their early years always brought him back to her. Regardless of how hard some of those memories were, especially when he'd get fixated on discussing special times with her parents, it'd kept them close during her visits. She wanted nothing more than for him to live out the rest of his days knowing she'd gotten the inn back—before he couldn't remember anything at all.

"Well, I can't make the bank move any faster on your loan, but I *do* have the perfect thing to take your mind off it."

Lana groaned. "Is this about that friend of Nathan's again?"

"Come on, this guy is perfect for you!" Alicia insisted.

Lana rolled her eyes. "You always say that."

"Yeah, but I mean it this time. Just wait until you meet him. Besides, you can't stay cooped up in that kitchen for the rest of your life. You need to talk to people besides me and Nathan."

She knew her friend was right, but she still scrambled to think of how to tell her that she'd rather not. Alicia had texted Lana earlier about these dinner plans, but she'd held off answering, knowing this friend of Nathan's was a setup. It wasn't that she didn't want to date or settle down and have a family one day, but running her restaurant with only one extra chef took up all her time.

"I'm not cooped up. I'm just trying to maintain my restaurant all on my own. Besides, I talk to Heidi every day."

"Talking to your sous chef while hiding in the kitchen

doesn't count." Alicia sighed through the phone. "Would you just pop outside and have a quick bite with us? Tell Heidi you're taking a break. You know her, she won't mind."

Lana hesitated because Alicia knew her sous chef well and was right—Heidi would most likely encourage her to get out of the kitchen too. "I'm not trying to be a social drag, I'm just busy."

"Ugh! I'm busy too, but I don't go recluse on the world. Just give it a try. I booked us for an eight o'clock reservation on your patio tomorrow night. Make sure you put on something fun and flirty."

Lana chuckled. Alicia seemed to forget that chefs on duty couldn't wear "fun and flirty" outfits in the kitchen. She drew her eyebrows together. What reason could she give this time? When Alicia had tried to fix her up with a different guy over breakfast last month, a head cold had saved her from having to go. She truly had no desire this time either, but as her mind raced for an excuse, she couldn't think of one. She'd have to surrender. "Okay, you win. But I will be dressed how I always dress at work: in my uniform, which isn't fun *or* flirty."

"Lana! Come on! At least brush those gorgeous red curls into something presentable!"

"I make no promises," she said. They wrapped up their conversation a minute later, and Lana returned her phone to her pocket, stopping for a moment to just enjoy the quiet of the beach.

In the distance, the seagulls swooped up, drifting through the air, before landing in a new spot in the sand near the inn's old deck. She always felt comforted at the sight, remembering how hard her grandad had worked to build that deck. Like the shore's own melody, the birds called out to each other, strutting over the sand. Her grandad's words from the night before whispered in her ear as she watched them peck around, scrounging for any piece of food they could find.

"Is he still there, Lana?" he'd asked her.

Lana had pulled up his blanket, tucking it around him as if he were a little boy. "Who, Grandad?" But she already knew.

"That seagull. The one from that summer. Don't you remember?" His eyes drifted toward the ceiling, looking calm and clear in his thoughts. Lana bent down, kissing his forehead, unable to find the right words and trying to escape the feeling of wind rushing through her curls and the memory of her father's firm grip. *Of course I remember*, she'd wanted to say.

"There are always seagulls out there, Grandad. I can never remember which one is which." That was *always* her answer. In recent weeks, this memory had been resurfacing, and he'd replayed it over and over with her.

"I hope you take the pontoon out soon," he said, changing the subject as his thoughts shifted like they always did.

As if the seagulls from that last summer with her parents weren't hard enough to talk about, this was how he'd ended their conversations lately. It took everything Lana had not to crumble each time, knowing the family boat he was referring to would continue to stay on dry land.

Being out on the water was where Lana had always found the most joy as a child, but everything changed after she lost her parents. What had once brought reprieve only reminded her now of the stormy seas of her past. And no matter how hard she'd tried, she couldn't get herself onto a boat of any kind.

No good would come of getting lost in those thoughts, especially when she had so much to do today. Looking away from the inn, she refocused on the task before her.

With her attention on clam digging, she noticed there was still no one else clamming with her. That would change after the holiday weekend passed. Catching shellfish was a popular activity for both residents and tourists in Bluedale, so Lana couldn't help but soak in the tranquil start to her day.

After successfully filling her last basket, she stacked them, picked up all four by holding them under the bottom one and made her way to shore, easily walking along the soft sand flats that were now fully lit by the sun. Just down the beach, early risers had begun to show up with their coffee or books to sit and enjoy the quiet in the sun before crowds of people arrived. Reaching the parking lot behind her restaurant, she waved at some familiar faces who ran past, and brought all her baskets to the back of her bright-red Jeep. She placed them on the ground before peeling out of her hip waders and muck boots, then opened her trunk and tossed her wet attire in.

Now shivering without anything on top of her swimsuit to warm her, she quickly hopped into the driver's seat to fetch her sweatpants and zip-up sweater. The hot summer air was taking its time blowing in this year, but she didn't mind because soon enough, the salty humidity would make this job a little harder.

With her sweats on, her body began to warm back up, and she opened the car door feeling satisfied with the number of clams she'd collected. They needed to be cleaned, soaked, and put on ice before they spoiled. Her lobster order didn't need to be picked up until later, so she picked up the baskets again, and headed to the kitchen.

Wiping sweat off her brow a few minutes into scrubbing, she cracked a window to let in some of the cool, early summer air. Alicia's insistence on meeting this friend of hers crossed her mind again as she examined each clam, discarding the ones that were already opened and putting the cleaned ones in bowls to soak. Her job required a lot of focus and she bit her bottom lip, continuing to mentally justify her resistance to meeting someone new. Shaking off the guilt she felt for trying to dodge her friends' nice gesture, she pulled her full attention back to the clambake preparation.

Making it a successful kick-off party for the summer season was a much more important thing to worry about. Her reputation was riding on her future with On the Bay, and that reputation might determine whether or not she got approved for the bank loan.

That meant making sure every private party and the daily food preparation were the best she could provide. She needed no distractions or uncomfortable blind dates.

Tossing the last clam into the bowl, she thought again about all the possibilities of owning the inn. Perhaps she could remodel the dining area and expand it, not to mention finally having indoor seating. It would all depend on the loan amount, but her mind raced with ideas, and she prayed this would be the answer she'd been waiting on to grow her business. She could daydream all day, but for now she had a private party to finish getting ready for.

After the clams were all in bowls to soak for a couple hours, she cleaned and dried her hands and moved on to getting the night's appetizer prepped, when she heard a car pull up near the window. Peeking out, she saw Heidi get out of her adorable yellow Volkswagen Beetle. She tossed the towel down onto the counter and walked outside to greet her.

"Did you have a good dig this morning?" Heidi shielded her eyes, her short blonde hair, nearly the color of her car, flapping in the breeze as she shut the door.

"It was a success!" Lana said, while Heidi opened the back door and pulled out a giant plastic tub filled with unshucked corn. "How do you manage to fit anything in that tiny car of yours?"

"Hey now, don't start the day knocking my car!" Heidi said with an amused expression. Lana walked over as Heidi placed the bucket on the ground. Since the day Heidi had bought it, Lana couldn't help but poke fun at her, especially with how different her Jeep looked next to the little yellow car. "You'd be surprised what I can squeeze in here." Heidi pointed to the bucket, grabbing a handle. "Can you help me drag this in? It weighs a ton."

Lana gripped the other side of the bucket. "You sure got a lot. Did you clean out all the corn at the farmer's market? I'm surprised they had so much this early." Together the women lifted it up.

"Pretty much. It's not the sweet kind yet, but they sure had a good bunch. The potatoes are on the other side of my back seat and that bucket is even heavier. What time is the lobster order going to be ready?" Wobbling back inside, carefully balancing the bucket, they placed it down in the kitchen near the small island and went back to get the potatoes.

"Around two this afternoon, which is perfect. Then we don't have to ice them too long. Are you still up for gathering the rockweed?" Lana asked.

"Absolutely—you know that's my favorite." Heidi opened the other back door, and together they pulled out the potatoes, which were indeed much heavier, and brought them in.

"Besides, you did the dig this morning all by yourself, so it's no problem for me to get it."

"You do a better job of gathering it up anyway," Lana told her, nearly throwing her back out as she set the potatoes down next to the corn. "I think we're set for a while with potatoes."

"You can never have enough potatoes in a kitchen." Heidi dropped the other side down and brushed her hair off her face.

"Or enough dates. What was last night?" Lana twisted her mouth, pretending to think for a minute. "Date number twelve this month?"

Heidi grabbed one of the potatoes and held it up. "Don't make me use this on you!"

Lana raised a teasing brow. "Don't be mad 'cause it's true. You're like the 'one-and-done dater.'"

"Excuse me, but remember that guy we met at the tavern in Eastham? He got two dates." Heidi tossed the potato back in the bucket. "And I've only been on a few dates these past few weeks, thank you very much."

"Wow, *two* whole dates? He should get a prize. Tell him to come on down and I'll give him a free lobster roll."

"Says the woman who dates no one!"

Lana couldn't help but smile. Heidi may work for her, but the two had grown very close, and even though they were just having fun, she knew Heidi wasn't scared to be a little truthful either. "You're right. You win. But I will date again. Eventually. Once I hear back from the bank."

At that, they both laughed.

"I know you will." Heidi winked at her. "And he will be as perfect as your food."

"He'd better be." Lana nodded to the door. "The skiff boat is in the storage out back. Let me give you the key." She pulled out her key ring, twisting one off and handing it to

Heidi before glancing at her watch. It was already close to noon, and she wanted to run home to shower before coming back to get things ready. The event was for a fortieth birthday, and the family wanted to arrive a little early to decorate the patio. "I'll meet you back here around two-thirty, after I pick up the lobster?"

"Sounds good. There's an abundance of rockweed out there this early in the summer, so it shouldn't take me long. See you soon!" Heidi dashed out of the kitchen and headed off.

Lana grabbed the broom out of the supply closet, left the kitchen, and went out to the patio to begin sweeping it off. Muffled voices in the distance caught her attention. Following the sound, she leaned the broom against one of the tables and walked across the sand to the edge of the beach grass that divided her restaurant from the inn. Two men with clipboards were standing in front of the large outdoor deck. Perhaps they were from the bank and had been sent to appraise the property. She leaned her head in to try and make out what they were saying.

"I think there will be enough room for the proposed plan, but only on the east side of the building." Both men walked farther away, and she couldn't hear their conversation anymore, but something about what he'd said made her uneasy. She didn't have anything in her proposal about that side of the building.

Picking the broom back up, she swept around to the side, where she caught sight of the blue reusable cover that was stretched over her parents' pontoon. Lana swallowed a lump in her throat and blinked back her emotions. The men's voices from the inn echoed in the distance again as they started to come closer, pulling her attention away from the boat.

When she was finishing sweeping, she went back inside

the kitchen and put the broom in the closet. The voices could now be heard outside her kitchen window, which meant they were in the parking lot her restaurant shared with the inn. There was no time to ponder what they were doing, so she quickly checked the clams and hurried to her car to get home and shower. Forty-two people were not going to serve themselves.

A COUPLE HOURS LATER, Lana returned feeling clean and refreshed, and ready for the clambake. She and Heidi got the lobsters, clams, corn, and potatoes covered on top of the rockweed to steam in the firepit, before they went back to the kitchen to get the rest of the food.

When they reemerged onto the patio, the family hosting the party had placed a red velvet cake for the birthday celebration on a side table next to Lana's red, white, and blue macaroons. The hired bartender for private parties had just finished setting up the drinks, and Lana looked around, impressed with the family's choice of burlap table covers and nautical runners with red-and-blue lanterns on top—each table complete with a small bucket holding lobster bibs and napkins.

After a quick meeting with the servers, Lana headed over to sample both of the specialty drinks the barman had crafted for the evening, and gave him her approval before she disappeared into the kitchen. As she mixed the batter for the strawberry shortcake biscuits, her phone lit up on the counter with an incoming call.

Normally she would ignore it once she got started in the kitchen, but she froze when she saw it was the bank calling.

"Hello?" she said, trying to sound confident. Capable. Like

a woman who could—who *would*—take over the inn and make it thrive.

"Is this Lana?" a female voice said.

"This is she."

"Hi, Lana, it's Debbie from Bluedale Trust. Gearing up for the holiday weekend?"

"Hi, Debbie! We are. We're preparing for our first clambake of the season."

"Sounds wonderful. I really enjoyed experiencing that last summer." Lana heard her sigh and felt her stomach drop. "So I'm calling about your application for a loan to buy back the inn." Lana's heart was in her throat. This was it—the moment of truth.

"Yes?" she said eagerly.

"There's no easy way to say this, but your application has been denied."

The words were such a shock that Lana literally stumbled, banging her hip on the edge of the table. The sudden burst of pain forced her to gasp in air so she could reply. "Was there a problem with my business plan? With my financials? I thought—"

"The issue is with the property itself," Debbie cut in. "The bank can't approve the loan for you to purchase the inn because it's no longer for sale."

"Wh-what?" Lana stammered. "But it only went on the market a month ago."

"And right when your loan application came in a few weeks back, so did another offer—which was ten percent *over* the asking price. The owners sat with the offer for a couple weeks. They knew you wanted to buy it too and they really did consider it—but money has been tight for them lately. The extra funds were just too hard to say no to, so in the end they accepted this other offer."

"Is it too late to counter?" Lana knew she wouldn't be able to top ten percent over asking, but she was desperate.

"Unfortunately, it is. We just got word that zoning and planning approved phase one building permits already."

Lana's knees went weak, and she had to cling to the table to keep from falling as she struggled to push down the tears that filled her eyes.

"Not again…" she said, barely above a whisper, before it dawned on her what Debbie had just said. "Wait, did you say building permits?"

"Yes, the offer came in from a development company out in New York City. That's all I know about them." There was a pause, and when Debbie spoke again, her voice had a forced cheerfulness to it. "But you'll be glad to hear there is some good news. You've built up enough credit for a business loan. Maybe you can get building permits of your own, and extend the space you have now for the indoor dining area you originally hoped to add."

It was something Lana had thought to do a couple years prior, but she'd stopped pursuing the idea when she wasn't approved for a large enough loan. The space around the restaurant was very limited, with property lines from the inn taking up most of the land on one side—but it wasn't impossible to expand on the other.

"Maybe," she said, trying her hardest to sound appreciative of Debbie's suggestion.

"I know how hard this is, Lana. Everyone here at Bluedale Trust was rooting for you, and I'm sure the rest of our town will be sad to hear this news too."

"Except for the zoning and planning committee," Lana said sarcastically.

"You know them—all business and care for how this offer will enhance Bluedale's growth."

After a few more pleasantries, which Lana barely heard, she hung up. In the quiet of the kitchen, she hung her head, still in disbelief that she'd have to let the inn go... all over again.

CHAPTER 2

Hunter Graham turned the corner onto Park Avenue, sighing with relief when he saw Graham Property Development just ahead. Memories of walking up to this building as a young boy popped into his mind, and he felt so proud to finally be working alongside his father.

His grandad had begun this firm with very little money and had grown it from the ground up, starting with small projects. When his father had taken over the company, he'd expanded it by leaps and bounds, including their newest branch in Boston, where Hunter had relocated only months before so he could get the office up and running. Their first project: a brand-new luxury event venue and cruise line, right on the shore in one of Cape Cod's busiest tourist locations. They were setting their stakes high in the Boston area.

When he reached the large brass door, it stuck for a moment against a gust of wind, before he stepped inside and rushed over to the elevator, stopping it from closing just in time. Pressing the button, his thoughts ran through everything he'd prepared to show his father and their senior analyst, Simon, before heading off to the Cape.

This was his first solo project, and an important one. It was his chance to earn the promotion to Vice President of Business Development and prove to his father that he was the right man to eventually take over the whole company. Everything was riding on the success of this new development.

A few floors up, the door opened, and their front secretary, Janet, lit up with a wide grin when she saw him.

"Well, hello there, Mr. Graham," she greeted him, coming over to give him a hug. Janet had worked for his father since Hunter was a child, and she knew his family very well.

"Mr. Graham? Sounds strange coming out of your mouth." Hunter hugged her back, giving her arms an extra affectionate squeeze before letting go. He hoped she wasn't gearing up for a long chat. While he loved talking with her, he was already running late, and his father was not the patient type.

"Well, now that you're running a whole new branch, I feel it's only appropriate to stick to the formalities." Janet winked at him. "You better get on back there. He's stuck his head out a few times looking for you." She nodded toward the conference room, knowing all too well how impatient his father was.

Hunter winced. "Which means I'm even later than I realized." He waved as he hurried away from her. "Good to see you, Janet. Take care of yourself if I don't see you after."

"I'll be long gone by the time you and your father are finished with that meeting. Next time you come, though, I'd better be hearing about some beautiful Boston woman who stole your heart."

Hunter laughed and shook his head. Janet knew he didn't

have time for romance. Not with that promotion hanging over his head. With a deep breath, he pushed open the door.

"There you are, Hunter!" His father looked up from his laptop with a disapproving scowl.

Hunter walked to an empty chair around the large, oval meeting desk, across from Simon. He couldn't help noticing the amused expression on Simon's face. The other man was visibly smug about being more punctual…and was striving for the same promotion as Hunter.

"Sorry, Dad, there was traffic coming out of Boston this morning due to the holiday weekend." Hunter met his father's eyes, which continued to glower at him.

Philip Graham was not one to tolerate tardiness, and when his own son was late, his patience waned even thinner. His father's strict nature had taught Hunter how to stay focused and steadfast, but it came at a cost. Tough love might be what worked best to motivate his dad, but Hunter would have appreciated a gentler approach. Not that his father ever seemed to realize that. But even though it was always hard won, there was nothing that meant more than his father's pride in him. Even if the man never actually said the words, the promotion would prove he finally thought his son was good enough.

Before his father could offer a rebuttal, Simon put his pen down, clearing his throat. "We have a lot to cover, and we're already running behind, so let's continue. Phil, go ahead and finish what you were just saying." Simon looked over at Hunter with a haughty grin. "Your dad was just going over the latest pre-design that you sent him, before I plan to present some market conditions for Bluedale."

"Bluedale sure has a nice ring to it, doesn't it," Hunter said, looking evenly at his father and hoping it would calm the tension.

"Yes, it does, I suppose." His father pushed his laptop

aside, resting his hand on his chin, not looking entirely convinced.

Hunter swallowed. "And Bluedale is the first town after you cross the bridge onto the Cape, where we can advertise to tourists right as they arrive."

"Yet, maximizing market share would be easier in the location in Hyannis that you were prospecting," Simon said as he crossed his arms. "Being able to find us easily shouldn't be the only deciding factor."

"It's a big perk, considering how congested the Cape is in season," Hunter shot back.

"Gentlemen, let's pause the disagreement and look at the plans Hunter has for us," his father said.

Hunter turned on his laptop, connecting it to the large screen on the wall and bringing up the property layout. It showed a bird's-eye view of the bed-and-breakfast property in its current condition.

"Hmm." His father raised his eyebrows. "I know we've gone over the specs countless times and our engineers were there this morning walking the property, so I'll be interested to hear the report from them. Seeing the property from this angle still has me a little concerned it's a bit small for the additions we're creating on blueprint."

Hunter grabbed the remote on the table and brought up the slide with a technical drawing.

"Remember this area?" Hunter went up to the screen and pointed to the side of the building. "And how you weren't sure we could do the ballroom with the first design that was drawn up? Well, our engineers called while I was driving here and confirmed the space and ability to go ahead with it. They just emailed the reports."

His father quietly peered up at Hunter as he listened, before returning his focus to the screen above and sitting back. "I see..." He trailed off, evidently thinking it through.

"Based on the population, Bluedale looks to be much smaller than Hyannis. It'll have a limited local market for events. We need to get creative with how we'll compete with other established towns nearby. It might be too tough."

"You are correct, Dad—Hyannis is much larger with many other options—but try to look at it a different way. Unlike Hyannis, we're going to be on the more isolated north side of the peninsula, which means a different choice for weddings, for example, that won't be right next to other venues. And we're going to stand out, being away from the noise of the south side. Not to mention our cruise line." Hunter pulled up a map on the screen. "Keep in mind, we're going to cover different water too." He pointed to the bay side of the Cape where Bluedale was located, versus the Nantucket Sound where their steepest competition sat, with cruises that frequently sailed along the Atlantic and south of the Cape to the islands.

"Let me read those reports from the engineers," his father said, ignoring the map. Hunter clicked to open them. His father studied the screen and after a couple minutes, he leaned back. "I see there's a small restaurant blocking a lot of that space the engineers are referring to, including the beach."

"Yes, it's some sort of outdoor seafood place," Hunter said. "But I haven't looked into much more than that."

"And why not?" his father asked, peering up over his readers at him.

"What do you mean?" Hunter asked.

"If they're in the way, then let's fix that. Let's put together an offer they can't resist, well above what the current assessed value of that property is, and buy them out. Then we'll stand out nicely from all that competition you just rambled on about—with more beach, more room, more options."

"Your father is correct—you should have looked into that by now, Hunter," Simon cut in, and Hunter had to struggle to keep from rolling his eyes.

"I was too busy focusing on other areas of the project," Hunter replied through clenched teeth. Simon never failed to dig at him.

"Well, you're going to have your work cut out for you even more with that buyout," Simon fired back.

"And why is that?" Hunter looked at his father, who was unusually quiet as he focused on Simon.

"I did my own research. For starters, we wanted to make sure we understood what previously went wrong with that inn, for business planning purposes." Simon swiveled in his chair away from the screen, toward Hunter. "In doing so, we found out about the long-standing history behind it."

"I'm listening." Hunter hoped Simon wasn't about to blow all his plans out of the water.

"It was built in the seventies and did well for a long time, before the competition increased. There was an equity loan taken out for whatever reason, and the owner's health issues were also a factor. It was ultimately foreclosed on about five years ago. That was when the latest owners bought it," Simon explained.

"Okay," his father said. "Then why was it put up for sale again?"

Hunter held up his hand to pause Simon. "I can answer that." He looked at his father. "I did my research too. The couple who purchased it at auction—Mr. and Mrs. Carter—realized a few years in that owning a cute little inn on the Cape was more work than they bargained for. They're happy to sell to us. There's no drama there, and no real issue with the property." Hunter cast his eyes back toward Simon. The last thing he needed was for him to convince his father the owners were pushed out by the steep competition in the area.

"Oh, I know the Carters aren't a problem, but that doesn't mean you won't face issues with the *previous* owners, especially when it comes to that restaurant you want to buy out," Simon said, flashing Hunter a sly smile. "The owner is the granddaughter of the original owners of the inn. She lost her family's inn and now we're going to try and buy out her restaurant, which was probably the last piece of land she was entitled to."

"Then the probability of her accepting our offer will be low, so let's put that on the backburner for a moment and go over the rest of these plans," Hunter said, shooting Simon a look of warning not to interrupt him again.

"Yes, let's table that discussion for now." His father shifted in his seat. "What else do you have for me, Hunter?"

Hunter switched to another slide, opening the pictures of the cruise ship. He was so proud of this portion of the business model, knowing how well it would bump up profits for the venue—with events on land and at sea. "The remodels are complete. I know you got this same copy already, but here it is."

At the sight of the newly renovated vessel, Simon let out a low whistle. It wasn't massive, but it was impressive. All throughout the ship was decorated in ocean blues and greens, with a hint of champagne to balance it out, which made for a simple, yet clean look. The one main event room had updated flooring, big windows for natural lighting during the day, and a warm and neutral color palette to act as a blank canvas for individual events to incorporate their own theme. The small kitchen was also modernized, with additional storage.

Their cruise line would host weddings and other events, along with daytime tours along the Cape Cod Bay. They'd purchased the ship only a couple months ago at a low price, just as they began their property search, and now it looked brand new. Hunter's father studied the 120-foot ship pictured on the screen. Graham Bayview Events and Cruises would certainly be the new hit of the Cape.

"The wedding industry for receptions on the water is large enough in Cape Cod that it will make our venue stand out among others, with the added option of renting out the ship," Hunter said, feeling pleased.

"Yes," Simon said. "But we don't have a date set in stone to launch the ship, do we?" He shuffled through the notes in front of him as if to look for something. "What about a secured port?"

Hunter inhaled, trying to keep his composure. "Just keep your focus on market analysis and I'll handle the rest."

Philip cleared his throat. "Well, I'd like to know the answer to that, Hunter."

"A bid was made on one, but I still need to follow up," Hunter told him, feeling sheepish because he should have done that before this meeting.

"You need to get on that right away," his father said. "I'd like to see the ship launch soon, especially since the venue remodel won't be complete until this fall. The ship will be a great way to get the word out in town and throughout the Cape, and begin generating revenue since hundreds of tourists will see it."

"It absolutely will, and I'll lock down a port as soon as possible," Hunter assured him. There were a lot of details to keep track of and not everything was settled yet, but he was confident he'd be able to pull this off. Mostly confident, anyway. His father had sent him to Boston to watch his performance and the pressure was beginning to mount already, leaving little to no room for mistakes. So far, everything was going well. He just had to make sure he didn't hit any major roadblocks.

"I took some time looking into this myself since Cape Cod is filled with cruises and boats and I needed to compare financial models and growth, both with the cruise line and without it. There's another port I found that looks promising. I'll send you the information," Simon said.

"Well done, Simon. We need to always be one step ahead." His father looked relieved, and Hunter began to feel defeated. Simon then started to go over market value and event revenue with the remodel, without waiting for a response from Hunter.

His father was nodding along with everything Simon said, making Hunter wonder, for maybe the hundredth time, if he was being considered for the Vice President role only because he was Philip's son. His father often looked above him at his other employees, rather than directly at *him* for reassurance. This had been going on for years, even before he'd given him the opportunity to open the Boston branch. His father's tight grip on all operations was no surprise because that's how the Graham men were with business—except him, who had a tendency to see things from a softer angle and with more flexibility. It had never stopped him from getting the job done, but still, Hunter knew it wasn't the way his father preferred to operate. It was why he'd had to wait so long to get his first big solo project.

"Looks like I'll be staying in Bluedale full-time during construction." Hunter looked up at that thought. Now that he would be getting the cruise line ready for its opening day that summer, he would definitely need to stay close.

"Yes, you will, but this will be a big project for you to oversee, so let's see how it goes." His father gave him a worried look. "I'll be there a few times to check in, especially as things move along."

Turning his attention back to the screen, Hunter tried not to let frustration over his father's apparent lack of confidence get the best of him. The drive to keep growing was of course in the forefront of Hunter's mind, yet part of him questioned if he could really do it in the way his father expected. And more importantly, if that was the only way Graham Property Development *should* continue.

AFTER THE LAST sip of what was probably his fifth coffee several hours later, Hunter pushed his chair back to stand up. "What a day this has been. We've accomplished a lot. What do you say we wrap up now?" His whole body was stiff from sitting for so long, and when he raised his arms to stretch out, his father held up his hand.

"Hold on." His father gestured toward Hunter's chair.

Feeling both annoyance and hunger, he lowered himself into his seat once more, rubbing his aching shoulder. "Can we possibly talk about this later? I need to eat. The only thing I've had since I've left this morning is about a gallon of coffee."

"Relax, I have reservations for us and your mother at a new restaurant in the financial district in about an hour."

His parents had long been separated, but they were good about getting together for family dinners every now and then. "Okay, what is it?"

"We need to circle back to the buyout of that restaurant next to the inn. There's no way around it—it has to be done." His father gave him a hard stare.

"Based on what Simon told us earlier, it doesn't seem likely the owner will accept," Hunter said, holding back irritation.

"Make it happen. It's what we do in this line of work." His father closed his laptop.

"I have one more bit of info to add," Simon said.

"Of course you do," Hunter said, crossing his arms.

"Lana Kelly is the name of the restaurant owner, and you should know she put in a bid to try and buy back the inn. Locals may know this—and that we're the reason she didn't get it—so she'll probably have a grudge against you before you even make the offer. Be careful how you present it to her. Try to smooth things out first. If things go badly with her, we won't just lose the chance to buy the restaurant property—we could alienate the whole town."

"Smooth things over?" Hunter grimaced, not looking forward to the prospect. In the past, while working as a property coordinator, he'd become good at getting the surrounding town on board with whatever the company had in mind. There was always some resistance to change, but their projects brought in new jobs while construction took place, and when the construction was over, the new business would boost the town's economic growth. That was usually enough to get past the "don't trust the outsider" mindset he ran up against in small towns, in particular. But the charm offensive may not work as well when there was someone on the other side arguing against him—someone the townspeople already knew and liked. If he made this Lana Kelly woman upset enough, she could sure make it harder for him to get cooperation from the rest of the town. And things moved way too slowly on projects when the town wasn't cooperating.

His father frowned. "Is that a problem, Hunter? Simon is right. Tread carefully before you present the offer. But make sure you close the deal. And remember, business is business," he said, his face stern and chin held high—the same look his father always gave him when he was defensive.

"I'll be honest—this will be tricky and may leave a bad mark on our reputation, making it difficult to continue building in Bluedale," Hunter pointed out.

"Look," his father cut back in. "Just introduce yourself and talk it out with her. The first thing you need to do is contact her for an in-person meeting. Bluedale is small-town friendly, which means we will be too, so you will need her support in order to start this project with happy and excited residents. And more importantly, we need to try to avoid rumors about us being the big, bad outsiders who ruined the local girl's plans. We want everyone happy about our project moving forward. Got it?" His father stood up over him.

"Got it. I can handle this," Hunter said, still feeling skeptical. It would be a tough balancing act, making the restaurant owner happy while also putting pressure on her to sell the last piece of beachfront her family likely had left.

"We'll see. Smooth things over, but don't let yourself get distracted. Your grandad did not get this company to where it was when I took over by backing down to avoid hurt feelings." His father stepped toward the door but turned back once more before leaving. "I'll see you at the restaurant at seven. And remember… this is your chance to show us your leadership skills, Hunter."

Simon trailed behind his father, and once they were out of earshot, Hunter let out a sigh of frustration. Something told him that meeting with Lana Kelly was going to be the hardest part of this project—even harder than the renovations.

"*L*ana?" Heidi came to her side where she was leaning against the kitchen counter after hanging up with the bank. "Are you feeling sick? You're looking a bit pale."

Lana straightened up, offering a smile to ease Heidi's worry. "Not sick—just a little stunned. The bank called, and…" She let out a defeated sigh.

"And by the looks of you, it didn't go as planned."

"That's exactly right. The owners accepted another offer." Tears glistened in her eyes, and it took everything she had not to cry. With a full house of guests on her patio outside, it was not a good time to fall apart.

"Lana… I don't even know what to say. 'I'm sorry' sounds so lame compared to what you must be feeling."

Lana couldn't help but chuckle. Heidi's sense of humor always made her laugh, even now when she'd just found out the worst possible news. "It really does."

"Then I won't say it, but you know I am."

"I know. Thank you for always being such a good friend and partner in the kitchen."

Heidi leaned over, putting her arm around her. "Take a deep breath. We will get through this party together. Then you can cry."

Lana mustered up a weak grin. "Let's go give our guests a great party."

WHEN THE LAST of the guests and staff had left, and the kitchen had been cleaned up, Lana yawned, plopping down into her office chair. She never felt the fatigue while she was busy in the kitchen, but the exhaustion always hit her as soon as the day was over. Usually, it was a good tired—a thriving restaurant kind of tired.

That's how it should have been tonight, given that the party had been a complete success. Heidi had popped out a few times and came back to report that their guests were laughing, dancing, and complimenting the food all night, reminding her of all she'd accomplished with her father's old fish market.

Now in a quiet moment, her binder filled with remodel plans for the inn stared up from the desk, reminding her of all she'd *hoped* to achieve that was still out of reach. Picking it up, she leafed through a few of the pages and drew in a long breath before putting it back down. A picture of her parents that she kept on her desk caught her attention. In it, she was a toddler, with her mom holding her on her hip and her dad behind them with his arms spread over both of them—a happy trio smiling back at her.

All she wanted to do was pick up the phone, call her parents, and ask them what to do next. She hadn't told her grandad that she was trying to buy the inn again, and now she wasn't sure telling him would be wise. She'd just wanted him to live out the rest of his life happy with the memories that he still held onto, despite his disease. Picking up the picture, she couldn't help the emotions that were building in her heart, and without the ability to stop them, she bent over and let the tears fall.

A few minutes later, she was breathless as she put the picture back on her desk, their happy faces still staring at her. She inhaled deeply and straightened her shoulders, letting the setback from today's phone call with the bank shift into fierce determination. Without knowing what her next step was, she did know that sitting in memory lane wouldn't help anything. Standing up, she went to the bathroom to refresh herself.

After splashing her face, she went outside to make sure the outdoor lights were off. The silence of the patio that had been filled with laughter and happiness only minutes before pulsed against the headache that had formed in her temples. She needed to get home and get a good night's sleep.

She went back inside and got her purse, turned off all the rest of the lights, and walked out into the cool, early summer night air again. *Dry the tears*, she told herself. She had a restaurant to run, a reputation to uphold, and goals to meet in order to keep her small restaurant going on the growing Cape. Now without the inn as an option to expand, she'd need to refigure how to do that and keep the customers coming back.

"And," Lana whispered out loud to herself, locking the door, and heading to her car, "I have parents looking down on me." She was certain that if they were standing next to her in this moment, they'd encourage her to rise above this.

"ARE we late for the beach, Mama?" The little girl's voice sounded muffled outside her bedroom window, stirring

Lana awake.

"No, we're not late. We have plenty of time to get there," the girl's mother answered.

Lana opened her eyes, squinting against the sun beaming through her curtains. *I've got to get blackout shades.* She groaned and sat up.

"Don't forget my sand toys, Mama!" the girl called to her mom, louder this time. Lana recognized her neighbors' voices and smiled. The little girl, Sara, lived in the condo right next to hers with her parents, Kristen and John. Getting out of bed, she threw a sweatshirt over her T-shirt and went to the kitchen to start the coffee.

Walking back out to the living room, she opened the sliding door to her deck and stepped outside, instantly hearing the shallow waves of the descending high tide spilling onto the shore below. The view of the ocean from her deck never got old.

The early morning welcomed her with serene warmth, but that also meant packed beaches all over the Cape for a very busy opening day. Memorial Day weekend was always so exciting in Bluedale. Tourists were beginning to mix in with the residents, and Lana crossed her fingers for a busy season.

As she slid back inside to get her coffee, the nutty aroma of the fresh, hot brew awakened her senses. Once she had a steaming mug in hand, she took it outside to enjoy on the deck. Leaning on the railing, she closed her eyes against the sun for that first sip. Feeling the hot liquid perk her up, she looked down at the beach, laughing when she saw little Sara running way ahead of her mother toward the gentle waves. Low tide was the best for kids to play in.

Living in a small condo, boxed in between others, could feel tight, but you couldn't beat being able to sit on your private deck and watch the ocean—not to mention, Lana's neighbors made it a wonderful place to be. She wasn't one to socialize much, but Lana had known Kristen and John her whole life, making it easier to confide in Kristen. Having them next door brought comfort, and little Sara's voice loudly carrying on outside her window made her feel less lonely.

She couldn't imagine living anywhere else than Bluedale. It was all she knew, with every corner of town holding memories for her, especially her younger years with her parents. Taking the last sip from her mug, she decided to get ready for the day. Heidi was prepping this morning for the dinner service, so she had the day to herself.

An hour later, Lana was showered. To combat the summer heat, her red curls were thrown up on top of her head, and she wore a pair of jean shorts with a green, cotton halter top that matched her emerald eyes. Trying not to think about yesterday's upsetting news, she turned her thoughts to something else and decided to call Alicia. It was Saturday after all, which meant she was not at her office and was hopefully free.

"I was just about to call you," Alicia said when she answered. "Nathan and I are looking forward to introducing you to our friend tonight."

Lana squeezed her eyes shut, having forgotten about the setup. "Oh, right. I totally forgot."

"Of course you did, which is why I was going to call you to remind you." Alicia paused. "Okay, I sense something is wrong. Forget about dinner. What's going on?"

"I didn't get the loan for the inn." Lana held her breath, trying not to cry all over again. She didn't want to dump all of her work issues on her friend so early on a Saturday morning, but Alicia had been waiting on the answer from the bank along with her.

Walking back onto her deck, she looked out to the sea,

waiting for her friend's response. Alicia was silent on the other end. The seagulls excitedly filled the silence, squawking down below on the sand. Lana's gaze lingered on them for a moment, watching them wait for all the beach-goers to start opening their food.

"I'm shocked," Alicia finally said. "I really felt good about this."

"Are you free to meet up? I could use my best friend right now."

"I'll meet you at Bluedale Bakery in ten minutes. Wear some good walking shoes!"

OUT ON THE PIER, with summer berry Danish pastries and caramel iced coffee in hand, the two women found an empty bench to take a break from walking and eat their snack.

"Yum," Alicia mumbled between bites, her blonde hair catching in the ocean breeze. "This pastry never fails to remind me why I moved out here after law school."

Lana smiled. "And I thought it was the idea of living closer to me that brought you here. But I don't blame you." She took another bite, the rich, sweet flavor melting in her mouth. Bluedale Bakery had been around since she was a little girl and their pastries never let her down. "I used to dream of these when I was away in school. I remember when I started my first baking class, I tried to mimic them and failed miserably." They both laughed.

"All right, spill it. What exactly did they say? Was there a reason they said no? Something wrong with your application that you can fix?"

"They can't give me a loan to buy the inn, because the inn is no longer for sale."

Alicia raised her eyebrows. "Explain."

Lana filled her in on the other offer that was accepted. Getting all of this off her chest helped to release the tension she didn't realize had built up in her.

Alicia munched on her pastry and sipped her iced coffee, listening intently, before her eyes narrowed as she looked into the distance. Lana knew what that meant—the lawyer in her friend was emerging.

"Too late to counter it?" Alicia asked, turning to face her again.

"Yes, it is, and I wouldn't be able to anyway. Believe me, I thought about it, but the amount this offer went over the asking price is beyond what I could even dream of countering."

Alicia nodded. Without any answers, the two of them fell into silence.

Lana lifted the empty pastry bag and fanned her face against the hot sun, watching the sparkling Atlantic water gushing waves onto the shore.

Families and groups of friends were walking past them—teenagers laughing and making jokes, their excitement for the impending summer break evident. Normally, Lana would be just as thrilled to spend the summer season here, but today felt different, as though everyone around her got to enjoy it except her.

"I know this is a huge loss, but On the Bay is such a great restaurant, Lana. You've really done a fantastic job. You should be proud... inn or no inn."

"I am, but—" Lana hesitated. Tears stung her eyes, and she took a sip of her coffee in an attempt to relax. "I can't keep going with the restaurant as it is. I *need* to expand—or to make some other kind of change to bring in more of a profit. Losing the inn for a second time was hard enough on an emotional level, but it also would have made it so much easier for me to grow the business. Prices are rising and competition is exploding around me."

She was worried her small, outdoor seafood restaurant wouldn't be able to turn a profit much longer. Getting the inn back had felt like the answer, and given her personal connection and her family's history attached to it, it had all seemed set up for a great comeback in Bluedale.

Alicia shifted in her seat, looking her directly in the eye. "A little competition should not stop you."

"Who says it's stopping me?" Lana asked.

"You're wallowing."

"What do you mean? I'm just stating the facts."

"The fact is that you've worked so hard to transform your father's tiny little fish market into what it is today," Alicia reminded her. "I've always been so impressed with that. Not all restaurants start with so much history to live up to."

"Thank you," Lana said, her mouth curving into a smile. She appreciated Alicia's support and encouragement. "But for the last couple of years, it's been hard to keep up. Two new seafood restaurants opened in Bluedale last year, and I've noticed this week leading up to Memorial Day weekend was already a little slower than previous ones. With this latest setback, I'm feeling lost."

"Lana," Alicia said gently. "You've operated that restaurant for five years without the inn. You have the passion and the skill to keep it going for a long time coming."

"I hope you're right. It's just that..." Lana trailed off and looked down, searching for the right way to say it.

"This is more than just normal business competition?"

"Exactly. The inn is who I am." She met Alicia's eyes again.

"No... *you* are who you are. Every part of you went into that restaurant, all without the inn."

Lana nodded her head, taking in her friend's words, and

blew out her breath. She faced the blue sky. "So, what now? I don't know how to make sure I can increase my customers and keep the restaurant going." Not wanting to get too emotional while sitting out on the boardwalk, Lana pulled the focus back to the business side of things.

"Those new seafood restaurants you mentioned—are the owners from Bluedale?"

Lana shook her head. "I don't know where they're from, but—"

Alicia stopped her, reaching over and giving her hand an encouraging squeeze. "You are known and loved all over this town."

Lana scrunched her nose against the bright sun, trying to follow what Alicia was getting at. "Being from Bluedale doesn't get me more customers…"

A hush fell over them again before Alicia broke the silence. "Maybe it hasn't so far—that you know for sure. But what if we used that angle to make On the Bay flourish even more than it already has?"

Lana turned to her friend, studying her a second. She could tell Alicia was just building a wall of defense for her against the hard news she'd gotten from the bank. "Thank you for being so supportive, especially during a blow like this. But I feel like I'm going to need more than just the fact that I'm a hometown girl to bring in the money."

A smile slowly spread across Alicia's face. "Take a breath —everything will work out. What happens with the inn is out of your hands now. I've got some ideas brewing. Let me stew on them a bit more."

"Okay, and in the meantime, I'll try to stay optimistic." Lana couldn't imagine what Alicia might be cooking up, but she wouldn't bring down the mood anymore. "And I certainly don't want to start things off with any unnecessary tension with the new owners of the inn. I just don't know how I'm going to be able to be a friendly neighbor."

"It's okay to be angry, Lana. I'm upset too," Alicia said as she stood up. "But for now, let's have a little fun and go walk around the shops before you head back to the restaurant."

Lana stood up with her, playfully rolling her eyes and knowing that once her friend got started with a plan, it was quickly executed. "You're not going to share any of these ideas you have?"

"You'll see! I'll get Nathan up to speed on everything. He's going to have some work ahead of him. You may have lost the inn, but Bluedale hasn't lost you! Now come on, let's go shopping!"

The look on Alicia's face told Lana things were about to get interesting. Growing more curious, Lana followed her friend.

"YOUR GREEN EYES are literally sparkling against that red dress. You have to get it," Alicia said, as Lana emerged from a changing room a little while later.

"It fits you like a glove." Jackie, the shop owner, was standing next to Alicia.

Lana faced the mirror and twisted around back and forth. "You know, I think you're right. I really like it. It's not something I'd normally buy and I'm not sure where I'll wear it, but who cares. I'll take it."

"Good choice," Jackie said. "And those dark-red curls make it pop. I've always been jealous of your hair. It's just so gorgeous."

"Thank you, Jackie." Lana popped back behind the curtain to change out of the dress.

When she met Jackie at the counter to pay, the shop

owner quietly watched her before she pulled out a bag to put the dress in.

Lana shifted on her feet against the uncomfortable silence. "So how have summer sales been so far?"

"Not bad actually. Today's been steady. A great start to the tourist season." Jackie glanced at her again. "That'll be $67.20."

Lana swiped her card.

"How's everything going over at On the Bay? I can't wait to get in there again—especially for your stuffed clams. You'll have to let me know when they're back on the menu."

"I sure will," Lana said, picking the bag off the counter. "And everything's great at the restaurant."

"Lana…" Jackie hesitated, coming around the counter to get closer. "I just wanted to let you know how proud I am of you."

"For buying a dress out of my comfort zone?" Lana said, and Jackie grinned.

"Well, yes, that—but also for what you've done with your restaurant, despite losing your family's inn… and now losing it for a second time." Jackie lowered her eyes.

Lana looked over at Alicia, who shrugged. "So you've heard then?"

"Yes, but only because my husband's cousin is the branch assistant manager. She told us the inn was bought before your loan application could even process. Everyone at the bank was feeling down after they had to tell you the bad news. I'm sorry you didn't get to buy the inn back. I wish you could've. The Carters are nice enough folks, but the place hasn't been the same since your family left it."

"Thank you, Jackie. Your support means a lot," Lana said, not in the least bit surprised that word was already trickling into town about the loan.

"Don't let this setback keep you bottled up. Bluedale loves you more than that inn."

Baffled, Lana didn't know how to respond. *Keep* her bottled up?

Before she could respond, Alicia tugged at her sleeve. "Come on, Lana, let's hit some more shops."

When they left the store, Alicia waited until they were safely a few streets down before exploding. "See what I mean?"

"About what?"

"Bluedale loves you." Alicia stopped at another entrance to a store, opening the door for them with a mischievous smile.

Lana shook her head. "I don't know what you're drumming up, but it better make sense soon."

As Lana followed Alicia into the next store, she knew it would take more than the town's love to get her through meeting her new neighbors at the inn.

CHAPTER 4

*L*ooking past the hostess, Hunter spotted his parents, who were already seated, and when he got closer, his mother broke out in an excited grin.

"Hunter!" She waved him over, then stood up to wrap her arms around him in a tight hug once he reached her. "You look so good. Boston seems to suit you." She pulled back, her eyes moving up and down his face.

"Nice to see you too, Mom. And yes, I'm really liking Boston so far." Hunter looked tenderly at his mother and genuinely grateful to see her. Laura Graham's warm and loving personality was something Hunter had clung to as a child, and in a way, it still brought him comfort. His father's workaholic nature—inherited from his grandfather—often left him uncomfortable and out of his element when they weren't at the office. Having his mother there as a buffer should make things go a lot more smoothly after such a drawn-out meeting.

Pulling out his chair to sit down, his father wrapped up a phone call and shifted his attention to the exchange between Hunter and his mom. For as long as Hunter could remember, his father never seemed fully present and was always taking calls, which had bothered him growing up—yet he often found himself doing the same now as an adult.

Over the years, the pressure of working for his family's development company had trickled into many of his past relationships, and he found himself just as distracted as his father. It was why his parents' marriage had eventually collapsed—and why Hunter himself never seemed to be able to make it work when he tried dating. He didn't let the idea bother him too much. There was plenty of time for him to find the right woman and settle down: *after* he nailed this project on the Cape and secured his position with the company.

"Have either of you two eaten here before?" Hunter asked, moving on from the curt nod his father greeted him with, in contrast to his mother's loving embrace.

"I haven't, but your mother said it was delicious." His father placed his menu on the table, reaching over to pick up his Old Fashioned and taking a sip. "I ordered one for you as well," he said, keeping his eyes down, studying the menu. "Figured you could use it."

Disregarding the remark, Hunter glanced at his mother. "Anything you recommend, Mom?" He located the second whiskey on the table and picked it up to take a sip. The rich bourbon flavor relaxed him while he scanned the menu. He couldn't stop replaying his father's insistence that he find a way to buy out this Lana woman. There was a promotion riding on this, so he needed to figure out the best way forward.

"The roasted short ribs are popular here, and I've personally enjoyed the papaya pork chops. I've also placed an order for an appetizer that I think you'll like," she told him.

"Sold on the ribs," Hunter said, closing the menu.

His father cleared his throat and looked evenly at both of

them. "You'll be proud to know that our son has finalized a location on the Cape for Boston's first big project," he cut in, turning to Hunter's mother.

Hunter eyed his father with a straight face, attempting to mask his confusion. He'd questioned Hunter's choice of Bluedale from the start, so why was he offering his praise now?

"That's wonderful, Hunter!" His mother beamed at him with pride. "Cape Cod is such a prime area to invest in. What's the project?"

Hunter enjoyed seeing how happy his mother looked at the news. Before he could respond, the waiter came over, took their order, and refreshed their waters. When they were alone again, he began: "It certainly is a prime area. The project is going to be an event venue, and it'll be a wonderful addition to the town of Bluedale. The property is located right on the water—it's an old inn that we're planning to transform—and even though the remodel will take some time, we're also adding a cruise line, which will start running much sooner."

"How amazing!" she said, looking at both of them with delight. "Phil, that sounds like the venue you opened out on Lake Erie with a cruise line. Wasn't that a big success?"

Hunter noticed his father's expression harden, and he wondered again if he regretted putting his son in charge of this job. "It was," was all he said.

"Well, I'm so proud of you. I know you'll do a fabulous job," his mother said.

Hunter met his father's irritated stare. "There're going to be a couple obstacles to get started, but it's nothing I can't handle."

"Obstacles?" his mother asked, as her expression shifted to worry. Hunter instantly regretted mentioning it, knowing he shouldn't bring up any work stress with her.

"It's nothing that can't be handled, and Hunter has been advised accordingly." His father picked up his drink as the waiter arrived with the appetizers. "Let's not get into that again."

Hunter couldn't stop his next words before they came out. "I'm not *getting into* it, Dad, but I do want to carefully consider how to approach the situation so there won't be any unnecessary tension or rumors spread in town. Bluedale needs to be excited about what we're going to offer, not pissed that we're trying to further push out one of their own."

"Hunter," his father said, as he shifted in his seat and placed his drink back down. "I can see you're too concerned already. A simple conversation with the owner will suffice. Our company should be the only thing you're worried about." His father glanced at his mom, whose eyes were wide as she listened. "Sorry to bring you into this business matter, Laura."

Hunter pushed his seat back. "Excuse me, I'm just going to use the bathroom."

He needed a minute to calm down and, besides, his father was right—his mother did not need to listen to any more of this.

Reaching the bathroom door, he paused. He knew he needed to stop letting his emotions get the best of him and keep his head in the business. Success for Graham Property Development was important to him, so he rolled the tension from his shoulders and mustered up the determination to ignore his concerns.

He had a job to do and big opportunities ahead of him. He would meet with the restaurant owner and find some way to make peace, present an offer, and move forward with their plans… he hoped.

"LEAVE it to you to pack like a kid going off to college," his mother said, shaking her head while they stood together in her building's parking garage early the next morning. Hunter closed the trunk with a grin. He'd been so busy scheduling contractors, checking on permits, and working with his team to prepare for construction that he'd hardly had time to pack, and knew he'd be heading straight to Cape Cod after the meeting with his father the day before. Throwing as much as he could into the trunk was about all he had time for.

"Doesn't everyone travel with their clothes shoved into laundry baskets?" He shrugged, making her giggle. "I couldn't find my other suitcases, so this will have to do."

"If you want to live out of laundry baskets for the summer, feel free."

"Don't worry, I'll put it all away in drawers once I get settled. I know it'll make you cringe if I don't."

Laughing harder, she looked at him with her familiar doting stare. "I'm so proud of you. I can't wait to see pictures of it all. And, Hunter"—she paused, holding his arm— "remember who you are. You know how your father is, and that is not who *you* are."

Hunter put his hand on top of his mother's. "I'm sorry you had to be in the middle of that discussion at dinner last night. I know it's hard enough for you to be around Dad, but making it worse with a heated business discussion doesn't help. It must bring back some unpleasant memories for you."

"Your father is who he is, and I'm okay with that. It's you I'm concerned about. Stand your ground, Hunter, and make decisions based on what *you* feel is best."

"Don't worry, Mom, I can handle Dad. His hard nature may have pushed you away—and understandably so—but I won't let him push me around too much." He winked at her and held his arms out.

His mother leaned into his hug. "You better get going. It's a holiday weekend so there's bound to be traffic."

"Thanks, Mom. Maybe you can get away for a few days and come see the area once the renovations at the venue are all complete. It's a really nice town."

"You know, I just might." She looked up at the sky that was beginning to awaken.

Hunter gave her a hug goodbye and got in the driver's seat, waving one last time as he backed out. His mother always saw him off when he came to stay, no matter how early it was. Checking the time, he figured he had about two hours until he could start his follow-up calls—starting with the port.

He'd remembered the port Simon had researched and given him information on, but he wouldn't need it—he'd accomplish that himself. This was his project, and his father needed to see him take the lead with all decisions. This was how he'd show that he was VP material. Simon had been after this position for a while now, even before the prior VP of Development had retired, and his father insisted he wouldn't favor family so they would both be considered—making tensions between them high. That didn't slow him down or worry him... too much. He just needed to stay focused and make sure this project was a success across the board. If that meant dealing with the restaurant owner next door, then that was what he'd do. Nothing would impede his progress.

The sunrise radiated a soft yellow light across the New York skyline behind him. Traffic was still light crossing the bridge as he exited the city. As he turned up the music, the fresh new day awaited him—and so did Bluedale.

CHAPTER 5

The nurse was laying another blanket over Lana's grandad when she walked into his room, holding a bouquet. The Sunday morning sun beamed brightly through the window, creating a peaceful glow while he slept.

"Good morning, Casey," Lana greeted his nurse, recognizing her instantly. She was newly assigned to her grandad's room, but since she spent so much time here, it wasn't hard to remember names.

"Hi, Lana," Casey said. "Going for a morning swim?" The nurse looked at her one-piece bathing suit and shorts.

"Planning on it. High tide is expected in about an hour. It's my favorite way to wake up."

"I might need to try that too sometime." The sunlight moved across Lana's grandad's weathered face. "It's looking to be a beautiful day. He's been having a good morning, so I'm thinking he might enjoy time outside once he wakes up."

Lana nodded. "His favorite place to be."

"I love those early summer white daisies." Casey looked at the flowers in Lana's hand.

"My wife's favorite." His familiar and fragile voice was barely above a whisper.

"Good morning, Mr. Kelly. I'll be right back with your meds."

"Which is why I got them for you." Lana went over and kissed his forehead. "How'd you sleep, Grandad?"

"Pretty well. I love a good nap, but waking up to see you here is even better."

Lana smiled affectionately at him before she took the vase that sat empty on the window ledge over to the sink and filled it with water. She put the daisies in the vase and brought them back to the ledge, catching sight of a bluebird that landed on a feeder box on the large tree just outside the window.

"I hope Casey takes you outside soon before it gets to be too hot. I know how much you like to watch the birds out in the garden." She moved to sit by her grandad and picked up his hand. She'd learned that holding his hand brought him comfort—always keeping them linked—even on the bad days when his mind drifted somewhere else.

Something shifted in his worn, blue eyes that still shone as serene as the ocean. She'd always loved that she looked like her mother, but she wished she had those same sapphire eyes as her dad and grandad. *Our eyes are like land and sea, Lana.* Her father's words shuffled through her mind, and she looked out the window, watching the bluebird fly away and swallowing a lump that had formed in her throat. Out of the corner of her eye, she noticed her grandad watching her silently.

"Your dad loved that great black-backed gull who came to be with us that summer. Don't you remember, Lana?" he asked, squeezing her hand as if he had read her thoughts.

"Of course," she whispered, trying to keep her composure. She'd prepared herself on the way over to be ready for this conversation, but it was becoming harder. His dementia made her feel like she was being robbed of a future with Grandad as it naturally unfolded, since they were always repeating the past. Of all the days for him to get stuck on, why did it have to be *that* day—the last one she'd had with her parents?

"I had a dream last night that you were an eleven-year-old girl again, and we had our arms stretched out toward that gull. Just like you did with your father. That gull was quite a brave one, always coming to you with such ease," he said, his gaze following the sunlight that sifted into the room from the window.

Shifting in her seat, Lana wasn't sure how to respond, so she quietly stared down at her grandad's hands in hers.

A soft knock on the door interrupted the silence. Casey poked her head through the doorway.

"Hello again," she said, pulling the med cart in and parking it on the other side of the bed. "After you take your pills, what do you say to a nice walk outside for a bit, Mr. Kelly?" Casey turned to face him, holding his medicine in a cup.

"That sounds like a great idea, Grandad. I better head home to get ready for my day of food prep at the restaurant anyway," Lana said. "But you enjoy your walk with Casey. I'll be back soon."

Grandad stared at her, not letting go of her hand. "Have you gotten out on the water yet, Lana?"

Casey gave him the cup, which released his grip, and Lana watched him take his pills, knowing exactly what he meant. One of the things he had come to completely forget was that ever since the accident with her parents, she'd never gone out on a boat again—and she didn't have the heart to remind him.

"Not yet, but the summer season has just begun. Plenty of

time still to get the pontoon out," she answered, ignoring the pang of guilt for her lie by omission.

"Well, get yourself out there, Lana girl. The water is where you're meant to be."

Lana felt the words sink right into her heart. Leaning over, she hugged him but didn't respond. Casey must have sensed her hesitation and immediately took over, helping him out of his bed and up to his walker.

"There you go, Mr. Kelly. Let's get you outside to enjoy this beautiful day," Casey said, throwing a small smile over her shoulder as she walked out of the room.

Outside, another bluebird sailed by Lana, and while she watched it land on the feeder box, all she could see was the bay. For a moment, she let herself imagine the feeling of drifting on the pontoon through clear, wide-open water. It was something she missed dearly—yet couldn't find the courage to face. Maybe one day...

SUNDAYS at the restaurant didn't slow down, but her week always began with a coffee and some donuts for her and Heidi. She decided to grab her weekly order first before heading home to grab her chef uniform she'd forgotten before she left earlier. The drive from the nursing home took longer than usual with all the extra tourists on the Cape for the holiday weekend, so she cranked up her music to give herself a reason to smile as she inched down Main Street toward the bakery.

When she finally arrived, she was pleasantly surprised to find the line was shorter than she'd expected. One of the clerks waved at her, holding up the box to show her they'd already started on her regular weekly order. Just as she stepped into the back of the line, a breeze brushed up against her and two male voices boomed through the door behind her.

When she turned around, she didn't recognize them as locals, nor did they look like tourists. They each wore black, short-sleeved work shirts, and when one stepped to the side to hold open the door for another customer, she read *Graham Property Development* on the back. They came over and stood directly behind her. Pressing her lips together, she turned and gave them a quick nod.

"Good morning, Lana," the clerk greeted her when she reached the counter. "Your donut order is all set. I filled the box with your favorites. Let me just grab your coffee. The usual?"

"Yes, please. Thank you," she said, noticing the two men stepping up to the other register beside her.

"Good morning!" their cashier greeted them, and she saw the manager make his way over to the counter, a normal gesture in a small town like Bluedale.

"New construction in town?" he asked, reaching out his hand. "My name's Joe. I'm the manager here."

"Yes," one of the men answered, shaking Joe's outstretched hand. "My name's Kevin and this is Steve. We work for Graham Property Development. Our company just bought the old inn over on Barrier Beach Boulevard."

Lana couldn't believe it. It had only been two days since she'd received the news, and the competition that had beaten her out for the inn was already in line with her at her favorite bakery.

Joe noticed Lana staring, but quickly looked back at the men. He didn't have to say anything, but she could imagine what he must be thinking. Many people in Bluedale had already found out what had happened.

"The new owners of the famous inn that Bluedale has

loved for so long?" Joe asked, sneaking another glance her way.

"Yes, that's what we've heard. Except we're going to be completely transforming it."

Lana froze. *Transforming it?*

"Oh yeah? What are the plans?" Joe asked. "You're not tearing it down, are you?"

"Well, not exactly. We're taking what the inn is now and expanding it into a brand-new event venue with updated suites on the second floor, including a bridal suite for weddings. I've heard they're also going to offer events on the water with a two-story cruise ship."

Lana clenched her jaw. *Two-story cruise ship?*

The manager whistled. "Wow! That sounds awfully ritzy. Seems like a shame to change everything up, though. Plenty of folks in this town like the inn just the way it's been for all these years." He quickly eyed Lana again with a look of sympathy. Lana nearly burst into tears right there. No part of the inn's legacy would be kept intact with a brand-new remodel. "They have you working on a holiday weekend?" Joe asked.

"Just some final things to prepare for the crew that's starting bright and early with us on Tuesday morning. You'll probably see more of us here soon—especially our boss. His name is Hunter."

Lana searched behind the counter for her barista, who was still working on her coffee. She couldn't bear to hear much more.

"I'll be sure to look out for him. A two-story cruise ship sounds impressive. How large is it?" the manager asked, and Lana held her breath.

"Not terribly big—maybe enough to hold a couple hundred passengers at most. I've only seen a few pictures of the inside, but it's not on the same scale as the cruise ships you see on the south side of the Cape," Kevin explained.

"Well, Bluedale may not be very large, but luckily the bay is vast enough to offer something like that. Good luck with the remodel." Joe walked away, and Lana wanted to cry, imagining her grandparents' beloved family-style inn completely changed into something so impersonal. How would she even begin to tell Grandad?

The clerk finally returned with her coffee, pulling her attention away from the men. "Here you go, Lana. Sorry for the wait. Enjoy!"

Lana forced a smile, thanking her again, and quickly made her way out.

Instead of the slow crawl through traffic again, she decided to leave her car and keep moving to shake off the shock of what she just heard. The short walk to her condo from the bakery felt good, helping to clear her mind. Little Sara was riding her tricycle around their shared driveway when she got back. She stopped to wave at Lana before continuing on with her mother.

The girl's innocence always touched Lana. She didn't have a care in the world as she pedaled up and down the driveway. Lana enjoyed Sara's enthusiasm for life and her uninhibited zest for learning new skills. Watching her with her mother always brought happy memories of her own mom. With all that was going on at the inn, she missed her mom more than ever.

The humidity was already settling in, and her condo felt stuffy when she opened the door. Clicking on the air conditioner, she went to the dryer where her freshly cleaned uniform was, and paused as the tears from the bakery burned her eyes again. This time, she let them fall as she stood there, feeling defeated. *Stay strong,* she reminded herself. This was no time to buckle.

CHAPTER 6

Hunter slid his sunglasses off as he stepped out of the car, and squinted against the midafternoon sun in the parking lot of the first restaurant he spotted in Bluedale—The Chowder House. After spending hours in the car, the slight breeze that rushed over his skin felt good. Summer finally felt like it was here, and being out of the city, standing next to the beautiful blue ocean, was a good start to this new adventure.

Heading over to the boardwalk, soaking in the salty air, he enjoyed the flawless scenery. Children were squealing with delight as they ran from each wave that crashed ashore, with protective parents standing nearby. The child in him wanted to kick off his shoes and run out there with them, but the smell of buttery fried seafood that drifted past him brought his focus back to The Chowder House and his grumbling stomach.

It was packed when he got inside, which wasn't a surprise for Memorial Day weekend. Most people were tanned from hours on the beach, relaxed, and enjoying what the Cape was known for—seafood. His mouth watered when he saw today's specials of lobster rolls or crab cakes.

He spotted an empty stool at the bar, so he squeezed his way through the crowd of people waiting for tables and made his way over to it. "Is this seat taken?" Hunter called over the laughter and noise to the couple next to the chair. When they offered it up, he sat down.

The bartender acknowledged him with a nod, and after finishing the drink order he was working on, he came over and handed Hunter a menu.

"I already know what I want." He gave the man his order of clam chowder, the lobster roll special, and a cold summer ale.

A few minutes later, the bartender came back with a filled pint glass and placed it down before leaning over. "Here for business?"

Hunter laughed. "Is it that obvious?"

"Well, the clothes gave it away." The bartender cast his eyes up and down, pointing out Hunter's light-colored pants and polo shirt.

With amusement in his eyes, Hunter took a sip of his beer. "Okay, you got me there."

"I'm just messing with you, but I'm pretty familiar with the locals, and all the tourists are usually in beach attire. What brings you to Bluedale?"

"My company just bought the old inn off Barrier Beach Boulevard. I'm here for the summer to plan for the extension and conversion we're doing to it, transforming it into an event venue."

The bartender's eyes widened. "That sounds like a big project. A little fancy for Bluedale," he said, pulling out two new glasses and preparing a couple of cocktails for other patrons. "Have you met Lana Kelly then?" He poured vodka and a mixer into the shaker as a waitress reached around him to hand Hunter his chowder.

"No, I haven't." He picked up a spoon and stirred the soup, shifting in his seat at the mention of Lana.

"Well, you should. She owns On the Bay, right next door to where your venue will be. One of the best seafood chefs on the Cape, in my opinion." He gave the drink mixture a shake and carefully poured it out into the glasses.

Hunter took a large swig of his beer. "Yeah, I heard about the restaurant. Looking forward to meeting her."

"Rumor in town is she wanted to buy the inn," he said, placing the drinks on a tray for a waiter to take to a table before pulling out more glasses to fill. "Well, buy it back, that is."

Hunter nervously brought the chowder to his lips, unsure how to respond. He didn't know how well this bartender knew Lana, but it was a small town and people talk. The last thing he needed was everyone thinking he didn't care about her feelings when it came to her family's old inn.

"I heard about that as well," he said, hoping that was enough to stay neutral and end the conversation.

"Kind of sad." The bartender filled the shaker with ice, rum, and lime juice, and vigorously shook it again before pouring the cold drink into glasses. Topping it off with club soda and garnishing with mint, he handed the drinks off. "Nothing like a cold mojito after a hot summer day."

"Yeah, those looked good," Hunter said, watching another waiter take them away. "What did you mean it's sad?"

"Oh, right, Lana's inn." He quickly bent down, pulling out some beers. "Just meant it's sad she won't get to have the inn again. Her grandparents ran it for decades. It was a hit, especially when her grandma was still alive. I swear, that woman made the absolute best clam chowder in the world. Much better than what you have in front of you, but don't tell the manager." The man laughed. "I remember going there for a bowl every week as a kid with my parents. The whole town is still waiting on Lana to serve that family recipe at her restaurant. Not sure why she hasn't."

"Sorry to hear her grandma passed." Hunter picked up his beer again, feeling worse by the second listening to her backstory. It took willpower not to chug the rest of the glass down.

"Yeah, it had to be tough. Especially after losing her parents." He walked down the bar, handed a seated couple their beers before returning to Hunter, and noticed his was getting low. "Another?"

Hunter nodded. "Don't worry about a glass. I'll take it in the bottle. You said after she lost her parents?" A waiter appeared next to him with his lobster roll.

Pulling out another beer, the bartender popped it open and slid it toward him. "They passed away a long time ago, followed by her grandma a short time later. Now it's just her and her grandad left. He's struggling with his health in a nursing home, though, so perhaps owning the inn would've been too much while trying to run her restaurant and care for him." A few more people came up to the bar and flagged him down. "I better get to them. Good luck with Lana if you do meet her. You might need it." He wiped his hands on a towel. "And enjoy Bluedale!"

Hunter wanted to pull the bartender back and ask him what he meant, but he was slammed with customers and Hunter didn't want to make his job any harder. The warning still wasn't sitting well with him when he took his first bite of the lobster roll, hardly noticing how delicious it was. As he continued to eat, he listened to the easy conversation all around him and began to relax.

Maybe this Lana Kelly had a strong personality—that was nothing he hadn't dealt with before in this line of business.

He'd just need to win her over by hanging an irresistible offer in front of her.

AN HOUR LATER, Hunter pulled into the white cobblestone driveway of the one-bedroom cottage his company had rented for his stay this summer. It sat adjacent to the main house, about a half a mile from the beach, and was surrounded by trees. It was the perfect place to be for a summer project.

The main house was Cape Cod's classic English-style, one-story home, painted neutral gray to mimic the weathered wood look that he noticed was a popular color for most of the homes he passed on his drive in. The gardens surrounding the property were clean and simple, but filled with a mixture of bright-blue hydrangeas and pink climbing roses along the sides of the home to offset the gray.

An older woman came out from the back of the main house, her short, gray hair tied up off her neck. She wore a friendly smile as she pulled off a pair of gardening gloves. Hunter turned the car off and got out, waving hello. "Are you Mrs. Huxley?"

"I sure am, and please call me Margaret. Hunter Graham?"

"Yes, that's me. What a beautiful property you have." Hunter gestured at the gorgeous landscape.

Margaret's face lit up at his compliment. "Thank you so much for your kind words. My gardens are my favorite pastime."

"Well, it certainly shows." He admired a row of gardenias.

"Let's get you to your cottage so you can settle in."

Hunter followed the woman to the back of the house, and the same white cobblestone walkway brought them to a firepit encircled by Adirondack chairs. Another small pathway led to what looked to be the cottage.

"You'll be staying over there." Margaret pointed to the cottage. "And as you can see, the firepit has pathways to both houses, so please, feel free to use it. At my age, I'm typically in bed by the time the sun goes down anyway, so you won't see me out here much after dinner."

"This is all wonderful, Margaret. Thank you. Being by a fire during the summer nights sounds so relaxing." Hunter stopped when he caught sight of a glimmer of blue through the trees. "Wow, I can see a tiny bit of the ocean from back here."

"The property is positioned just right to catch a glimpse of it." She put her hands on her hips and squinted toward the trees. Then, with a smile, she continued, "Shall we?" She led him to the cottage, pulling her keys out to unlock the front door. "And wait until you see the view from your bedroom."

"I can't wait." Hunter already felt like he was on vacation, rather than working.

Margaret opened the door and grabbed a set of keys that hung on the wall, handing them to Hunter. "These are yours, but there's also a digital alarm for the place. You can set your own code and, after your stay, I'll reset it for the next person. The instructions to do that are on the kitchen counter."

Hunter took the keys. "Thank you. I'll have to remember the alarm when I take my early morning runs."

She shut the door behind them. "You'll love running here. If you follow this street to the end, you'll reach the ocean. There's a boardwalk alongside the beach. It's a lot sunnier than these shaded streets."

Hunter walked into the space. The first thing he noticed was how impeccably clean and uncluttered it was for such a small cottage. Instantly feeling right at home with the large, blue sofa that sat in front of a fireplace with a flatscreen TV above it, all he wanted to do was kick off his shoes and settle in. The interior walls and crown molding were painted white against dark-stained wooden floors. Curtain panels of navy blue matched the couch, and the room displayed all kinds of wooden beach decor, with a rustic style to it, giving the atmosphere warm coastal vibes. Just on the other side of the living room was a kitchenette with white cabinets, a small dishwasher and oven, a microwave, and an under-cabinet refrigerator.

Margaret took a step back. "I'm off to finish tending to the vegetable garden. Your company already paid for June through August and sent over the paperwork, so you're all set to settle right in."

"Great. Thank you again for providing such a beautiful place for me to stay while I'm here for the summer."

"Bluedale is a wonderful place to have to be for business," Margaret said with a smile, stopping at the door. "What kind of work brought you here?"

"My company bought the inn over on Barrier Beach Boulevard. We're remodeling it into an event venue."

"Oh…" Margaret's smile quickly faded. "I see. Well, I'm off. Let me know if you need anything."

Hunter watched her leave. After learning all he had from the bartender, he wasn't surprised by Margaret's reaction. Simon had been right to think that the town would be on Lana's side, sympathizing with her over having lost the inn. That made it all the more important that he find a way to win her over. Once he got her on board, everyone else would surely follow.

He made his way upstairs to the tiny bedroom with adjoining bathroom. He was impressed when he saw a king-sized bed fit in the room. Putting his bag down, he lay flat on his back, facing the ceiling. *This will be a good summer.* He was already thinking about changing out of his long pants and into shorts and taking a walk when his phone buzzed in his pocket.

A text from his father:

> Give me a call when you get to the cottage.

Propping himself up on his elbow, he tapped to open a video call.

"I assume you made it okay?" His father's face appeared on the screen.

"Yeah, I'm here now in my bedroom. It's a great little place. I'm looking forward to scoping out Bluedale and other parts of the Cape this summer. You'll be impressed with this town."

"I do anticipate getting there in about a month to check on progress," his father said, ignoring his remarks about Bluedale. "Anyway, I wasn't actually calling about your accommodations, but to let you know that our lead surveyor, Kevin, just called."

"Yeah, he and another surveyor were out on the property earlier. I had them on the list to check in with today."

"Well, since it's the weekend and both of our offices are closed, he just tried reaching you, and when he couldn't get ahold of you, he called me to see if I happen to have the most recent specs on the layout of the land."

"Sorry he bothered you. I have a copy; I'll send it to him." Hunter swiped up and saw the missed call from Kevin, which must have come through when he was talking to Margaret.

"Don't apologize, just be more available," his father said.

Hunter drew in a breath to keep his patience.

"Anyway, he's planning on talking to Lana Kelly shortly."

Hunter sat up fully on the edge of the bed. "He is?"

"Yes. He has a question about the property divide on the

beach. He did leave a message with the town last week about it, but he's still waiting on them to return the call."

"If you saw the town, you'd understand why. It's rather… quaint. I'll bet they have odd business hours."

"Great," his father said dryly. "That'll make this job more interesting for you."

"It just has a sleepy beach feeling, is all. But that doesn't worry me." As soon as he said it, he remembered the bartender's words: *A little fancy for Bluedale.* Despite the confidence he displayed to his father, their plans suddenly felt a bit too extravagant.

"Hope it's not too sleepy for our venue," his father said. "And if those property lines on the beach are too tight, buying out the restaurant's side really will make this a better investment. Anyway, just give Kevin a call when you have a chance to send him over those specs. Also…" Hunter heard a sigh through the phone. "He shared that he's been hearing around town that this inn was very well loved when the Kelly family owned it. So you might be right about how hard it will be to convince this Lana Kelly to sell. Just get it over and done with."

If only you'd listened to me before. Hunter kept his thoughts to himself, not ready to start another argument. After they hung up, Hunter stood and walked over to the double French doors in the bedroom and opened them, stepping out onto a small deck with one chair. The view was even better from up there, just like Margaret had said, and for a minute he watched the small specks of sunlight dance off the water. Pulling his phone back out, he looked up the number for On the Bay and hit call, before sitting down to get comfortable. *Might as well get this over with.*

CHAPTER 7

*L*ana dipped down under the surface, and the greenish-blue water wrapped around her as she glided forward. Coming up for air, she slowed down, letting the moving current of high tide carry her. One last dive under before she called it quits. The muffled underwater noises drowned out her thoughts, making it a perfect break before she did her Sunday food prep.

Swimming laps was a habit she'd begun in high school when she felt stressed, and the bay offered much calmer waves for longer swims—which she needed after the encounter she'd just had with Graham Property Development at the bakery.

Wading back onto shore, she picked up her towel and wiped her face before drying herself off. Even though she wanted to know who'd made the other offer, she wished she'd never eavesdropped on that conversation in the bakery because she hadn't been able to get it off her mind since.

The laps helped perk her up a bit—enough to get back in the kitchen at least. Wrapping the towel around her waist, she walked back to the restaurant to change before dinner prep, and the comfort of the hot afternoon sun blanketed her shoulders, soothing her. Just as her mind was able to put the morning behind her, a man appeared just ahead, waving at her.

Lana shielded her eyes to get a better look, but she didn't know him. As he got closer, she noticed the black shirt—the same one from the bakery earlier—and stopped walking. She closed her eyes briefly to steady her nerves. "Graham Property Development," she whispered out loud, realizing it was one of the men she'd seen while standing in line at the bakery.

When the man got close enough, he waved again. "Hello there," he greeted her, but stopped when he noticed her standoffish demeanor. "I, um, noticed you swimming, and I wanted to see if you had any idea how to reach the owner of On the Bay right over there?" He pointed behind him toward her restaurant as she continued to watch him in silence. "I think they're closed."

Lana realized how rude she was being, but she couldn't believe she had to have two encounters in one day with this company. "I'm sorry, you caught me deep in thought," she lied, in an attempt to be more amiable. "My name is Lana and I'm actually the owner. We're open on Sundays for dinner, but I was just taking a swim before I get in the kitchen."

The man stepped closer. "Oh, well, it's a nice day for a swim. My name is Kevin," he said, reaching out his hand.

"Nice to meet you, Kevin." Lana took his hand with a dubious look, feeling unsure of what he was going to say next.

"I'm the surveyor for Graham Property Development. We just bought—"

"The inn," Lana cut him off, feeling her patience waver with the mention of the inn. So much for the recharge from her swim.

"Yes, that's right." He paused, his eyebrows rising as her stare bored into him. "We're the ones giving it a much-needed facelift."

Lana caught her breath, trying to swallow past the sting from his words. *Facelift?* They weren't giving the inn a facelift—they were converting it into something unrecognizable. Complete with a cruise ship.

"It's sounds to me like you have a completely new business model." Lana tightened her towel around her with defiance, her heart beating against her growing irritation.

Kevin narrowed his eyes. "Yes, well, my bosses are the ones making those decisions. I just have a quick question about the exact property lines on the beach. I called the assessor's office a few days ago, but still haven't heard back."

It was a rather simple question, but it left her with loaded feelings. From the expression Kevin gave her, it was clear he didn't care how she viewed their project. Annoyance gave way to full frustration, and while a part of her wanted to unload it all on him, she had a small clambake party booked tonight to prepare for, so she needed to just wrap this up. Besides, what could this surveyor say to make it easier anyway?

"See the tall sea grass just over there?" She pointed, and the man turned to follow her instruction. "It's just past my patio and down a bit. I know it's not very much of a dividing line, but that's what it is."

Kevin nodded. "Okay, that clears up that question. And I'm guessing it just splits right down to the water?"

"Yes." Lana pointed again to the area where her rock pits were used for the clambakes. "My beach space is rather small next to yours. It's just over there where we offer clambake parties."

"I see." Kevin observed her setup for a moment. "Thank

you for your time." He nodded and turned to walk away, leaving her to quickly make her way back to the restaurant.

Flicking the lights on inside her office, Lana put the towel down and changed into her uniform, before taking one of the bakery's summer specialties from its box—a lemon-glazed and cream-filled donut. She checked the restaurant's voicemail and took a bite, the sweet citrus awakening her senses as she jotted down a note from one of their vendors, confirming that they could switch an order she'd placed. Just as she was about to bite into the donut once more, she stopped short at the next message.

"This message is for the owner, Lana Kelly. My name is Hunter Graham of Graham Property Development. As the new owners of the building next door, I'd like to schedule a time to discuss the new developments and get acquainted. I look forward to meeting you in person."

Lana went still, completely missing his number, and had to torture herself through the message again to write it down. She just couldn't escape this nightmare today. She sat back, staring at the phone number. He sounded so calm about everything, which felt like a punch to the stomach. Did he not know or not care that this inn meant everything to her? *It's not his responsibility to worry about that,* she thought, looking up at the ceiling with a sigh. He hadn't done anything wrong, no matter how personal this felt.

For a second, she considered ripping up the paper with his number and tossing it, but she remembered what she'd said to Alicia the day before about not wanting unnecessary tension between them, and forced herself to calm down. Putting the paper down on her desk, she walked out to the kitchen. Hunter Graham would get to meet her all right, but she knew she needed to have the right words to convey what was in her heart.

Lana pulled out the bowl of clams from the dig that hadn't been used for the party on Friday night and began to check them. It was the last day she could use this batch, and luckily tonight's clambake was small—only eight people—and there were plenty of clams to use. Discarding the few that looked dead, she covered the rest and refilled the second bowl with fresh ice underneath, before putting them back in the fridge.

Heidi was gathering the rockweed again and making a lobster run early this afternoon, so Lana had more time to prepare. Pulling her hair back, she secured her long waves before beginning. The kitchen once again came to her rescue with a perfectly timed distraction. She began with the cherry tomato basil sauce over scallops and chopped the onion, garlic, and fresh basil before moving on to the pistachio-crusted salmon. Turning on a handheld blender, she started to pulse the pistachios, grinding them faster than necessary.

The more she thought about Hunter Graham's message, the angrier she got. Shaking her head, she clicked off the blender and added ground Dijon mustard and maple syrup to the pistachios for the sticky coating. The mixture was thick and difficult to stir, but she was grateful for a task that took some arm strength, burning off the irritation that just kept building.

This developer might want to create an elegant new event venue, but the inn had its stakes here for decades with her grandparents, bringing people years of enjoyment with Bluedale traditions and a warm friendly atmosphere—which was exactly what she'd wanted to save. How could he possibly compete with that?

Wiping her brow with a towel, she went over to the thermostat before she got started on the mango panna cottas for tonight's dessert special and switched the air conditioning on to cool the kitchen down. Footsteps outside caught her attention.

"Lana? You in there?" a male voice called from the doorway.

"Hey, Rob!" Lana pulled out the milk and heavy cream from the fridge.

Robert, one of her fish suppliers, came into the kitchen. "It's a hot one today. Summer is in full swing now." He placed a large ice cooler on the floor next to her. "Here you go. Fresh scallops from the dock right to your door. They've been on ice for a bit, so they should be ready to open."

"Thanks! Just in time," she said, bending down to get a saucepan to make the cream layer for the dessert.

"Okay, well, I'm off," he said, starting toward the door. "Hey, listen, I know this may not be the best time to say this, but I wanted to let you know how sorry I am that you didn't get to buy the inn back."

"I see the news has trickled to you now?" Lana peeked up at him, noticing the concern on his face, and measured out the sugar, cream, and milk into the pan. "Don't worry, I'll be okay. You know me. I'll carry on."

"That's what I'm worried about."

Lana stopped and turned from the dessert mixture. "What do you mean?"

"Just don't want you hiding behind your food back here. Bluedale is here for you, Lana. Don't forget that. Whoever bought that inn has big shoes to fill."

"Thank you, Rob. That means a lot." She wanted to press him further about what he meant, but she needed to finish her dinner prep. The clock was ticking. "I better get back to the food prep."

"I'll leave you to it. But I'll be back Monday with your other salmon order."

"Great, thank you. See you then," Lana called over her shoulder.

A quick check of the time told Lana it was a little past two. She was making good time, so she finished the cream mixture and put it over heat, moving on to marinate the scallops while she waited for it to boil. After opening, washing, and removing the scallops from their shells, she stored them in a container in the fridge.

Continuing the dessert prep, she kept her focus on the task at hand, trying hard to ignore the phone call from Hunter Graham that she needed to respond to soon. Cooking had a beautiful way of freeing her mind from the present moment, but she couldn't shake off what Rob had just said. She didn't *hide* behind her food, she just poured herself into it. There was nothing wrong with that, was there? Surely it was good to have an outlet that brought her a sense of peace. Cooking had always provided that for her. And so did the ocean. *The water is where you're meant to be...* Her grandad's words echoed in her ear. Brushing away a sweat-plastered piece of hair that fell down the side of her face, she pushed her focus back to her work. Whatever relief cooking brought was surely needed.

An hour later, the fridge was lined with mango panna cottas in dessert cups, next to three freshly made blueberry cheesecakes, and she pulled open the freezer door to make sure she had plenty of sorbet, popcorn shrimp, and chicken tenders for the kids' menu.

The door to the kitchen opened again, and this time Heidi came in, holding a large Styrofoam container.

"The lobsters and rockweed have arrived!" She placed it on the counter. "Please tell me ten lobsters are enough. Tonight's group is small, correct?"

Lana nodded.

"And I also grabbed us both some late lunch because I know you're probably running on coffee alone."

"And a donut. They're in my office." She smiled at Heidi. "What would I do without you?"

"Starve. Which would be a really ironic way for a chef to die." Heidi winked at her. "The lunch is in my car. I'll go grab it."

"I'll get it," she offered. "Some fresh air would do me good."

"The sandwiches are in a bag on my front seat. I got chicken salad."

"Sounds delicious," Lana said, wiping her hands on a towel and reaching for the door.

"You go ahead and get started. I'm going to get these lobsters on ice, and then I'll join you out on the patio."

It felt anything but fresh when she walked outside as the hot, muggy air instantly pressed against her face. Retrieving the bag from Heidi's car, Lana moved slowly from the parking lot to the patio, and the frustration she'd been able to ignore while cooking began to mount again. Everything she had encountered in one day with Graham Property Development, particularly Hunter's voicemail, felt more oppressive than the heat.

Her entire childhood was vanishing with this event venue —and she worried she might disappear alongside it. More importantly, she'd lost the chance to give her grandad back something he could still clearly remember when everything else that had mattered to him was fading into forgotten memories.

Voices next door pulled her out of her thoughts, and she put the sandwiches down on a table, walking back to the parking lot to see what was happening. A truck labeled Bluedale Building & Remodeling and a black SUV with a

New York license plate were parked on the edge of the lot. Lana shook her head. *They're sure moving fast.*

"Lana? What are you doing?" Heidi called by the side door, shielding her face with her hand against the sun.

Lana jumped, realizing how silly she must look spying on the new neighbors. "Nothing. I thought I heard a funny noise back here." It was the fastest excuse she could think of.

Back at the table, they put up the umbrella. She tried to forget about the construction next door and dove into the sandwich.

"It's amazing that you feed dozens of people weekly, yet you often exclude yourself." Heidi gave her a playful look.

"I get so engrossed in my cooking that I don't realize how much time has passed." Lana shrugged, even though she knew Heidi was right. What she'd really been consumed with the past few weeks was waiting on the call from the bank, all while juggling the restaurant and taking care of her grandad. Taking any time for herself seemed harder and harder.

After a few more bites, Heidi put her sandwich down. "I saw the vehicles pull in behind me when I got here. Is that what you were looking at?" she asked with concern.

"Yes," Lana admitted.

"You must feel terrible seeing that. I'm sorry that we haven't had the chance to talk about it since you found out."

Biting her lip, she cast her eyes down to the table, trying to hide her disappointment. She didn't want Heidi worrying about her. "Oh, I'm fine. I was just curious, is all. Looks like they're getting right to it."

Heidi nodded but didn't look convinced. "It doesn't matter what they're reconstructing over there. You have something they don't—a lifelong reputation here in Bluedale," she reminded Lana, reaching over and giving her a reassuring pat on the arm. "I think the residents who have known your family will remember what you did there and how special it was. Can't build over that, no matter how hard they try."

Lana stared down at her half-eaten sandwich, taking in what Heidi had just said and remembering her conversation with Alicia the other day. *You are known and loved all over this town...* She smiled, looking back up at Heidi.

"What are you smiling about?" Heidi asked.

"Oh, just that my two closest friends think alike. Alicia said something similar. She even has a 'plan.'" Lana smiled. "Though she refuses to tell me what it is yet."

"Well, from what I've learned about Alicia, she's amazing in a pinch and her plans are usually pretty good," Heidi said.

"Yes, they are. Remember that day you walked by and saw the restaurant in shambles with the original design I had?"

Heidi nodded, bursting into laughter. "How could I forget? I saw the sign: 'On the Bay Coming Soon. Outdoor seafood by the water. Now hiring.' And I thought, 'Wow, this is perfect!' Until I walked in, and you had bright-blue paint all in your hair and were nearly in tears. I needed to put my shades on it was so vibrant."

Lana put her hand up, stifling a grin. "Okay, in my defense, I was trying to capture the ocean vibes!"

"You brought the entire ocean onto your walls! My favorite part was Alicia coming around the corner with her jaw dropped, yelling, 'Lana, this is not a color to stimulate the appetite!'"

Both women erupted into more laughter.

"Once we nailed the colors, Nathan got On the Bay launched all around town faster than I put the first menu together. So, whatever her idea is, I'm sure it'll be good," Lana said, picking up her sandwich.

"Based on the fact that Alicia and I have the same train of thought, I bet she's going to somehow utilize your upbringing and the fact that you're a Bluedale native."

Lana chewed her food quietly, thinking about Heidi's suggestion. She had a point. It was certainly the first thing Alicia pointed out. But what could that do to help her restaurant grow?

The men's voices from next door got louder for a moment, and Lana glanced over her shoulder. "Wait until you see what they're going to do," Lana said, looking back at Heidi.

"I'll be here for you, whatever happens," Heidi assured her. "Come on, let's finish our lunch, get out of this heat, and do the rest of our prep. If we just keep our focus on what we're doing over here, what they're doing next door won't matter."

As Lana followed Heidi inside, she wasn't so sure it would be that simple.

AFTER SHE'D GONE HOME to wash up, Lana returned to the restaurant an hour before the customers were due to arrive. A few of the guests for the clambake were sitting on the patio, enjoying the sunset. She gave them a wave and ducked into her office before it was time to fire up the pit.

When she put her bag down in her office, the note with Hunter Graham's number was the first thing she saw on her desk. Holding her breath, she picked it up. With all the prep she and Heidi had done earlier, there wasn't too much left to do besides start the clambake, and that didn't take much time. No better time than the present to get this phone call out of the way, especially since she had the excuse of dinner hour to keep the call short.

She dialed the number, and her heartbeat picked up its pace with each ring as she leaned against her desk. Willing herself to calm down, she nearly dropped the phone when he answered.

"Hello? This is Hunter Graham."

"Hunter, hi, this is Lana Kelly."

"Hi, Lana, thank you for calling me back," he replied, his tone softening. Something in his gentle voice relaxed her nerves slightly.

"I hear we're going to be neighbors now." It was all she could think of to say.

"Yes, we are, which is the reason I called you. I'd really like to meet up and talk in person about that. Would you be free any time this week to get together?"

Lana stayed silent for a moment too long. Even though she knew from his voicemail that he would ask her this, she still felt unsure and really didn't see the point.

"I want to make sure we start off on the right foot, seeing that we're in such close proximity," he continued.

His voice—not harsh or demanding, the way she'd imagined the big development company who'd swooped in and pulled her dream out from under her—distracted her from all the reasons she wanted to say no.

As Hunter patiently waited for her to answer, she knew there was no possible way to avoid him and all that was happening right outside her window. And what better way to avoid unnecessary tension than to meet Hunter face-to-face? "A meeting would be great. Thank you for such a kind gesture."

"Well, from what I've researched here in Bluedale, it's a tight-knit community. It's clear that you're well respected here. Let me buy you coffee. It's the least I can do with all the loud construction that's coming." Hunter chuckled.

Let me be the one to buy the inn and we will get along famously. She bit her lip so the words didn't slip right out. "Tomorrow's out because of the busy Memorial Day we're expected to have. I'm free Tuesday morning, though. It's my slowest day here at the restaurant. Does eleven o'clock work for you?"

"Works great for me. Where shall we meet?" he asked.

"How about Bluedale Bakery. They have the best coffee."

"Bluedale Bakery it is. Looking forward to it."

Lana hung up the phone, the mellow baritone of his voice echoing in her mind. He didn't sound like a dream-crushing monster at all, yet her heart still felt mangled by the recent turn of events.

Hunter might want them to get off on the right foot, but would his grandiose plans offer him the same start with the rest of Bluedale?

CHAPTER 8

The day dawned crisp and clear after a night of thunderstorms. The ocean stretched in an endless horizon as Hunter slowed his pace, soaking in the view. A thin layer of sweat covered the nape of his neck, sending a chill down his back against the lighter air that the storms had ushered in overnight. With lower humidity, it was shaping up to be a perfect beach day.

Hunter increased his speed again, turning away from the boardwalk and heading back to the roads leading up to the cottage. As he ran faster, the things he wanted to say to Lana circled around in his mind, repeating in a constant loop. After a relaxing Memorial Day, eating lunch at a little waterfront bistro in Chatham, and shopping to add to his selection of cooler work attire, he was ready for the renovations to begin and his meeting with Lana to be over with.

Pacing himself up a small incline, his footsteps ground against the loose gravel with even speed for the final stretch of his run. He enjoyed his early jogs in Boston, but out here in Bluedale, without the rush of people around him, he escaped deeper into each stride, letting all his stress go. His position in his father's company was something he truly loved and wanted to continue to grow, but sometimes the weight of his responsibilities sat heavy on his shoulders—like today. His meeting with Lana had kept him from sleeping soundly the night before and, much earlier than usual, he'd finally relented and laced up his running shoes just before the sun peeked into the sky.

Slowing to a walk, he turned into the driveway, waving at Margaret, who was up and already crouched in her rose bushes pulling weeds. "Beautiful morning!" he called out to her.

"It sure is! Hope you had a good run." Margaret tossed more weeds into the growing pile behind her.

"The best! Can't beat running out here." He threw her another small wave before he disappeared down the short walkway to his cottage. To his relief, she seemed relaxed enough with him, despite her initial reaction to finding out he was the one who'd bought the inn.

Making his way inside and to the bathroom, he turned on the shower, grabbing his phone to check his messages while the water warmed up. The only one he had was a text from the lead carpenter telling him that he was there with the sewer company, and that he had the estimate for the additional septic tank they'd need. He quickly replied, telling him he'd be there early that afternoon. He hadn't mentioned to his crew that he was meeting with Lana and decided not to say anything just yet, especially to the local subcontractors they'd hired, who he had come to assume most likely knew her.

Once he was showered and dressed comfortably for the heat, he headed to the kitchen. The fridge and pantry were completely empty, and he was starving. His meeting with Lana wasn't until eleven, so he grabbed his keys to get some breakfast in town. Making a mental note to pick up groceries on the way home later that day, he did a quick search of places that served breakfast, chose one, and plugged it into his GPS.

Minutes later, he pulled into the parking lot of Bluedale's local diner, snatching the last open spot. The diner must be a popular choice this morning, which surprised him considering how fast and easy it was to get there. There was light traffic nor dozens of lights to get through—just a simple drive. It had been nice to actually enjoy the scenery, but it brought some worry. The venue needed steady traffic. It made him even more determined to win Lana over. The town was a pretty small market to begin with—he couldn't afford to alienate anyone. He got to the door and held it open for an older couple who were leaving.

The crowd gathered near the hostess station was so large that there was hardly any room to make his way through to put his name in. No wonder there weren't many cars on the road. . .everyone was already here at the diner.

"How many?" the hostess asked when he finally reached her.

"Just me," Hunter answered, looking around at everyone waiting. "This place must be a favorite to be so busy on a Tuesday morning."

"That's right! Welcome to summer on the Cape!" she said, giving him a friendly smile. Seeing so many people inside the diner helped him to relax more, and he was reminded that it wasn't just locals who came through the area. Tourists flocked to the Cape too, and surely some of them would have events they'd want to celebrate in a classy, modern venue.

After giving his name, he turned to go back outside and wait until his table was ready, since there was nowhere to stand comfortably inside. When he did, he collided with a sea of red curls.

"I'm so sorry, I didn't mean to bump into you," Hunter

said, his eyes darting to the floor, where a book the woman had been carrying had fallen.

"No, it was my fault. I wasn't paying attention," the woman explained as he picked up her book.

He straightened back up. "Here's your…" He trailed off, finding himself struck by eyes as green as summer leaves next to long, auburn waves that tumbled all around the woman's face. Her crescent-shaped eyebrows lifted slightly when he spoke, as if his voice had jogged something for her, but she seemed to dismiss whatever had crossed her mind, which only heightened his curiosity.

"Book?" When she gestured to it, he realized that he was still holding onto it.

"Yes, sorry." He handed it to her, yet was still unable to pull himself away from her eyes.

"Table for Lana Kelly!" the hostess called out from behind.

"That's me," she answered over her shoulder, shifting away from him.

"Lana Kelly?" Hunter asked, touching her arm.

"Yes," she said, curiously tilting her head.

"I'm Hunter Graham," he told her.

She blinked, clearly surprised. "Oh… Hunter, hi." Lana fumbled with her words, looking suddenly uneasy.

"Sorry to have bumped into you this way. I was just grabbing something to eat before our meeting."

She nodded but didn't seem to know what else to say.

"Looks like half the town had the same idea. Busy place." The crowd had only gotten bigger since he'd arrived.

"It's always like this once Memorial Day comes and goes." Lana started to turn toward the hostess, who impatiently called her name again. Holding her hand up to let the hostess know she was still there, she looked back at him. "Let's free up a table for someone else. I've requested an outside table that I'm sure has plenty of room for both of us. Would you like to join me and start our meeting early?"

Hunter smiled, momentarily forgetting the reason he'd called for their meeting to begin with and the offer that loomed over his head that he was supposed to present her. He couldn't help it, though—the way she chewed her lip as she waited for his response charmed him. "Of course I'll join you. Thank you for the invite."

The hostess brought them outside to a wide deck and led them to their table, which overlooked the sweeping views of the coastal wetlands that led to the ocean.

"Wow, I didn't expect this view in a diner." Hunter gestured toward the salty marsh, admiring the light that sharply bounced off the winding bodies of dark water within the tall grass.

"Yeah, the view is one of the main draws for me. It's one of the most beautiful spots on the Cape, where the land meets the sea. But also, the food is really good." Lana opened her menu just as the waitress approached them.

"Good morning! How about some drinks to start?" The waitress pulled out her pad and pencil.

"Well, I saw fresh-squeezed orange juice on a sign up near the hostess station, so I'll try that. And a coffee please," Hunter said.

"Same for me," Lana added. The waitress dashed off, and Hunter looked out to the marsh again.

"What's the wooden bridge over there for?" he asked, pointing to it.

"That's part of the sandy walk through the marsh that runs parallel to the beach. It's a long way, though, so have some sneakers on if you decide to try it." Lana peered down at his feet. "I'm not sure those fancy loafers will hold up." She glanced at him before turning her attention back to the menu, her expression still closed off.

"Well, it's a good thing I brought my sneakers then." Hunter swallowed, scanning the food options and feeling his nerves pick up against the awkwardness.

Lana didn't answer, but continued to read the menu for another couple minutes before placing it back down. He wasn't sure where to even begin this conversation, despite spending his entire morning run going over what he wanted to say, which truly surprised him. He'd had conversations like this before, on previous projects, but somehow, this time felt different. As he sat there at a loss for words, he realized that it wasn't the situation that rattled him, but rather her. He'd forgotten all of his points as he sat there watching her hold tightly to her defensive body language, yet something sparked in her eyes underneath her guarded expression. He wanted to learn more about her, rather than just the fact that she was a chef.

The waitress came over, put their drinks down, and took his order first. When she turned her attention to Lana, he sipped his orange juice, carefully eyeing her as she shared some small talk with the waitress. It didn't surprise him that they knew each other.

"I hope I'm not intruding on your breakfast," he said, attempting to start the conversation again when the waitress left. He noticed the book that she'd placed on the table. "Looks like you were ready to dive into a good story."

"I sometimes like to start my day here and catch up on some reading when I don't have to be at the restaurant early," Lana answered evenly, picking up her mug. "But it's okay, you're not intruding, especially since we'd planned on meeting today anyway."

Hunter took a sip of coffee and decided to keep the conversation easy a little longer, staying positioned back against his chair in an attempt to make her feel more relaxed.

"So On the Bay sounds like a really good restaurant to try

out. According to a local bartender I met, you are one of Cape Cod's best seafood chefs," he told her, figuring a nice compliment might ease the awkwardness. "Was cooking something you always wanted to do growing up?"

"Yes, it was."

"And what made you choose Bluedale to start your restaurant?" he asked, pouring cream into his coffee and taking another sip.

"Bluedale is all I know and love. I couldn't imagine anywhere else I'd want to be," she said without missing a beat.

Hunter noticed something apprehensive in her eyes as she said it, like there was more she wanted to say. Meanwhile, he scrambled in his mind for how to begin the imminent conversation that hovered heavily over him.

"Wow, that's great. How wonderful for everyone here who has known you to see you doing what you enjoy."

Silence again. Hunter took a deep breath, trying to carefully navigate what he needed to say next. Lana hadn't softened one bit despite his efforts to make her feel more comfortable. He struggled to keep his own defenses from bubbling up as they locked eyes. The sun had moved behind her, making her beautiful red waves glisten and reflecting her natural beauty. He had never seen anyone as striking as her.

"Here we go." The waitress appeared and Hunter exhaled. "Grilled biscuit with sausage patties, scrambled eggs, home fries, and gravy." She set Hunter's plate in front of him. "And avocado toast, one sunny-side egg, and bacon for you, Lana." Putting the second plate down, the waitress's gaze flickered between Hunter and Lana.

Lana smiled up at her. "Thank you, Sandra."

"Enjoy!" The waitress dashed off again.

"This all looks delicious," Hunter said, picking up his fork.

"So I know Bluedale is a special part of you, and so was the inn." He noticed Lana pause for a second, saltshaker in hand over her egg.

"The inn *is* a special part of me." She picked up her toast.

"Yes..." Hunter stopped, wondering if she even knew of their plans to remodel the entire structure of the building.

"I'm sorry," she said, lifting her chin up a few minutes into their meals. "I hope I don't come across as rude, but can we cut to the chase? You asked to meet with me and so here I am. I understand you are expanding the inn into an event venue and adding a two-story cruise ship, is that right?"

Hunter quickly finished chewing his bite, surprised by her sudden directness. That answered that question—she clearly did know the extent of their plans. Perhaps this was what the bartender also meant when he'd wished him luck with her.

"Yes, that's correct," he answered, pushing around the eggs on his plate, knowing it was time to come out with it. "I wanted to meet so we could talk about the plans."

Lana peered silently at him for a minute. "What about them?" she asked.

Hunter shifted uncomfortably in his seat, avoiding her stare and feeling like she was ready to pounce. "Well, knowing your family's ties to the inn, I wanted to personally share some of the specifics, especially since you're right next door and will literally see firsthand all the changes as they happen." *And present to you an extensive buyout offer that could give you enough funds to start over in a larger restaurant at another location.* At this rate, he wasn't sure how to even say that out loud to her.

Lana quietly chewed her food, while Hunter waited patiently for her to gather her words. In contrast to how calm she appeared, her bright-green eyes flickered with something different, fiercer, when she met his. He suspected there was more to the story about her connection to the inn.

"I appreciate the consideration, but I get the sense that you still don't really understand *my family's ties*, as you said." She shook her head. "To you, Hunter, it's just a building that you can scope out, make an offer on, and then mold to your liking. As a businessperson myself, I can certainly understand that. However, as the granddaughter of the original owners, who offered my town over forty years of memories that will never be forgotten and welcomed tourists with a personal touch that you'll never replicate, I don't think I'm ever going to appreciate your plans."

Hunter leaned back, trying to keep his cool, and noticed that a few diners nearby had glanced their way. "You're absolutely correct that your grandparents offered many years of wonderful experiences, but as time passes, people and places adjust to accommodate change. Change isn't a bad thing. Our event venue and cruise line will offer Bluedale experiences as well, but new and different ones. It'll boost the town's economic growth, which in return… helps you."

Lana's face turned as crimson as her hair as she kept her focus directly on him. A light breeze picked up, blowing one of the loose curls across her face, and to his surprise—and despite the heat of their conversation—he had to work hard to resist the sudden urge to brush it away.

"And what makes you think your fancy event venue could offer what Bluedale wants or needs?"

"In one of our meetings about the town, we discussed how small and intimate it was. So we wanted to make sure to tailor what it offers to our customers the right way, which means we certainly did a lot of research. In doing so, we learned that people come to Bluedale to avoid the stress that larger vacation spots have out here. The location will be easy to find just off the bridge coming onto the Cape, and it'll offer the same stunning beauty the rest of Cape Cod has with less overwhelm," he explained, trying to ignore how impassive her facial expression became once again.

This was turning out to be as challenging as he could have imagined, but every time their eyes met, all he saw was decades of her past mixed with a present sadness that began to root itself within him.

"As a lifelong resident of Bluedale, I'm glad you did your research," she said, looking out at the tall grass in the murky marsh with the sun now behind a cloud, as if to match how she was clearly feeling. "But you obviously missed the mark. Please explain to me how your remodel and business plans, including a cruise line, will be less overwhelming than the small, family-friendly inn my grandparents ran?" She kept her gaze on the marsh for an extra beat before she turned to him again.

It was evident that no matter what he had to say, this was even harder for Lana than he'd initially guessed. He'd originally wanted to steer the conversation toward what her plans were for her restaurant, so he could make sure their offer would suffice what she had wanted to do, but instead he was met with a strong emotional resistance. It was quickly becoming clear that proposing a buyout to provide her with the financial means to pursue her goals somewhere else was a lost cause. Lana's walls of defense were much too thick.

"The cruise line will make this tiny town stand out against all the competition. The slower pace on the bay side will now have another option for water tours and events, making Bluedale shine on the map."

"We already shine, Hunter, in ways you just don't understand. The history of not just my family's inn, but Bluedale itself, is what makes us... us. What you're doing takes the traditions we fight hard to keep here and makes them... soulless."

Hunter clenched a napkin in his fist under the table. He needed to fix this tension between them so he could at least *try* to make the offer, at least to appease his father—but he knew one conversation wouldn't accomplish that with how poorly this first meeting was going. "I'm heading up this remodel myself, and I'll make sure everything is up to Bluedale standards. Something your family will be proud of. I—"

Lana held her hand up. "No need to explain further. I appreciate your effort in taking the time to say all this to me face-to-face," she cut in. "But with all due respect, Hunter, completely transforming my inn is not something I will ever be proud of."

He wanted to say more and try to find a common ground, but he held back, and wasn't sure what to do next. The sun reemerged from the cloud, reflecting off the emerald glow in her eyes, and he suddenly wished they hadn't met under these circumstances.

"Thank you again for inviting me to your table for breakfast," he said, seeing her bend down to pick up her purse and reach inside for her wallet. "And I really hope I can show you and Bluedale what we have to offer and how we'll fit right into this wonderful community."

Lana stood up, squaring her shoulders and gazing down at him. "Perhaps Bluedale is going to show you instead." She put cash down to pay for her half of the meal. "If you'll excuse me, I have to get going with my day."

As he watched her walk away with her head held high, he could tell that Lana Kelly had something more behind the fiery stance that matched those red locks—and despite the current event taking place between them, it left Hunter hooked.

CHAPTER 9

The late-morning sun fell gently on Lana's shoulders, wrapping around her like a warm blanket and causing her to slow her step as she walked into the nursing home. She'd spent the past couple hours helping Heidi prep for the evening's special of rosemary skewers with prosciutto-wrapped sea scallops.

Normally Thursday was her day off, but her nerves wouldn't settle since meeting with Hunter. And since the kitchen was her favorite place to zone out, it was her first stop before she'd visit Grandad. It had been two days since their breakfast meeting, and she was still sorting out how she felt about it.

By the time they were done, they had all the dinner selections prepped, as well as the scallops sorted onto trays to pop into the oven later. She had even made fresh fruit tarts with lemon mascarpone cream filling—an addition she whipped up last minute, which would be a clear indicator to anyone who really knew her that she'd really needed the distraction. Before she could cook anything else, Heidi noticed her demeanor and practically shoved her out the door to get to lunch with her grandad.

When she reached the entrance to the nursing home, she paused and rolled the stress off her shoulders before opening the door. The last thing she wanted was to appear distracted during her time with Grandad—not to mention, she knew that telling him about the inn was a bad idea. It had been hard enough for him to lose the inn the first time. Luckily, due to his condition, the nurses kept all visitors at bay except for her, so there was no chance someone else would spill the news. With her head up, she walked in and went to the front desk.

"Good morning, Lana!" the friendly lady at the front desk greeted her. "Your grandad is waiting on you in the dining hall already."

"Thank you." Lana waved and headed in that direction, brushing off some leftover food splatter. The staff in the nursing home were wonderful and had become so familiar that it was easy to forget all her troubles when she visited her grandad.

The dining hall was buzzing with conversation and a good number of visitors eating with their loved ones. Grandad was seated at his usual table near one of the windows, quietly looking outside. The sight of him made her smile and she hurried over to him. Nothing beat her Thursday lunch dates with him.

"I'm here," she said when she reached the table. "Sorry I'm a few minutes late—got caught in the kitchen."

Turning to face her, he studied her for a moment.

"They don't make it like your grandma did," he said, pointing to the back of the room where the door to the kitchen was.

"Make what, Grandad?" she asked, pulling out the chair across from him so she could sit down.

"Clam chowder. It's on the menu today," he said.

"Is it? Well, that sounds good. Even if it's not Grandma's." Lana saw something cast over his eyes and immediately knew. She took a deep breath, willing herself to meet him wherever his mind had taken him.

"You can tell your professor when you reach the part of class about seafood that you have Cape Cod's secret recipe." He laughed. Lana felt her heart drop, regardless of how prepared she was.

"I sure can," she replied, keeping the fact that she was done with school to herself. The doctors always informed her to stay present, no matter when that was for him—yet some days she could easily guide him back to her. Today wasn't one of them.

"Bluedale became known for miles for her clam chowder. Don't you remember?" He peeked out the window again, chuckling to himself. Lana loved watching him smile, even if he couldn't always get his bearings.

"I do remember. That chowder was incredible," she agreed, feeling her stomach clench in preparation for what was coming next. This wasn't the first time he'd brought up her grandma's clam chowder either. She hoped that would be the only thing he mentioned about it and that he wouldn't bring up the second part of the memory that seemed tied to it, but when Grandad looked at her, she braced herself for more.

"And remember how mad she would get when you brought bowls of it out to that seagull? All the rest of them would flock around you in droves to come get some too, driving Grandma nuts." He laughed and his eyes glistened against the memory, before he fell silent for a moment. "No wonder you connected with them, especially that one gull before..." he finally said in a low voice.

"Yes, they loved Grandma's chowder," Lana said quietly.

This time, she lost control and was bombarded by a mental image of her younger self dashing away from her grandparents after they broke the news to her about her parents' accident.

"I often think of that day too, Lana," her grandad said knowingly. This was the first time in many months he had said something so direct about her parents' death. "I'm glad the gull was there that day."

Lana smiled through the wet tears that pooled in her eyes. She could still see the leftover chowder on top of the stove that had stopped her in her tracks, as she filled up two bowls with it before running off to find her special seagull. It was the last bowl of her grandma's chowder that she ever ate. For what felt like hours, she'd waited for the great gull until she finally spotted him diving in and out of the water, flying higher with each dip. She'd wished she could fly far away with him.

"Me too, Grandad." It was all she could say, as she tried her hardest to stay steady against the pain of her past.

"You know, my sweet girl, maybe one day that chowder will be your specialty," Grandad said, and Lana saw his face brighten at the idea.

I'll never be brave enough to serve it, she almost said, but stayed quiet.

"One day I'll tell you the story behind that clam chowder and why it was so special. But right now, I'd like to eat."

Lana stood up, wiping her eyes. "I'll go get us some lunch. You stay put and enjoy the view of the lovely day out the window."

With a deep inhale, she made her way to the lunch selections. He didn't need to hear that every time she tried to make her grandma's clam chowder for the restaurant, it ended before she could even finish. Or that, even though the town had asked her numerous times if she could replicate it, she just couldn't bring herself to serve it. Thinking about the chowder brought him happiness, taking him back to the old days with her grandma. It was hard to always know how to respond to her grandad, considering his ailment, but she knew one thing—loving him through every moment, good or bad, was what he needed most.

THE DRIVE back to her apartment after lunch was a blur. Even though she and Grandad had enjoyed a pleasant visit, all she could think about now was the future of his beloved inn. She was still consumed with guilt about not telling him what had happened, like she was holding this important secret from him.

After she got home, she decided to dump some of this heavy load onto Alicia, and she pulled out her cell phone.

"It doesn't matter how good-looking he is, Alicia—I wasn't even paying attention to that." Lana flopped onto the couch a few minutes into the call.

"Okay, sure, but thinking back on it now, what would you say? Hot or not?" Alicia asked again.

Lana rolled her eyes. Leave it to Alicia to be focused on what he looked like before hearing anything else. Staring up at the ceiling, she found her mind drifting to Hunter's enticing, chocolate-brown eyes and dark-brown hair that swooped down onto his face. Not to mention the way his voice quickened when he spoke of the inn. No matter how hard she tried to ignore it, his concern for her family's history was clear, and she'd liked that more than she should. Lana shook her head and turned to her side, keeping all of that from her friend. The fact is, she didn't trust his intentions or why he'd bothered to even meet her.

"Can we just stick to why I called?"

"All I'm saying is, he's got to be handsome. He's a city guy in development," Alicia pressed her. "Besides, the bartender at The Chowder House ran into Nathan and told him a young, slick businessman was in town with big plans. Why else would you invite him to join you for breakfast?"

"Alicia!" Lana couldn't help but laugh at Alicia's insistence. "Fine. He was handsome. Now, can we move on?" Irritation replaced her grin, because in a matter of ten minutes, they still hadn't moved on from his looks. She knew her friend was just trying to make light of such a heavy situation for her, but no matter how attractive Hunter Graham was, it didn't change anything. "And no, I didn't invite him to breakfast—not the way you're implying. I happened to run into him at the diner and felt obligated to invite him to the table since we were planning on meeting anyway."

"Well, if we're going to be his enemies, then all I'm saying is, at least he's nice to look at," Alicia replied with a playful tone.

"No one said anything about being enemies." Lana appreciated Alicia's continued attempt to cheer her up, but she wasn't in the mood to keep joking around. "If I don't find a way to tolerate the transformation of the inn, then it will just be a constant headache for me. So I refuse to be enemies with him." She sighed, standing up to get some lemonade from the kitchen.

The cool air from the fridge kissed her face as she bent down to retrieve her drink. The humidity was back and expected to stay through the weekend. She poured the cold liquid into a tall glass and added some ice cubes.

"You're meeting with Nathan on Sunday morning, right?" Alicia asked.

Taking a sip, Lana walked back to the living room and sat down on the couch, remembering that Alicia still had an idea stirring behind the scenes. Nathan was planning on coming to the restaurant to go over it with her.

"Yes, I am," she answered.

"Good. I shared my idea with him right after we talked on Saturday. I wanted to get his input before I told you, and he really liked it, but you know Nathan—he has to think through everything at a snail's pace."

"I can't handle any more hints. Please give me some specifics." Lana looked up at the ceiling again, bracing herself because her friend could certainly whip up some wild ideas.

"I don't want to give it all away because Nathan put everything together on his laptop for you to see. We know how visual you are. All I'll say is that I think we need to take what I said the other day on our walk, about you being a Bluedale native, and utilize this for a rebrand."

"Rebrand? How would that help exactly?"

"We just think that in order to stand out from all the options around you, you need to bring in more of… you. Your history. Your family's special touches that Bluedale has always loved." Alicia grew quiet, waiting on a response, but Lana was deep in thought. "Lana… you don't need the inn to create the magic of who you are as a person and a chef."

Lana felt the impact of her words jolt her. The inn was something she always thought she needed to succeed, but more importantly, to keep what little was left of her family intact.

"I don't know, Alicia. I just don't understand how any of that will matter in the long run." She paused, circling the ice in her glass, watching the cubes swirl. "Besides, there's not much more I can really do with the little space I have. You know, last night, on a whim I looked up all the commercial listings that are currently for sale to possibly up and move the restaurant to a bigger location, so I could bring my customers inside and have room to grow, but everything that's for sale is on the other end of the Cape—not where I want to be—and they're also out of my price range."

"Don't even bother doing that. You've already built up your name here in Bluedale, and besides, since this is one of the first stops into the Cape, that has always worked in your favor. With the advertisement for the restaurant right in the rotary after the bridge, it always brings in lots of hungry tourists."

"Yeah… I guess you're right. But watching what's being built next to me is just reminding me that Cape Cod is continuing to expand, change, and it's only going to get… fancier. I just want to keep my name strong in the pool of competition."

"You will, and remember, it's not a seafood restaurant going in next door—it's an event venue. So there is no competition there."

Lana put her glass down and got up, walking out onto her deck. The beach below was filled with side-by-side umbrellas and children splashing in the water. Putting her phone call on speaker, she leaned on the railing and let the mesmerizing view of the ocean ease her worry. The truth was, she just wasn't sure she had it in her to stay right next to Hunter and his big plans when they were destroying an important part of her past.

"Lana? Are you okay?" Alicia asked, and she realized how long she'd left her friend hanging.

"Yes, I'm here. I'm just contemplating what you said."

"Look… despite how hard it'll be to see Hunter and his company make such drastic changes to the inn, you don't need to move, Lana. It's your food that has people coming back, not fancy dinnerware, event space, or even indoor seating. You offer way more than many of the other alfresco seafood places on the Cape, and that makes you stand out," Alicia firmly told her.

A bright reflection from the sea caught her eye as the sun bounced off the water. This wasn't the first time Lana had thought about moving her restaurant to a bigger location, but every time it had crossed her mind, her attention was brought right back to the ocean.

On the Bay was the only oceanfront that she would be able to afford for her clambakes, which was a large proportion of her business—and this beach was the only piece of her family she had left now that the inn was gone. She couldn't let that go.

"Thank you for the encouragement. Standing out as a restaurant owner on Cape Cod is a constant stress." Lana closed her eyes, willing away the million thoughts that circled in her mind.

"My husband is brilliant. You know that. He will angle this new marketing plan of mine perfectly. Just you wait," Alicia said.

Lana nodded. "Yeah, you're right about Nathan."

"Listen, I need to finish up the work I have here, but please try and relax tonight. You need it," Alicia said.

"I'll try."

When they hung up, Lana felt much better after their conversation, her mind now swimming with curiosity over her upcoming meeting with Nathan. Down below, she watched the soft current murmuring onto the shore with hypnotic grace around all the laughing children. Maybe now she could move forward. But just as soon as she thought that, Hunter's words interrupted her focus: *Something your family will be proud of.*

Shaking her head, she pushed off the railing and made her way inside. In a business sense, letting the inn go was the next step that she needed to take, yet something unfinished tugged at her heart, locking her in place.

CHAPTER 10

With a cold beer in hand, Hunter watched the clambake party from the inn's deck, which was just outside the old lounge area—a perfect ending to his Friday. Set higher than Lana's outdoor patio, he sat tucked away at one of the tables watching all the fun on the sand below. The sun was just beginning to set, its golden globe radiating above the water.

He watched the guests around the intimate clambake. They were all talking, laughing, and enjoying themselves. Even though he knew Cape Cod—and most of New England —loved this old tradition, he'd never experienced a clambake before. Lana was smart to specialize in it, something he hadn't considered when creating his business model and personalizing it to fit the atmosphere here in Bluedale, and the people he'd met so far seemed to be questioning it too.

"Hey, boss, I'm heading out for the night. Need anything else?" A male voice behind him startled him out of his clambake party viewing.

Hunter glanced over his shoulder and saw Kevin standing

in the doorway. "Nope, I'm all good. Thanks for another day of hard work. I'll see you tomorrow."

"Bright and early."

"I know working all these weekends is tough," Hunter said. "Thank you for all your hard work."

"It just comes with the job expectations in the beginning of these new projects, but thanks." Kevin nodded in appreciation. "Hopefully the foundation will be good to go sooner rather than later, although it's been really nice staying here in Bluedale. It's such a great place. I'm meeting some of the guys in town at the Yellowfin Tavern for a few beers. Care to join?"

Hunter considered it, but laughter from below pulled his attention away and that's when he spotted her—Lana making her way to her guests around the clambake, holding a tray of food. "That sounds like fun, but I think I'm going to call it an early night," he said, keeping his eyes on her.

"Okay, next time then," Kevin said, pausing before he left. "Oh, wait, before I leave—one of the local carpenters, Bob, pointed something out today and I wanted to show you. It's about Lana, the restaurant owner next door. He said they were childhood friends, and he was hoping we'd be willing to keep this bit, for her sake." He walked over to the other end of the deck and pulled his phone's flashlight out, angling it down. "Come take a look."

Hunter walked to where Kevin was standing and followed the light, seeing what appeared to be a name engraved in the wood. Crouching down to read it, his stomach clenched when he made out the words: *Lana Kelly, age eleven.*

"Thank you for pointing this out," Hunter said, standing back up.

"No problem. Just figured you'd want to see it before the deck is ripped up. I know it shouldn't be a concern of yours, but it looked so personal. Anyway, I'm heading out now. Good luck with tomorrow's test cruise with the ship coming in. Glad you secured that port."

"Thanks, Kevin," Hunter said, remembering Simon's suggestion about the other port he'd researched and glad he didn't have to use his contact.

"See you Monday."

Hunter turned back toward the beach, catching the sun as it showed off its last rays of red beauty. The group was still circled around the clambake with plates in hand. Lana maneuvered away from the crowd, heading back inside to her kitchen, her auburn curls as vivid as the sunset.

For the past few days since their awkward breakfast at the diner, he couldn't get her off his mind. Not once had she returned a smile during their meeting, yet her passion for her restaurant and her family's inn inspired the utmost respect. Hard work was certainly something they shared. The more he thought about her, especially while observing her now, the more intrigued he was, and he found himself wanting to know more about her restaurant, rather than offering her money to move it somewhere else.

A burst of laughter from Lana's patio where her regular diners were eating pulled him out of his daze, and he took the last swig of his beer and went inside. It was quiet walking through the inn with the construction crew now gone. The entire layout was going to be unrecognizable in a matter of weeks. He thought about Lana's name engraved on the deck when he looked around the room with all the demolition debris and tarp everywhere, suddenly understanding a little more how hard this must be for her to witness and wondering what memories she'd made in this room too.

Inside the kitchen, he flicked on the lights, his eyes widening at how much was already done. A recycling bin sat near the pantry and, after tossing his empty beer bottle into it, he walked around the large center island that was getting replaced. All the old appliances were already ripped out to make way for the new. Luckily, all this kitchen needed was a facelift. For a small inn, it was a sizeable room already, so with new appliances, including a second oven and a commercial-size fridge, it would serve the venue well.

He headed through a different door out of the kitchen and into the small, old dining room across from the lounge. The wall in between the lounge and dining room was nearly demolished, and he was pleased with how much bigger the space was already by joining the two rooms. This was where the largest construction would happen, with the addition they were building to allow up to a hundred and fifty guests. He sighed, knowing how long it would take, but he wanted the ballroom done right since it was the center point of the venue.

For now, his focus was the cruise line since they could begin accepting bookings immediately, and just as the image of the ship came to his mind, so did the image of Lana by the water only minutes ago. She seemed to mesh beautifully with the sea out there.

He walked over to a window to see a full moon rising, taking over the sky, and he decided to walk along the beach. The clambake party was still in full swing outside as he walked right by them. Taking his shoes off, he let his feet sink into the sand with each step, the gritty sensation tingling through his toes. The tide was lapping onto the shore and the rhythmic sound of each wave settled him. Stopping for a moment, he looked up, soaking in the twilight sky as it whispered of the stars to come. The night view out on the Cape was just as magical as what he'd witnessed during the day, and for the first time, he really appreciated the beauty this area offered.

He looked ahead at the sea and pictured the cruise line

pushing its way through those waters, trying to muster some excitement for tomorrow. Now that they had the port secured, they were planning on getting the ship there to be docked and ready for bookings, and he couldn't wait to see all the changes in person. Voices from the clambake carried over to him, and he turned to peek at them but didn't see Lana anymore.

Moving the sand with his feet, he looked down, remembering her face when he'd told her who he was at the diner. He had to push past the angst he felt with every part of this project, but that seemed easier said than done, knowing how disappointed she was. Turning to head back to his car, he shook off all these feelings and decided he just needed a good night's sleep. Tomorrow was a new day and there was a lot more work to get done.

THE WAKE FOLLOWING behind the ship rippled smoothly as it slowly pulled into the dock the next day. Hunter slipped on his sunglasses to shield against the strong rays of sunlight peeking out of the gray rain clouds that had covered the sky all morning. The storms that had rolled in overnight were a vast difference from the bright full moon during his walk last night. As the last of clouds broke apart, humid steam floated up from the upper deck where he stood.

"Everything looks to be all set." Max, his event manager, came up behind him. "I just took another walk-through in the main reception room, and they did a terrific job with the remodel. I just know this ship will fill up fast in no time."

"I think so too. You mentioned in an email yesterday you already have a wedding booked?" Hunter asked.

"Actually, as of yesterday, three weddings have booked for next summer. Inquiries are also coming in for smaller, everyday water tours for this summer, and prospective clients have called and asked for information on when construction will be completed at the venue, according to Charlene," Max announced proudly, looking just as pleased as Hunter felt.

"Wow, that's great. I'm so impressed with the marketing push right here in town." Hunter could never figure out how Max and Charlene did it, but they were the best he'd ever worked with. Charlene had been promoted from front desk manager in their New York location to a marketing position, and then transferred to help Max get Bluedale organized.

"Yes, as well as on social media. And a few days ago, I stopped off at the Bluedale Information Center and dropped all kinds of brochures."

The two men started to make their way down the ship. "Great. This will be a huge hit here." Hunter looked behind him, admiring the beauty of the large vessel.

"It sure will, boss," Max agreed. "Okay, I'm off to the mobile office on site to catch up on some stuff before I head back to Boston."

Hunter waved him off and stepped onto the platform toward his car, while the crew finished docking the ship. Things were off to a really good start. Hunter pulled out his phone, dialing up his father.

"Hello, Hunter, how was the test cruise?" his father answered.

"Wonderful. It was overcast with rain showers earlier, but they stopped and the sun came out, so it made for a good ending. The remodeled bathrooms and event room on the lower deck look perfect now. I'm also impressed with the size of the kitchen that we were able to fit in there."

"The construction team was one of the best. I'm pleased to hear it all came together. Looking forward to a ride myself. Any more updates?"

"As far as the inn goes, the bathrooms in some of the original rooms on the second floor will need a complete remodel, but we should have most of that done by late fall. And the sewage upgrade will be done Monday, with a much larger tank that will be up to code since there will be additional guests for the sizable events we're anticipating." Hunter stopped walking, trying to think if there was anything missing from his report.

"Did you get ahold of the woman who owns the restaurant next door?" his father asked.

"Yes…" Hunter hesitated, picturing her green eyes again. "I did."

"Uh-oh, that doesn't sound good. Did you manage to get her to say more than two words, unlike Kevin?"

Knowing his father might take it the wrong way, Hunter decided to avoid explaining how they'd bumped into each other at the diner and had an impromptu meal together. The last thing he needed was pressure from his father implying he was getting too involved, so he kept his answer simple.

"Yes, we spoke, and it's all good." *Or, rather, it will be good.* Hunter clenched his jaw, thinking about how defensively she'd left the table. "We had a very cordial first conversation. I didn't make the offer, but no… arguments were had."

"I see. Make the offer soon, but make sure it's the right timing."

Hunter considered his father's insistence and thought back to his encounter with the bartender. He hoped he would be the only skeptical resident they'd run into. He stayed quiet, not wanting to give his father any reason to doubt him. Somehow he had to make this all turn out in everyone's favor. "I will."

"That's what I like to hear. I was growing concerned because Kevin reported back that he spoke with a manager in some bakery in town, who seemed a little taken aback by what we're creating. Buying out the property next door could very well rattle the locals even more, but if this Lana Kelly is open to change, everyone else should follow suit."

Hunter swallowed. *That's two wary residents then...* Not to mention Margaret's facial expression when he'd told her why he was in town. "It'll just take the town some time to adjust to us. I'll update you with more soon."

After they hung up, he finally reached his car, drove back to the inn, and parked. Walking past the construction and around the building to the beach, he decided to take a moment by the water, thinking about the conversation with his father. Perhaps he should have been more truthful about his meeting with Lana, letting him know it hadn't gone as well as he'd hoped. But what good would that do? His father would just blow off his efforts, telling him he wasn't trying hard enough.

As he got to the beach, he saw the figure of a woman watching the waves down by the shoreline, recognizing her red curls blowing behind her in the wind. Each step closer he got, the more his conversation with his father vanished from his mind.

Taking a deep breath, he called out to her. "Lana!" He waved when she turned, but slowed his step when she looked back at the water without returning the gesture.

"That is quite the ship," Lana said, as he finally made his way up to her.

He followed her gaze out toward the ocean to see what she was looking at, but he didn't see any ship in sight. She then held up her phone and he saw a picture of his ship only minutes ago at the dock. Not knowing what else to say, he agreed with her. "Yeah, it is."

"I have a friend who docks his boat at the same port, and they all saw the new ship come in this morning. He heard about us being new neighbors and shared this picture with me." Lana turned and looked at him. Something in her eyes seemed different than the other day, her defense a bit softer.

"It's not the biggest ship the Cape has to offer, but it's a perfect size for weddings and other events," he told her.

"It sure is." She glanced at the screen one more time. "Well, I better get back to the kitchen. Saturday is my busiest day."

"Good luck with the food prep," he said.

"Thanks. Are you heading back to the ship?"

"No." Hunter put his hand to his stomach as they turned to walk back. "I'm off to get some lunch before I meet with one of our decorators. I forgot to eat earlier."

Lana looked up at him out of the corner of her eye as they walked a few more steps in silence. "How about I save you a trip? Would you like some shrimp sliders?"

"Sliders?" He raised his brows.

"One of tonight's specials. I just put them together, and I think I have way more than needed," she explained.

His stomach grumbled at the mention of them, and even though he felt like he should pass on the offer, he couldn't. "I'd love some, thank you."

Hunter followed her up to the side of her patio and into her kitchen. Looking around, he noticed how impressive it was. Everything was updated and commercial size, even for a small outdoor restaurant. He wasn't sure why, but he'd expected a homier feel.

"What a nice kitchen you have here," Hunter complimented her, feeling his shoulders relax when she appeared pleased. "What was this place before you bought it?"

"I didn't buy it because it was already mine. It used to be my father's fish market before I remodeled it and turned it into what you see now." She opened the door to exit the kitchen and he followed, not mentioning that he'd already known about the fish market. "I offer finer food than the typical seafood shacks on the Cape." Lana led him through the door to the back, where her office was. "Wait here." She disappeared behind her office door and came right back out holding two sliders on a paper towel.

"These look delicious," he said. "Well, I'll leave you to it in here. Thanks again for these."

"You're welcome." The tension between them didn't feel as intense as the first time they'd met. She pointed to a door behind her. "If you head out the door right there and take a quick left, it'll lead you to the parking lot."

Hunter nodded and made his way out. The last thing he wanted was to linger and crumble the small progress they'd just accomplished. Reaching the door to his mobile office, with his food in hand, he glanced across the parking lot at her restaurant. His father's words from before echoed through his head: *make sure it's the right timing.* Shaking his head, he stepped inside the office. There wasn't ever going to be a right time.

CHAPTER 11

The birds were calling to one another in the beautiful way they do, with the songs coming from different trees as Lana carefully led Grandad down the walkway for an early Sunday morning stroll. She'd gotten up early to prepare for her meeting with Nathan and noticed a last-minute clambake reservation had come through. After Heidi volunteered to do the clam dig, she realized she had some spare time and went to pay her grandad a surprise visit before the meeting.

"The birds are loud today, aren't they?" Lana asked her grandad, who stopped and leaned against his walker to look up, catching the trees just as they swayed slightly in the breeze. The gust felt nice against the hot haze. Luckily the path was mostly shaded. "That wind feels good, but is it too hot out here, Grandad?"

"Never too hot for your old grandad," he said, winking at her. "Besides, the nursing home keeps their air conditioning so low I can hardly feel my fingers, so it's wonderful out here. But I can feel a storm brewing soon against this humidity. One of those quick summer ones."

Lana looked up and saw nothing but blue skies, yet she knew better than to question him—he was usually spot-on with the weather. "I hope not, because I have a couple errands to run before I get into the kitchen. I don't like being out in the rain."

"Nonsense." Grandad lifted an arm, waving it in her direction. "How about all those trips out on the pontoon in the rain? A little storm won't slow you down. It's been good weather this past week. How's it out on the water?"

Lana's stomach dropped. "I bet you miss being out there, huh, Grandad?" She decided to turn the focus away from her. While she was away in school, she knew that her grandad had spent many days on the water, but since he'd moved to the nursing home, the pontoon had stayed docked and tucked away.

"Every day. Especially with your dad. Boy, he sure loved to show me all he knew about sea life as a young boy. I knew then that he would grow up to be out there doing something to soak up all that knowledge." Grandad studied her. "You didn't answer me… about that water."

All she could do was put her arm around him and give him a reassuring nod. "I've been busy, but the summer's just begun. Plenty of time." Tears burned her eyes, knowing that was her response every time and he never remembered. She sat him down on a bench nearby to take a short rest.

Grandad closed his eyes, tilting his head back up toward the trees. "Oh, my Lana, my sweet girl. Let's go down to the beach after lunch and spread our wings together by the water's edge. Think the gull will be there today? Maybe your mother will join us too."

The tears in Lana's eyes continued to build, until they finally fell down her face. Grandad was slipping into a moment of relapse.

"Maybe sometime soon we'll go to the beach," she gently said, bracing herself for more.

Grandad stayed quiet, still facing up and resting his eyes. The sun traveled through the branches, lighting up his face. He looked so peaceful. Following his stance, she leaned back, looking up just as two birds chased each other from one branch to the next, and before she could will it away, the distant memory that was so present in Grandad's mind began to take hold. She could almost feel the rhythm of the pontoon gliding across the water, unsteady under her seat, and the heat of the late-afternoon sun caressing her back— her parents' faces in view.

"Being out on this boat with you both means everything to me," she'd told her parents, breathing in the ocean air, her curls bouncing behind her in the wind as her father steered the boat. She knew how much the pontoon meant to them, and she soaked up every minute she got to spend on it.

"I know it does, Lana." Her mother smiled, putting her arm around her. "Which is why it'll be yours one day."

"Really?" Lana nearly jumped with excitement. "Daddy?"

"It sure will, sweetheart! It is yours to dream on and do whatever your heart desires with it." Her father took his eyes off the water for a moment as he beamed down at her.

"Didn't you tell me once that you met Dad on a boat tour here on the Cape?" Lana asked her mother.

"That's right. I think we fell in love by the end of it." Her mother blushed, her eyes squinting against the sun, looking up at her father. "Then he took me to the inn, and I met your grandparents that same day. Grandma sat me down with a bowl of her delicious clam chowder. We both better learn how to make that, so the recipe is never lost." Her mother leaned in, resting her head on Lana's shoulder.

"Yes, you better!" her father joked from the wheel, and looked ahead again. "What a fantastic day it is. Look how clear the water is for miles."

"I could be out here all day!" Lana looked out across the blue sea.

"The ocean is who you are, Lana. You're meant to be out here," he told her.

"And I'll master it! Don't worry, Dad. I'll catch all the best fish like you do. But digging for clams is my favorite. I want to learn how to make Grandma's famous clam chowder for all of Cape Cod! And maybe learn how to cook all of our favorite seafood!"

"Sounds like a plan," he said, glancing down at her. "But whatever you do when you're grown, Lana, don't forget to find time to be out here. The sea is where you can always fly free, no matter what life brings."

LANA BLINKED, letting go of the memory with a sharp inhale. Grandad was still enjoying his rest and didn't notice.

She patted his hand, and he opened his eyes. "Come on, Grandad. Time to go back in."

When she got him standing and holding his walker, they locked eyes. For a moment he didn't move, watching her as if he somehow knew what she'd just remembered. Grandad might not always be aware of the present, but as he looked at her, she had no choice but to exist in the parts of her heart that she never thought she'd face again.

A SHORT WHILE LATER, Lana popped into the bakery to get her weekly donuts, and when she got back into the car, the first rumble of thunder echoed in the distance. Grandad was right once again with his weather prediction. Her phone buzzed with a text and she saw it was Nathan telling her that he was running about fifteen minutes behind, which gave her just enough time to make one more stop. It was her turn to do the lobster run, and after she swung through and picked them up, she still pulled into the parking lot before Nathan arrived.

When she got out of the car, she opened her back seat to get the bag of lobsters and felt the first drops of rain bounce off her head. Pushing the door shut with her body, she picked up her pace toward the restaurant and made it inside just as a sheet of rain fell from the dark sky. Heading straight into the kitchen, she knew Nathan would guess where to find her. After putting the lobsters on ice, she washed her hands, and was ready to tackle dessert prep.

Opening her dessert fridge to check on the raspberry coulis she'd made the other day, she noted that it had cooled and set enough for the coconut cakes she'd planned as a dessert special for that night. The clambake party was sure in for a treat. Throwing her eyes to the ceiling and counting off how many people were reserved for that night, mixed in with the average number of regular Sunday evening diners, she began to calculate how many cakes to make.

Just as she pulled out all the ingredients to begin baking, the kitchen door swung open, and Nathan came in holding his laptop under his soaking wet coat.

"Good morning! Sorry I'm a bit late—beach traffic was worse than I thought."

"No worries. You know me, I'm always cooking away and keeping busy around here. There are some clean towels in the closet behind you to dry off." A crackle of thunder erupted above them. "Sounds like the storm is on top of us now. Would it be all right to bake and talk?"

"Sure thing." Nathan went to the closet to retrieve a towel. "What's on the dessert menu?" His eyes darted to her prep station, as he dried his face, and he sat down at a nearby empty table that was used for shipment deliveries.

"Coconut cake with raspberry coulis." Lana pulled out a large mixing bowl from under the counter and measured out the flour, sugar, baking powder, and salt into the bowl.

"That sounds delicious. I'm here for any taste testing you may need," he said, opening his laptop.

Lana smiled as she cracked eggs into the mix, remembering all the previous times Nathan was caught in the kitchen over the years checking the dessert fridge for leftovers. "So any hope for my little ol' seafood shack?"

Her sarcasm amused Nathan, and he chuckled while clicking through his documents.

"Yes, there is, and this is more than just an outdoor food shack, Lana. But I will say, Graham Bayview Events next door is going to be hard for people to ignore." He paused with an empathetic look. "I'm sorry you didn't get to buy the inn back."

"I am too, but I'll be okay." Lana clicked on the mixer and moved it around the bowl for a few seconds. "Even the name sounds luxurious." She glanced over at him. "And yes, they will certainly be a presence, reminding me just how deep their pockets are compared to mine and why I couldn't buy it back."

"But what you offer here is pretty unique and stands out in its own way. Fine dining with a casual, yet intimate twist. People come here and get to taste some of Cape Cod's most delicious seafood out on your relaxed patio."

"True, and I know he's offering an event venue, not a

restaurant," she said. "And he also has a ship." She knew she sounded pouty, but it all just felt like a slap in the face.

"An event venue is not direct competition for you," Nathan said, when she turned the mixer off again.

"Alicia told me the same thing, but—"

"Competition is all around you in a place like Cape Cod," he cut in. "But I know this is bothering you because it's the inn."

"Partly, yes," she admitted and sighed. "I just don't know what my future looks like now that the inn is gone again. I could've really grown there."

"The inn only went back on the market a little over a month ago, so let's backtrack and recenter. This is not about what they're doing next door—this is about you, Lana." He paused as if he knew he was about to push a few buttons. "You need to allow yourself to expand and flourish. You do not need that building to do so. And what I'm about to show you was Alicia's idea. I just needed to sit with it before presenting anything to you because I know it'll stir up some emotions."

"Leave it to Alicia," Lana said. She knew her friends meant well, but she braced herself for what he was about to show her.

Nathan read his screen, scrolling down the page. "Just getting some images up."

"I like a visual." She began pouring the batter into cake pans.

"I know. I want to really highlight how to personalize this place more through photos. Just keep an open mind."

When she was done filling the last coconut cake, she transferred all of them into the oven and began to mix some more batter. "Fine, I'll try. I'm assuming getting bigger signs won't cut it then?" she asked jokingly, adding more dry mix into the bowl, then some eggs, and clicking on the mixer again.

"Ha! No, although I wish it were that simple. Okay, here we go," Nathan said, angling the computer to face her. "Come take a look."

After she'd poured the second batch of batter into more pans and popped them into the oven, she wiped her hands and went over to the table, pulling a chair around to face his laptop.

"Okay, I'm all ears," she replied, as he began to scroll through the slideshow he'd put together.

Lana listened and watched the slides move across the screen as Nathan explained how to build a stronger connection to her customers.

"So, unlike whatever is happening next door, opening yourself up to your customers can resonate with them, especially in a place like Bluedale. You've already done that somewhat by really tailoring parties like your clambakes to your customers, but they want to know *you*, not just your food. So, for example, coming out of the kitchen to greet your customers... *that* sticks in their minds. So let's amp that up. I'm going to show you with pictures." He pointed to a few images on the screen he had created for their social media channels of behind-the-scenes snapshots and introductions for both her and Heidi. "See, sharing how the business got started—particularly about you and your family—really makes you stand out." The slides paused.

"My family?" she asked.

"Yes, your family and the timeline of events for how On the Bay came to be. I truly believe sharing how you got to this point will make you shine, especially to new customers. Word of mouth is one of the best marketing tools a business can have, especially in small towns. And your story will be easily remembered."

"I don't think sharing how my parents died in a boat fire will win over my customers." Lana knew her defenses were building, but he was right, this was definitely stirring her up.

"No, Lana, breathe for a minute." Nathan scooted his chair a little closer when he saw how upset she already was. "And think for one second about how, if you had managed to buy back the inn, what would have happened. Everyone would have known you were trying to continue your family's legacy. Your entire past would have come right back into the spotlight."

Lana grew still, realizing just how truthful his statement was as it hit her heart. That was something she had overlooked entirely once the inn was up for sale again. Now she questioned her real motive to even try and buy it back. Was this about creating her own legacy or protecting Grandad's?

"You're right, Nathan. I wasn't even thinking about that." Lana drew in a deep breath, trying not to get herself more flustered so they could finish this meeting. "When my grandad lost the inn, I guess I had a drive in me to buy it back. To make up for what he lost."

"Lana." Nathan gave her a reassuring smile. "Everything he did was so you could carry the torch toward your own dreams that he knew you had since you were a little girl. And I have personally loved learning about your dreams as a child, growing up here in Bluedale, and going out on your parents' boat..." He hesitated, studying her face for a moment, knowing he had touched upon another sensitive subject with the pontoon. "And helping your dad fish, clam, and bring in some delicious seafood for the market that is now On the Bay. I can't believe I didn't think of this when we first did a grand opening."

Lana looked away, her emotions bubbling up all over again. "Nathan, I'm just not—"

"Before you say no," Nathan cut her off, reaching over

and putting his hand on her shoulder. "Just think about how being authentic creates a vibe here that is not only more intimate, but as I just mentioned, it provides your customers with something to talk about fondly around town." He reached over and gave her shoulder a small squeeze before he returned to his laptop.

"Connection is what we all want, and big fancy corporate businesses like Graham Property Development can't offer that. Just thought I'd give a punch to our new neighbors." Nathan winked at her, calming her nerves. Hunter's attempt to meet with her in person came to mind. Perhaps just being in Bluedale, he was already picking up on that.

Lana stared at the last slide on the screen. "Share your past." She repeated the idea in her head, trying to let it sink in.

"This really is an interesting angle, and one I never thought to use here at my restaurant. I guess anytime I thought about my family history, I always associated that part of myself with the inn. Let me think this through," she told him.

"Of course. Take some time to reflect on it. Also, I'm going to have our website designer make the site more user-friendly, easier to navigate, and with updated visuals—so I'm going to need to take some fresh food shots this week. And when you're ready, we can give it that personalized touch too." He hesitated for a moment. "And I even thought that if you still have it, we could bring out some of the decor your mother had in the fish market that I've seen in old pictures. Bring the past to the present."

"That's a lot to take in."

Nathan leaned forward. "You are the face of this restaurant. And..." He trailed off, shifting in his seat to face her better. "The inn isn't lost. It can be brought back to life in part of the marketing. Think of this like a rebrand for who you are moving forward, which includes your *whole* authentic self and utilizes what *you* have created for yourself." He waved a hand around the room. "This restaurant is all because of your talent and passion, not a continuation of your grandparents'—the way it would have been, had you taken over your family's inn. Let's keep going with that."

When Nathan left, Lana kept busy finishing up the cakes and appetizers, but her mind ran circles around everything he'd shared with her. She pulled out her to phone to text Alicia:

> I just ended the meeting with Nathan and I'm feeling all the emotions right now, so I will need time to really absorb all this. But thank you… I'm so fortunate to have you two in my life.

Nathan's words jumped into her mind just as she clicked her phone off: *I have personally loved learning about your dreams as a child.* She'd forgotten what it was like to dream new dreams, to feel that same vibrant zest for life that she did as a child. The restaurant had given her enough to get through each day, but was she living… or staying hidden behind her cooking? Lana could almost feel her father's secure grip around her from that last day, frozen in time— and for the first time, she realized… so was she.

CHAPTER 12

The seagulls flew in circles around the bread a little boy kept tossing over to them. Hunter chuckled at the boy's joy as he chased the birds, teasing them with the bread. His mother called out for him, and he threw all the bread in his hand and ran to her. Turning back to the water, Hunter peered down at the harmonious waves as they gently caressed the side of the dock, and mentally prepared for the day.

"Ready for the big day?" Max jogged up behind him and the two of them walked down the dock. "It's pretty exciting for a regular Thursday."

"Sure am. I'm looking forward to getting something started. It's looking less likely we can get any events booked by early fall, and more like winter before the venue will be in full swing. We ran into a mold issue under the carpets in one room when we pulled them up." Hunter shook his head and Max nodded.

"Yeah, but I think it'll be a bigger grand opening with the longer wait," Max said, giving Hunter a pat on the shoulder. "It'll all be great, but good things take time. Let's keep our attention on the ship, so the residents and tourists of Bluedale can start to learn who we are. Especially with the pushback I got from one of the residents."

Not another one. Hunter grimaced. "What do you mean?"

"I was in town early last week picking up some more print materials for today, and the gentleman who helped me flat-out asked about the venue."

"Is he mad about it?"

"I wouldn't say he was mad, but… he brought up the owner of the restaurant next door. Lana?"

Hunter nodded. "Yes, that's her. Very well known in Bluedale."

"That's what he said. He's known her since she was a little girl, and he said he would've loved to see the inn back in the hands of her family again." Max gave him an apologetic look. "I didn't mean to get into such a personal conversation like that, but it just sort of happened. I reassured him that we will do our best to make this venue something the town will love just as much."

"I actually met with her, you know," Hunter told him.

"Did you? How'd that go?"

"Terrible. We didn't see eye-to-eye on anything, but that's to be expected with the first encounter, I guess." Since he couldn't tell his father the full truth of how that meeting went, it felt good to get it off his chest—although he didn't mention the fact that he was supposed to make her an offer. He didn't want to share that with the company until the deal was made.

"I could have guessed that would happen. The man in the print shop told me how her grandparents started that inn and how well loved it was. I imagine it'll just take some time with her. I'm sure everything will work out. Can't stay enemies forever," Max said.

"No, hopefully we won't. I did reach out again to see if

she was interested in catering for the ship's kick-off day, but no response." Hunter sighed. Another flop. He thought about her fixed expression from across the breakfast table. And those eyes. He'd admired her passion, but he sure hoped Max was right.

"Like I said, it'll all work out, boss."

"Thanks, Max," Hunter said. "And just so you know, I haven't heard anything negative about you or the company specifically. This small town is sure protective of their people, but I think in time we will win them over too. Especially once we start hosting special events. Speaking of: any new inquiries for the ship?"

"We actually just had one come in for a fiftieth wedding anniversary that I'll be getting back to today. They're looking to invite seventy-five people for mid-August," Max informed him, as they made their way down the dock toward the ship. "And our day tours are filling up faster than I thought."

"Great. Today's soft opening for the cruise line will be fun for the community and really help get the word out. How many tours again for today's kick-off? Three?" Hunter stepped back to allow Max on board first. The cleaning crew was finished, and everything was ready to go.

"Yes, three tours for today. The DJ should be here soon, which will be fun for the kids. I'm going to go check on the caterers," Max said, nodding his head toward the kitchen.

"Speaking of caterers, we have some leads for a temporary chef for the ship, hoping to zero in on someone permanent soon." Hunter pulled out his phone and snapped some pictures to send over to the office in New York. His father had wanted to make it for this opening but got caught up in a new development they had eyes on, so the pictures would have to do.

"Great, send me those leads. For some reason, that's been the hardest part about launching this ship. It's been tough to find a chef, with all the competition around us snatching the good ones before we could even interview them." Max leaned over to look at the photos Hunter had taken. "Well, I'm off to get a few things done at the venue, but I'll be back here at the port soon for the opening introductions."

After making his rounds on the ship, Hunter stood along the side, watching the sparkling sunlight bounce off the ripples in the water. The mention of chefs took his mind off the busy day ahead and slowed right down to focus on Lana.

After not hearing from her about the catering, he also hadn't seen her all week, except for a few passing moments in the parking lot, but she always had her hands full and got inside quickly. It was as if she was trying hard to avoid catching sight of him. When he wasn't pulled in a million directions with the construction crew, all he could think about was trying to smooth things over with her—especially now after hearing Max share another story about a disgruntled local.

He sent over the pictures to his father's secretary and put his phone in his pocket before heading back to his car. The first tour was scheduled to start in an hour, which gave him time to get back to the venue and check in with the construction manager about the mold inspectors that were coming at some point later in the day.

A short drive later, he parked his car and was relieved to see that Lana's red Jeep was not there. She didn't need to see the big temporary sign that his assistant had put in the parking lot informing anyone who was mixed up about where their port was for the cruise. He hated rubbing it all in her face. He headed inside and tried to will himself to stop worrying about Lana, but no matter how hard he tried, he couldn't. Despite the pressure looming to win her over *and* to seal this offer with her, everything about her intrigued him. It was becoming more than just business.

His lingering thoughts about her were quickly drowned out by the noise and chaos of the construction inside. Locating the foreman, Bob, he got a full update on the progress with the mold inspectors, along with new hiccups that had come up. Despite the growing list of new things to check or fix, the day was running smoothly. He also informed Hunter that they'd found a box with what looked to be glassware and left it in his office to have a look. So before he got pulled into another discussion, he ducked out to take a peek.

On his desk was a large box, and inside were only four flute glasses. When Hunter reached in to pull one out, he saw words engraved on it:

Bluedale, 1998

Sliding it carefully back in the box, he stood there thinking what they could have been for. Before his curiosity took over too much, his phone rang, snapping him out of his thoughts. He saw Max's name on the screen and realized the time. The introduction ceremony was in ten minutes.

"I'm on my way," he said as he answered the phone.

"Okay!" Max's voice sounded distant against the noise in the background. "There's a great turnout here. See you soon!"

He hung up, put the box under his desk, and dashed out the door.

When Hunter got to the port, a rush of exhilaration filled him when he saw the crowd gathered around. Jogging across the parking lot, he made it just in time for the opening speech.

Max stood in front of all the guests and waved Hunter over to him before he began speaking. "Welcome, everyone, to Graham Bayview Events and Cruises! We are very excited to have you all on our very first tour!" Everyone applauded, and Hunter looked around, noticing more people were arriving. He couldn't have been more pleased. "Here with us today is one of the masterminds behind all of this, Mr. Hunter Graham of Graham Property Development." More applause as eyes turned to him, waiting on him to speak.

"Thank you!" Hunter smiled at Max, gesturing toward him. "Max here is my right-hand man in our Boston office, handling all events for our latest developments. And he's put together a really nice kickoff with music and complimentary food and drinks. We're so happy to be here in Bluedale, and we look forward to making memories on the water for years to come. Our venue will open later this fall, offering a beautiful place to host many special events as well. Now let's get on that ship!" Hunter led everyone onto the dock and aboard, feeling a sense of pride. If he could make Bluedale just as proud, the promotion would be within his reach. He just needed the locals behind him too.

As soon as the first tour began, the day cruised by quickly. Hunter stood next to Max outside his car and shook his hand. "Today was a success. You and the team did a fantastic job. I'm so impressed with how many people you managed to get for opening day."

"Thank you. It was a stretch to get the word out with less than a month to advertise, but small towns like Bluedale make the job easier. Most of the reservations for today's tours seemed to be from tourists in the area. I'd really love to push for Bluedale residents. That'll help get a good reputation going."

"I agree. Today was only day one with the ship, so we'll just keep forging ahead. I'm headed out for a run, but I'll see you tomorrow."

Making his way back to his cottage to change into

running gear, Hunter decided to explore somewhere new to run. Still on a high from a successful day, his mind went through the highlights and all the many wonderful tourists he'd got to meet. He wished more residents had come, but it was a good start. Everyone had a good time—the tour guide they hired did a fabulous job and the kids came off smiling with balloons and painted faces, which was an extra activity Max threw in last minute. When he walked out the door for his run, he remembered what Lana had told him about the trail by the marsh and decided to try it.

Gliding through the trail an hour later, he agreed it was the perfect path, offering many twists and turns to help him wind down after such an exciting day. He kept an even pace, enjoying the late-afternoon jog—a nice change to his usual early morning runs. It was a two-and-a-half-mile course, which brought him along the beach, through the marsh, and ended in a park. All he could hear was the sound of his feet shuffling as he quickened his stride once he hit an even stretch along the marsh.

In the distance, the diner where he and Lana had first met came into view, but he didn't need that reminder—she was already on his mind. Now, in the quiet, he wondered where she'd been all day. Her Jeep was still missing from the parking lot when he'd driven by the venue after the tours. He had no reason to call her, yet it was all he wanted to do. As the sun broke out from behind the trees, he tried to push away all the silly reasons he thought of to contact her—none of them business focused.

Another bend and Hunter could see the park ahead, which meant the end was close. Once he got to the final stretch of the park, Hunter slowed to a walk, pulling his shirt off and wiping away the sweat that drenched his face. The parking lot was just ahead, but something in the corner of his eye caught his attention. It was a sign with an arrow that said *Butterfly Garden.*

He must have missed it when he'd first got there because he was so focused on reading the trail route on the board at the entrance. Still feeling winded, he decided to check it out and walk a little more to cool down. When he got into the park, beautiful pink, yellow, purple, red, and white colors surrounded him. Butterflies swooped in every direction, landing on all the flowers and shrubs, and plenty of benches were placed around the garden.

He slowly walked through and admired all the natural beauty before noticing someone up ahead who was bent down close to one of the flower bushes. A few steps later and he recognized the deep-red braid down her back.

"Lana?" he asked as he got closer.

Lana turned and looked up, her eyes wide. "Hunter? What are you doing here?"

"I went for a run along the marsh trail that you told me about at breakfast and saw a sign for this garden," he said, wiping his face again. "The humidity sure picked up this afternoon."

She stood up to face him, her eyes gliding up and down. "I see that."

"Yeah, sorry about the shirt. I wasn't expecting to see anyone I knew out here. Do you come here often?"

Turning back around, she looked out at all the flowers. "This was one of my favorite places as a child to visit with…" She trailed off, shaking her head. "Yes, I come here a lot. It's a peaceful place to be, especially on my day off." That answered where she'd been all day.

Hunter watched her bend back over to smell a pink flower, and he'd wondered what she was going to say before she stopped herself. He wouldn't intrude, though.

"It's a very pretty garden, I agree. I'm glad I noticed the

sign," he said as she peeked up at him. "Is that one you were bent over observing a favorite?"

"I love all flowers, but no, that one isn't my favorite. Purple calla lilies are." Lana stood up again and began to walk down the path. Hunter fell in step beside her. "So, Mr. Graham, how was opening day with the tours?"

Trying not to stumble over himself in surprise that she'd asked, he took a second before answering her. "It went very well, thank you for asking." They walked a few more steps. "I know it's probably hard to talk about, especially since you ditched my offer to cater it." He gave her an amused look.

"I think I'm getting used to the changes, so it's fine." She matched his smirk. "But yeah, I did kind of ditch you, didn't I. Sorry about that."

"It's okay, I can take the punches."

"Good. 'Cause I have more to give." Lana playfully held up her fist.

"Whoa! Watch out then!" Hunter ducked, making Lana chuckle.

"In all seriousness, I wasn't sure how I felt about the offer, and I guess I dropped the ball on calling you back to decline." She gave him a sheepish shrug.

"Or you're afraid of the punches that *I* can throw!"

This ignited full laughter, and he lost himself as he watched her toss her braid behind her shoulder. The more she loosened up with him, the more he felt drawn to her.

"Oh, look! A red admiral." She pointed to a bush where a large black-and-red butterfly had landed.

"Wow! Look at those colors," he said, as the butterfly popped off and flew to its next location even closer to them.

Lana put her arm out. "Wait, let's watch for a minute. They're friendly butterflies, but we don't want to startle him." The butterfly sat perched on a flower, showing off its striking colors.

"You seem to know your butterflies." Hunter continued to observe it. "How do you know it's a male?"

"Well, he's small. Females are larger than that usually."

"I'm impressed." They locked eyes before she broke the stare and looked back at the garden.

"My grandma was an avid gardener. She told me all about the butterflies here on the Cape."

"Well, then I can understand why you're here on your day off," Hunter said, sneaking another glance at her while she watched the red admiral. When the butterfly flew off again, they continued their walk.

After a full circle around, they exited the garden, walking toward the parking lot.

"I'm glad everything went well for you today, Hunter." Lana stopped when they reached the entrance to the parking lot, and she looked up at him.

Hunter's nose crinkled. "Thank you, but I'm not so sure you mean that," he said gently.

"No…" She hesitated for a moment. "I do actually. As a business owner myself, I too understand the pressures of it all and the work that goes into it."

The late-afternoon sun cast a shadow behind Lana, giving her face a soft glow, and he felt his pulse pick up as her striking eyes pulled him in. She quickly looked down, giving him the chance to collect himself again.

"I better get myself to the shower. It was nice running into you here." He waited as she kept her eyes to the ground.

"Enjoy the rest of your day. I'm sure I'll be seeing you soon," she said, finally lifting her gaze.

Hunter watched her walk away and, just before he started for his car, she glanced back at him, and he caught a smile flicker across her face. Something was shifting between them. He absolutely would see her again. He'd make sure of it.

CHAPTER 13

The black clouds rumbled in the distance, threatening a downpour any second. Lana hurried to her car, balancing two big, brown paper bags in each arm, and was glad to cross that errand off her list. The seafood market had its normal Friday morning crowd, with customers filling up on their favorites for their weekend meal plans, making it hard for her to maneuver her way through.

A few drops of rain began to fall, and she put the bags into two coolers on her back seat, shutting the door and hopping into the driver's seat. There was a special on the shrimp in the market, so she made the extra trip, adjusting her own weekend special at the restaurant: lemon and herb shrimp skewers. With a salmon delivery coming that afternoon for salmon burgers, everything was now ready for the weekend ahead.

Lana began to drive off, and lightning lit up the gloomy day as rain beat down on her windshield. Turning her wipers on, she carefully made her way to her favorite outdoor lunch spot on the days she made trips to the seafood market—The Captain's Shack. As she pulled into the parking lot, she saw the staff lowering the sides of the awning around their deck filled with customers, which prompted her to call Heidi.

"Hey, how was the market?" Heidi answered.

"Great! I got a lot of shrimp, and they also had a special on their jumbo crab meat." Lana unfastened her seatbelt and reached down to grab her purse.

"Yum! I have a great salad recipe we can use that in," Heidi said.

"Sounds good to me. Is it raining there yet?"

"About to. I just heard a rumble."

"The storm is over my head, so it'll definitely be there soon. Can you pull the awning out now? It's always a pain to dry all the tables when we forget."

"Sure thing. I have some good news. A reservation for a small birthday party just came through online. I'll push the tables together and set up for that. The rain is supposed to stick around through the evening, so that'll be guaranteed business for a bad weather night."

"That's music to my ears. I'm going to grab something to eat, and I'll be there soon."

The Captain's Shack made the best lobster bisque, and no matter how many times she tried to replicate it at her own restaurant, she couldn't. *But they can't beat my clam chowder,* she thought, remembering how happy her grandad looked when he mentioned it and feeling her stomach drop with disappointment at the thought of him finding out that the family recipe had yet to continue with her restaurant. Thunder rumbled above and she looked up at the storm clouds. Hopefully the rain would at least slow down by the evening because, even with the patio covering, it always put a damper on the night, reducing her customer count.

It was days like today that always sent Lana into a tailspin of worry. Perhaps now that she was coming to terms with the loss of the inn, she really needed to reconsider what the bank had told her about a loan approval to get an addition for an indoor dining room.

Grabbing the umbrella she kept behind the passenger seat, she got out and hurried into The Captain's Shack, thinking about Nathan's new marketing angle. When she opened the door, voices boomed around her. Seeing how busy it was in the middle of the day encouraged her to roll up her sleeves and do just what he suggested, despite the emotional challenge it required, and find a way to connect with her customers in a way she never had before. If Nathan was right and it upped her traffic, the increased business could provide the funds to finally open for lunch.

She had a strong reputation for building her restaurant from the ground up, and she had pushed through so many struggles to get this far—she would get through this one too.

LANA SET one of the coolers down, rummaging through her purse for her keys to the restaurant. Heidi had texted her that she was stepping out to run an errand but listed off all she'd done so far with prep, leaving Lana to focus only on the marinade for the shrimp skewers. When she found the keys, she quickly stuck the right one into the door to get out of the drizzle that had started up again.

Putting her purse down on the desk in her office, she carried the cooler to the kitchen. Luckily the shrimp wasn't frozen, so it would make prep work faster. She set down the cooler before heading out to retrieve the second one from the car, and winced at the loud saw that blasted off noise next door. While she was starting to settle into all that was happening at the inn, it didn't make it much easier to watch, and her already low mood from the weather quickly plummeted further. This was going to take more patience than she was willing to give right now.

"Lana!" a male voice she could already recognize called out behind her, just as she reached her car. When she turned around, Hunter strode toward her, and she couldn't help but notice his short-sleeved button-down that showed off his burly physique, their walk from the Butterfly Garden replaying in her mind. "I have to say that I love your red Jeep!"

More noisy saws cut in from behind him and she squeezed her eyes shut. "Hello, Hunter," she said, popping her eyes open again. "Thanks, I like the red too."

"Yeah, those saws are loud." He motioned behind him. "But I told my crew that when you open for dinner, they have to cut all the noise."

"That's considerate of you. Thanks." She waited until he was closer, watching him walk with a smile that lit up his face against the gray clouds. "Don't you look cheery on this dreary, wet day?" she said dryly, as the construction noise pierced her ears again. She just wanted to get inside and drown out her worries with her cooking.

"I don't mind the rain. It gives us all a break from the hot sun."

Lana wanted to be polite, but it was proving to be hard as she couldn't help but imagine her grandparents' years of hard work being sawn right in half.

"I came over because I wanted to show you—"

"Hey, listen, I hate to be rude, but do you think you can show me whatever it is later? I'm busy getting things ready for the weekend." She leveled her gaze at him and regretted the words as soon as she said them. It was unprofessional and, besides, Heidi had already taken care of most of the prep.

Hunter's eyes widened, clearly not expecting that sudden reaction from her. "Of course, this can wait."

His deep-brown eyes captured hers for a moment before she turned around, grabbed the second cooler from her car, and made her way back inside. Guilt bubbled up in her when she made it back to the kitchen. She really needed to keep her composure because the last thing she needed were rumors spreading around Bluedale about any tension between them. That would only make her anxiety worse, and she didn't need people talking.

Turning her attention to the fridge, she opened it to make sure the cod was thawed enough for fish 'n' chips and went back to the counter. Heidi had the flour and beer batter already spread out and ready to go for later. Glancing at the clock on the wall, she remembered Rob would be there any minute to deliver the salmon, so she got going on the lemon and herb dressing for the skewers.

Over in the pantry, she grabbed two bags of lemons and put them down before gathering all the spices to mix with it. As she began the mundane task of squeezing the juice out of the lemons, her exchange with Hunter in the parking lot clouded her concentration. By the time she got through all of the lemons, it took everything she had to blank out the shocked expression on his face. Taking a deep breath, she combined the spices with the lemon juice, finishing it off with olive oil before mixing it all together. Covering up the bowl, she transferred the mixture into the fridge and rinsed her hands.

"Incoming!" Rob's voice echoed through her kitchen door.

"Perfect timing as always! Just set them over on the counter," Lana instructed while drying her hands.

"Sorry for the terrible weather, but it's bringing a nice break from the humidity. Have a good evening!" Rob nodded before heading back out.

Lana waved and began to sort the salmon, putting some of it in the freezer and the rest in the fridge for the salmon burgers. Just as she finished, she decided she'd have to bite the bullet and go over to apologize to Hunter. Every part of her resisted, but she couldn't stop once she started walking out the door.

When she crossed the parking lot, she had the urge to turn right back around, but she didn't. After knocking on the mobile office with no answer, she continued over to the front door of the venue. The door was open, so she went inside, not knowing where he could be. Voices murmuring in conversation down the hall caught her attention, and it became clear that two men were discussing measurements of some sort. It smelled like sawdust, and before she headed over to ask them where Hunter was, she stopped, suddenly realizing this was the first time she'd been inside the inn since it was sold for the first time, five years ago.

Trying not to let her emotions get the best of her, she looked around amazed. In a matter of weeks, they'd already demolished what used to be her grandma's front desk and knocked down a wall to open up the reception area. Tears stung her eyes as she remembered how she used to love playing "receptionist" as a little girl. It was more than she could bear to see, but she'd come to apologize to Hunter and she wasn't going to back down now.

A little sign caught her attention out of the corner of her eye. It said: *Cruise Bookings,* with an arrow. Following the arrow, she made her way down the hallway to an office—the same one that Grandad had sat in for nearly forty years.

Calm down. She steadied her quickening pulse, pushing away the image of her grandad sitting at his big oak desk. The door was slightly ajar, so she quietly knocked.

"Come on in," a male voice responded. When Lana opened the door, Hunter was seated inside, but he stood up when he saw it was her.

"Hunter, hi, are you busy?" she asked, her stomach flipping around against her nerves.

"I'm always busy, but that doesn't matter. What can I help you with, Lana? I'm assuming you're not here to book a tour or a wedding for the winter," he teased, sitting back down. "Please, have a seat."

Pulling out one of the folding chairs from the front of the desk, she sat down and looked around the office that was still mostly empty with bare walls. No trace of her grandad was left. The oak desk was now replaced with a small, black metal computer desk. "You need some life in this room," she finally said with a small smile, hoping it would break the awkwardness.

Hunter did a once-over of the room before he looked at her again. "This is my temporary event director's office before we get someone here full-time to take over. Sure beats the mobile office out there in the parking lot with the broken air conditioning." The corners of his eyes crinkled, and his charming smile seized her full attention. "Decorating is clearly not on his list."

That explained no one answering the door outside. Breaking away from his gaze, she looked down at his desk, buried under a complete disarray of papers. "Well, he isn't very orderly, is he?" She raised an eyebrow at him, and he chuckled.

"It's not all his fault—a lot of the paperwork is mine. I haven't spent that much time in here since I'm always making rounds on site, but it's cooler in here until we fix the air conditioning in my office. This rainy day is helping me catch up… or, rather, make my way through this mountain of paperwork filled with numbers."

"This is what Excel was created for," she joked again, relaxing into her seat a little more, hearing him laugh. "Listen, I came by to apologize for how I acted out in the parking lot before. It was rude and uncalled for, not to mention unprofessional and—" She stopped when Hunter put his hand up.

"Lana, please don't feel the need to apologize, although I appreciate it. But the truth is, I understand why you did, and honestly… I would feel the same way if I were you. I can only imagine how hard this is." He locked eyes with her again and she fiddled with her purse strap.

"Not to mention how I'm forced to witness it all," she said with a smirk.

Hunter smiled. "Okay, I see your point. But I still get it. Being right next door just keeps all of this right in your face." He looked down at his desk and began stacking and restacking the same papers, which she oddly found adorable. It was touching how much he seemed to care about how she felt, when all he had to worry about was his own business.

"It's getting easier," she admitted. "Despite the way I acted just before."

"That's good to hear." He set the papers down one last time before his chocolate eyes found hers again. Lana remembered Alicia's insistence on needing to know if he was handsome, and she nearly found herself nodding in answer to that question. Hunter Graham was, no doubt, very attractive.

"What was it you wanted to show me before?" she asked, bringing them both back to the conversation.

"When we cleaned out the kitchen, we found some champagne flutes tucked away in the back of one of the closets.

There's only four of them inscribed with 'Bluedale, 1998' and I figured they were your grandparents'?"

"Yes, they must be, but I don't recall seeing flutes like that before."

"Let's go get them. I left them in the kitchen." Hunter stood up and she followed him out.

Lana held her breath as he led her out of the office and to the kitchen that she had fallen in love with as a child. When she got there, she didn't recognize it at all. All the appliances were ripped out. But as she stared at the empty walls, she noticed the center island was still intact. Her grandma's smiling face as she handed her a plate of pancakes while she sat on a stool across the island flashed before her.

Blinking out of the memory, she turned to find Hunter in a supply closet. A minute later, he came out carrying a box. Setting it down on the counter, he pulled out a flute and handed it to her. *Bluedale, 1998* was beautifully written against the glass in a shadowed dark-blue color.

"So you've never seen these before?" he asked.

"No, I haven't." She studied the glass. "They're beautiful. I'll certainly take them," she said, putting it back in the box. "I'm surprised the last owners didn't see them."

"Me too. But they were really hidden back in that closet. Easy to miss if you weren't cleaning it out like we were." Hunter looked down at the box. "May I walk you out?"

"You don't have to. It's not like it's a long walk." She flipped her hair over her shoulder, adjusted her purse, and picked up the box before noticing that Hunter was watching her.

"I want to," he said, keeping his gaze fixed on hers. Lana felt a tingle shoot down her back as they made their way out of the kitchen.

Hunter walked her all the way to the front door, holding it open as she looked up one more time at him. Her head told her to keep moving forward, but her feet felt heavy beneath her thudding heart as she caught the faint scent of his spicy aftershave. All the stress of everything changing so fast with the inn faded while she walked away, her mind now drifting into curiosity about this man and who he was outside his lavish event venue.

CHAPTER 14

After a gloomy weekend, with rain continuing off and on, Monday welcomed back the sunshine, helping the crew to finally remove the last of the old deck, leaving a wide-open space that dipped down to the sand. In its place would be a raised stone patio, featuring couches and other seating, firepits, an outdoor bar, and cooking spaces. A beautiful area for pictures and fun.

After seeing how much room they had to work with now that the old deck was cleared, more ideas flooded Hunter's mind while he watched from a window. From where he stood, he could picture a large stone fireplace stacked nicely along the side, and he made a mental note to go over the design again with his team.

Every time he walked through the construction site, he found himself making many reminders for himself; however, at the moment, the most pressing thing of all was the fact that his father was finally coming to Bluedale. He was due to arrive that afternoon, and Hunter had been scrambling to get things ready to show him—not to mention facing the question he knew his father couldn't wait to ask: had he presented the offer to Lana yet? He'd been bracing himself all day for it and was coming up short on how to answer him. The truth was, as he became more and more acquainted with Bluedale, he was becoming less and less convinced he should make the offer at all. He was barely making headway with winning over the town as it was. Slamming Lana with something like that, he'd come to learn, would spread very quickly around the town.

Stepping aside for the yellow tape that someone was spreading across the doorway to the old deck, he felt a tap on his shoulder.

"Hey, Mr. Graham." Bob was standing behind him.

"Hi, Bob," he greeted the foreman. "Good start to the week. It's looking great out there. Can't wait to see the new patio complete." Hunter nodded toward the doors that were now blocked by the yellow tape.

"Thanks. Glad excavation can get here now to prepare the ground for the retaining walls. It'll be gorgeous out there once it's all done. So, listen, we saved that piece of wood from the old deck that you asked for. The one with Lana's name engraved on it. I cut it down smaller and brought it to your office."

"Thanks, I appreciate it," Hunter said as Bob turned to leave. Hunter looked back toward the doors, thinking about the deck, when an idea occurred to him. Lana's name wouldn't have been engraved there unless it meant something to her. "Hey, Bob?"

Bob stopped. "Yeah?"

"You're from Bluedale, right? You know Lana Kelly?"

"Sure do. Known her my whole life."

"Do you think it could be crafted in a way for her to keep? Is that something you think you could do?"

"I think I could give it a try. What do you have in mind?"

he asked, and Hunter motioned for him to follow him to his mobile office.

"Don't worry, we got the air conditioning fixed."

A few minutes later, after going over the details with him and confirming he could get it to him by the next day, Hunter pulled out his phone, found the number, and hit call.

"On the Bay, this is Lana," she answered a little breathlessly.

"Hi, Lana, it's Hunter," he said, wondering what she was whipping up in that kitchen of hers. His crew couldn't stop talking about her food the other day and were discussing when to go back. He needed to get himself over there. Besides… he would take any excuse to be near her.

"Hi, Hunter, what's up?" She sounded perky, prompting him to sit taller in his chair.

"I called because I have something to give you, but it won't be ready until tomorrow. Think you can swing by in the afternoon to get it?"

"It won't be ready?" she repeated.

Hunter smiled, pleased he'd thought of this. "Yes, you heard that correctly. I'm putting something together for you that I think you'll appreciate."

"Do I have to wait until tomorrow to know what it is?"

Hunter laughed. "Not good with surprises, I see."

"I like surprises all right. But from you? I'm intrigued."

He could hear the playfulness in her tone. "You'll just have to wait. I'll see you tomorrow. Any time after lunch. I'll be here."

"See you then."

They hung up, and Hunter found himself still grinning a few seconds later when a call from his father startled him out of his daze.

"Hi, Dad, all packed?" Hunter asked.

"Yes, and I already left. I should be arriving at my hotel in about three hours, according to my GPS. I stayed in Connecticut last night to shorten the drive a bit."

"It was certainly a long drive coming here from the city. You're staying in the hotel over by the public beach, right?"

"Yes, and I saw there's a great place that we can meet for dinner close to it. Called Bluefish Grill and Bar. Let's meet around six?"

"See you then." Hunter hung up the phone, opened his laptop, and quickly began to double-check all the updates he wanted to share with his father. As he looked through it, he couldn't have been prouder with all they'd done so far with the renovations. The bumps hadn't been too big, so progress was still on track. The ship had made a good start for them with the day tours that were slowly but steadily increasing, and new events continued to book from July through September, with the first one coming up in a couple weeks: a retirement party right after the Fourth of July.

Feeling satisfied with what he'd prepared, Hunter got up to finish some last-minute tasks before getting himself ready for dinner. Walking through the soon-to-be ballroom, he pushed back some tarp and heard voices yelling outside. When he got to the double doors with the yellow tape, he glanced in the direction of the noise and saw Kevin surveying the area now that it was cleared, pointing out something to the crew. A beach cleaning machine drove in lines, picking up all the leftover debris in the sand.

Just before he turned to leave, he saw her. Lana was down the beach, closer to the water, but instead of enjoying the view, she was watching the construction of the patio area. She was too far away to make out her facial expression, but she stood motionless, observing the empty space that must have once held a special place in her heart. Clenching his jaw against the urge to run out there and stand with her, he put his focus back on his workday. He felt the weight of then and now sit heavily on his shoulders. If this was how she looked watching the deck come down, how could he possibly convince her to accept their offer and move her restaurant away from this property?

STEPPING OUT OF THE SHOWER, Hunter got himself dressed, and checked the time. He still had over an hour before he had to meet his father for dinner, so with nothing else to do, he decided to head out and stop in town. He thought about his mother and how much she loved little keepsakes from different places, so he wanted to venture into the souvenir shops that lined the center of Bluedale.

Grabbing the first parking spot he saw, he got out and began to stroll down the street. The first shop featured all the gear you would need to swim, surf, and enjoy a beach day. Sweatshirts of all colors with *Bluedale* written across them hung on the wall in the back, and Hunter made his way over to them. He knew by now that the nights could sometimes be cool, especially along the beach, and figured why not dress the part. He selected a dark-blue one, found his size, and started toward the register.

Back out on the street, he walked past a couple other shops, including one that had paintings of Cape Cod and sea glass sculptures displayed. When he got to a shop that looked promising for a gift for his mother, he went in and was overwhelmed by all the small mementos that filled the shelves. Everything from Cape Cod's famous saltwater taffy and fudge to various seashells, coffee mugs, custom jewelry, bath soaps, and more was all around him. Looking through the items, he stopped when he found exactly the right gift. Three small, wooden matching cheeseboards, in three different colors with the shape of the Cape Cod peninsula painted on the top. His mother loved to entertain, so he knew she'd get good use out of this. A small line had gathered at the checkout, and just as he got in the back, he saw a familiar face in front of him.

"Hello." It was the bartender he'd met his first day in town. He turned to extend his hand, and Hunter noticed another man standing close by. "Good to see you again."

"Hi there, good to see you too." Hunter shook the man's free hand, noticing the basket he was holding filled with stuff.

"Giveaways for a party at the bar tomorrow night," he explained, holding it up. "Anyway, I don't think we officially met. My name's Ross and this is my dad, Greg."

"Nice to officially meet you, Ross, and you too, Greg," Hunter said.

"So, Hunter, I heard you're bulldozing the inn and turning it into something fancy," Greg said.

Hunter nearly took a step back instead of forward as the line got closer to the cashier.

"If that's how you want to put it." He hesitated when he noticed both men's even stares. "Yes, we're turning it into an event venue." While racking his brain to explain some more, he saw them glance at each other before smiles spread slowly across their faces.

Greg nudged Hunter's shoulder. "I'm just messing with you. It's been the talk all over town. Ross and I were just saying the other day we wanted to try one of those day tours we heard about." The man grew serious again. "And just so you know, I think it's wonderful what you're creating. The inn needed a major facelift."

"It definitely needed some changes, but it's still a bit sad," Ross said.

"Yeah, but with Lana's grandad ill in a nursing home, it's time for new beginnings," Greg said to his son.

"I heard about her grandad," Hunter said, glancing at his feet, feeling like perhaps this conversation was growing a bit too personal about Lana.

"You hear all of it?" Greg asked.

"Bits and pieces, but not the whole story," Hunter admitted.

"Did you know the inn was sold at auction when Lana's grandad lost it?"

"That part I did know." Hunter looked up, curious as to what he'd share next.

"It was sad for many reasons when they first lost the inn. You see, Lana was raised there after her parents died when she was young." Greg shook his head, looking down. "Such a sad story that was."

Hunter felt his stomach churn. "I knew that part too…" He trailed off, holding his breath in anticipation of more details. Each time Lana came into conversation, the pieces of her story became clearer.

"Yeah, it was a terrible accident. Anyway, she spent the rest of her childhood with her grandparents at the inn," Ross cut in and explained, reaching the counter and putting his basket on top when it was his turn. "I hear her grandad was trying to get her through school and took out a second mortgage to pay her tuition. Once he started to fall ill, he couldn't keep up anymore and became so far in debt that poor Lana wouldn't have stood a chance with it anyway. It needed someone like you to come for it."

"Oh, I see," Hunter said, trying to absorb what he'd just learned. "I know she had interest in buying it again and I understand why, especially after what you just shared. That inn must've been a huge part of her comfort after she lost her parents."

Both men nodded in response.

"I've been working on trying to connect with her over this ever since."

"Have you succeeded?" Ross asked, pulling his wallet out.

"Getting there, but now I know why you wished me luck with her," Hunter said.

While Ross paid for his items, the man's father faced him again. "You did her right, Hunter. She just doesn't know that yet."

Hunter wasn't sure how to respond. He stood in silence, trying to make sense of Greg's words. The inn was everything to Lana, so how could he have done her right? That's all he'd been trying to do since he got here—figure out how to make things right between them.

"No, she doesn't," Hunter finally said.

"The inn was a beautiful part of her history and Bluedale's, and that's never going to change, no matter what you turn it into. I just hope she sees that too," Greg said, as Ross stepped away from the counter.

When it was Hunter's turn to check out, he put the wooden serving boards on the counter, still completely perplexed by what Greg had just said. He turned to both of them one more time. "Well, thank you for the support. I hope you do come take a tour."

Ross nodded. "We sure will. It sounds like a good time."

Hunter fought the urge to pick up the phone and call Lana, but what would he even say? He was looking forward to giving her the gift tomorrow, but he needed to do more. Ross was right—it didn't matter how much he updated and renovated it; the building would always belong to Lana's family. Offering to take more away from her was not something he could entertain anymore.

THE BAR WAS QUIETER than Hunter expected when he walked into the restaurant, holding his laptop. Despite it being a Monday evening, everywhere else he'd been since arriving on the Cape had been packed since Memorial Day passed.

He spotted his father seated at a small table next to the bar, already sipping on a beer. When he sat down across from him, his father nodded and slid over another bottle.

"Thanks, Dad." Hunter took a long sip of the crisp, cold liquid before setting it back down. "How was the drive?"

"Easy. Traffic was light, but it's early in the week so that's probably why. I couldn't imagine trying to get to the Cape on the weekends."

"It's not busy in here either, which is a nice change. Everywhere I've been the last few weeks has been packed wall-to-wall with people. The tours on the ship have filled easily." Hunter picked up the menu, scanning through the options.

The waitress came by and greeted him, going over the specials.

"The cannelloni sounds good." Hunter looked at his father. "Did you have a chance to look at the menu?"

"Yes, I already know what I want."

For a while after they ordered, they fell into what felt like forced small talk, discussing his father's golfing tips and Hunter's runs through Bluedale's beautiful scenery, before their food arrived.

They ate in awkward silence until his father sat back, putting his napkin on his plate and taking the last sip of his beer. "That was delicious. There's nothing like seafood on Cape Cod."

"I agree," Hunter said.

"So let's jump into some updates. I went over the design you're narrowing down, and I'm thinking let's keep this much simpler. Clean and chic for a more upmarket result, especially when we begin to open more seaside venues along the New England coast. Remember, the look carries the reputation, especially with the outdoor space being on the water."

The waitress came by and cleared their plates, and the only thing Hunter could picture while listening to his father's ramblings about design was Lana standing on the beach, watching the deck being demolished. His father must have noticed his distant stare because when the waitress came back with two more beers, Hunter blinked out of his daze and saw he was looking directly at him.

"Everything all right, Hunter?" his father asked.

Hunter gripped the bottle, tapping his finger against the glass, unsure of how to answer. Not because he didn't know how he felt about his father's decor input, but rather, *why* he was suddenly opposed to the idea.

"Bluedale..." He trailed off. *Perhaps Bluedale is going to show you instead.* Lana's words popped into his mind. "It isn't a chic type of town, from what I've gathered so far in my time here." Hunter swallowed against his father's even stare.

"Is that so?"

He thought about the comments from the townspeople so far. "It's just that, the building is well known in Bluedale, and is remembered for what it brought to the town over the years. I've experienced a homier feel here, and I think something more casual would fit better at the inn. Perhaps that's why tourists choose to come to Bluedale. Thinking back over the design for the new patio earlier today, I was picturing something a bit more relaxing and cozier to capture that same vibe."

His father narrowed his eyes. "You mean the venue."

"Yes, the venue. What did you think I was talking about?"

"Well, you just called it the inn."

"I was thinking about it, is all. Trying to get a good handle on a design that fits this town." Hunter looked past his father, noticing that the bar had filled up with more people. He had referred to it as the inn and hadn't even realized it.

"Just keep your focus on the project ahead." His father gave him a long stare. "And the offer? I'm getting the sense you haven't approached Lana Kelly about that yet?"

Hunter hesitated, but knew the longer he lingered on the question, the more his father would press him. "Not yet, but I am actually planning to approach her again very soon." *Except, it won't be about an offer*, he thought, keeping his eyes on his dad.

His father nodded and took a swig of his beer. They finished up their drinks, and when Hunter left the restaurant, he breathed out a sigh of relief. He wasn't sure how much longer he could hold off explaining why the buyout offer hadn't been presented yet, but for now he needed more time to think it all through.

Besides, the longer he avoided another potential buyout, the more he could get done with the venue and the more bookings he could secure on the cruise line, showing his father how well it was going—even without Lana's property. It would increase the possibility of his father letting the offer idea go.

Something had pulled Hunter into this town the minute he first arrived, and that same intangible something brought life to every area of this project in unexpected ways. And he had no idea what it all meant yet.

CHAPTER 15

"Lana?" Nathan waved his hand in front of her face. "Did I lose you?"

Snapping out of the stupor she was in, she looked at Nathan. "Sorry, I lost focus there for a minute. What were you asking me?"

Nathan narrowed his eyes. "Hmm, I'd say that looked more like daydreaming. I know it's Tuesday and you have a long week ahead, but what's going on in that mind of yours?"

Lana clasped her hands together on her desk. "Just thinking about how we're going to relaunch the restaurant with this angle," she lied. The only thing circling around in her mind was Hunter Graham and whatever it was that he wanted to show her that afternoon… along with those deep, unfathomable dark eyes of his that seemed so contrary to his all-business surface. "So, what do you have for me?"

Nathan was here for an early morning marketing meeting after giving her time to think it through. She still didn't have a set answer for him, so she needed to keep her focus on what they were discussing, and not Hunter's enticing charm.

"I've been thinking about this a little more and I have

some suggestions, but it will require you to dig deep to make this happen," Nathan told her, which immediately pulled her back to the present.

"Dig deep? How so?"

He faced her, and something in his expression told her to brace herself. "We could use old photos of you with your parents and grandparents. Particularly of you all at the inn, on the pontoon, as well as here when it was your father's fish market."

Lana felt her heartbeat double in speed. She eyed him carefully, seeing full well the enthusiasm on his face. "What do you have in mind?"

"Let's start with the website. I think it needs a bit of a... makeover."

Lana crossed her arms. "A makeover? You said you wanted to make it more user friendly, but I think it's designed quite nicely actually."

"It doesn't look bad, but hear me out and take a deep breath because I know this is a sensitive subject." Nathan sat back. "I'd like to use a photo of you and your dad on the pontoon, for example, and also of you two inside the fish market, to tell your story front and center on the site, while bringing the visual to life through those pictures."

"Okay..." Lana relaxed her arms, shifting in her seat and still feeling a little hesitant about how intimate this was getting. The mention of the pontoon made her stomach clench, but she needed to at least listen to what he was planning.

"What if we also took these photos, as well as some of you in Bluedale—since this is, after all, your hometown—and continue that storytelling here at On the Bay? Especially the pictures of when it was a fish market. We can even get them reprinted in black and white, making them look more clas-sic. Photos of you as a child with your parents and grandparents would bring instant connection to the customers coming in."

"Without a dining room, wouldn't it be hard to hang all those photos?" Lana asked, ignoring the knots that continued to tighten in her stomach. Nathan was certainly striking all the nerves.

"There's plenty of room where people order at the windows to hang a handful of the most important pictures that show the evolution of the restaurant. We could even get some new paper take-out menus for the regular items and incorporate the pictures there too."

Lana swiveled in her chair, her face contorted in thought. Nathan's plan had been sitting with her for days, and now envisioning everything in more detail made it feel fresh in her heart. "This would be a big thing for me to share." She stared past Nathan, her childhood flying through her thoughts like a movie.

Faint memories on the boat with her father clenched within her as tears began to swim in her eyes. Her past was something she'd never thought to publicly display, keeping it stored safely in her heart.

"I told you that you would have to dig deep," Nathan said quietly, reaching for her shoulder.

"I think I've always just assumed the locals who come in either already know about my history because they lived here at the time, or because they've heard about it through the grapevine. I've never thought to put it out there like this."

"It's what Bluedale is all about—vacation vibes with the comforts of home and family. You and yours are a big part of what this town represents. Let's show that off here and get people talking." Nathan pulled his hand away and turned his laptop around to face her.

"Well… you're spot-on about Bluedale. That is who we are." Lana looked at the screen.

Nathan leaned over to click on an image he'd brought up. "We can replicate this with ads and social media. Here I have an example so you can see." He pulled up another image. "See the small caption underneath this stock photo I found of a man and his daughter on a boat? It's not of you and your family specifically, but see how I'm telling the audience about the possible adventures they could have on the water? That's what we would want to recreate on your social media accounts." He sat up straight and looked at Lana. "I really feel that your business will grow through bringing awareness of your upbringing and what inspired you to transform your father's fish market to On the Bay—including what once was with the inn too, since that's also a big part of who you are."

"But look what the inn is turning into. Don't you think pictures of my family and me, and how we used to be connected to the inn, will seem irrelevant with the new venue?"

"No, I don't. It's the sentimental part of this that will bring more people in and send your reputation surging. You and your family have a solid stamp here on this property, including next door, even with the changes."

Lana turned away from the laptop, pulling up the reservations for that weekend on her phone, and saw only one clambake. This was the slowest season she'd ever had, and she needed a new way to stand out. Nathan's idea not only did that, but would introduce her restaurant to the public all over again.

"So are you thinking a relaunch?" Lana glanced up from her phone.

"That's exactly what I'm thinking. Your five-year anniversary is coming up and this would be a fabulous way to celebrate," Nathan said. "And with the fancy venue going up next door, more eyes will already be on this location. I personally think it'll be a great thing to relaunch alongside all that."

Graham Bayview Events wasn't the only shining new tourist attraction in Cape Cod, with deluxe businesses like his being put up all over the Cape every year—his just happened to be right in her face, all while holding a special part of her heart. Except, they didn't have her: she was the face of it all and *she* was the one who could bring in the love of Bluedale, not the inn.

"Fancy or not, Hunter Graham doesn't have the human appeal you're hoping to highlight in this new marketing plan," she said. But as soon as the words came out, the way Hunter had looked at her when they were observing the red admiral that day in the Butterfly Garden popped into her head. His professional demeanor had been suddenly over-shadowed by the tender way he'd asked about her interest in butterflies.

She picked up the picture of her parents on her desk, rubbing her thumb over it. Nathan had always been great at marketing, but was this the right thing to do? She wasn't sure, but it was the only plan she had brewing.

"Okay." She looked over at him. "I trust you, so let's go for it." Still feeling unsure, she forced a smile, trying to look positive for Nathan, but her heart felt like it was sinking—right along with the reservations. Putting her past on display was going to challenge her in a way she wasn't sure she was ready for, and as she closed her eyes, she saw Grandad's face. What would he think of this?

WALKING through the parking lot with the construction noise was getting a little easier, and it distracted Lana from the nervous tingle in her stomach as she made her way toward Hunter's mobile office.

When she got there, she could hear his voice mumbling in

what sounded like a phone call on the other side of the door. Not sure if she should wait, she hesitated but knew he was expecting her.

Knocking softly, she heard him pause his conversation.

"Come on in!" he called out, before returning to the call and motioning for her to have a seat in a chair next to his desk when she popped her head in.

Taking a quick look around the office, she noticed the same clutter from the office inside the other day when she'd come to apologize.

"Listen, Dad, I need to go. We can discuss the rest of this when you get here in a bit. There's something important I need to do right now."

Lana sat down. "Looks like the papers just keep piling up." She found that she enjoyed poking fun at him.

Hunter nodded sheepishly. "Yeah, you could say that."

"I hope this is an okay time. I can come back if you're tied up with something else."

"Not tied up. Well…" He laughed. "That's not true—I'm always tied up, but I assume you are too. So I'm glad you took the time to come here."

Lana watched him bend over and pull a box from under his desk. "More stuff you found?" she guessed. "I'm going to ask my grandad about the flutes. He might recognize them."

Hunter placed his hands on top of the box, looking right into her eyes. "I hope he does." Reaching in, he pulled out what appeared to be a round piece of wood.

"Is that a plaque?"

"Yes, but I didn't find it this way, which was why I couldn't give it to you yesterday. I had one of my carpenters create it for you."

Now he had her full attention. "Create it for me?"

Hunter leaned over the desk. "Okay, before I give this to you, I want you to know it's all right to let me know if I've crossed any boundaries. I just wanted you to have a piece of what was clearly special to you." He handed her the wood, and Lana could hardly contain the emotions that bubbled up to the surface when she saw it. The piece of wood that she'd carved her name into the summer Grandad redid the deck was beautifully shaved down and mounted on a darker piece of wood behind it. Flipping it around, she could see hooks in case she wanted to hang it somewhere.

"Is this—" She sniffed, trying to quickly stop the tears that immediately pooled. "I'm sorry, I wasn't expecting this." She paused to try and settle herself.

"Please don't apologize. I guessed this must be important to you, and I can see that I was right." Hunter came around the desk and leaned against it in front of her. "And if you're asking if this is from the old deck, it is."

"How did you even see this? It was in the corner and so small." She looked up to face him. Hunter didn't need to hear that this engraving was done in the same summer she'd lost her parents, only days before they died—when her father helped her carve her name.

"By chance. One of the guys on the crew happened to notice it. He also knew of you and your connection to the inn—his name is Bob—so he had a hunch to bring the wood to me." Hunter bent down next to her chair, both of them admiring the carpenter's talented work before turning to face each other at the same time, his gaze drawing her in.

Lana's heart hammered in her chest as she breathed in his cologne, and she forced herself to look back down at the plaque. "Yes... I know Bob from childhood. And I'm so thankful he spotted this and brought it to your attention. I love it. Thank you so much." She ran her finger along her name.

"You're welcome. When I saw you watching the demolition of the deck last week, it really struck home how hard all of this is for you. So I asked Bob if he could create this yesterday, and he did."

Just then, the door swung wide open and an older man with the same striking looks as Hunter walked in. He had on his readers, scanning over a document, but he lowered it when he saw Hunter near her chair.

"Hello…" The man eyed her before he looked at Hunter, who was now standing. "I didn't mean to intrude."

"Not intruding, Dad. Lana and I were just talking about something we found here that belonged to her." Hunter reached his hand out. "May I show him?"

Lana nodded and handed it to him, nervously glancing up at his father, who didn't look interested at all.

"Lana? Are you Lana Kelly from next door?" his father asked.

"Yes, I am." She stopped, waiting on an introduction, but his father continued to just watch her. "My family owned this place for a long time, and Hunter here found something that he thought I'd like to have."

"I see," he said, taking the plaque from his son, barely lowering his eyes to it before handing it back to her. "Well, this certainly is… a nice gesture." He turned his attention to Hunter. "We have the meeting with Bob in fifteen minutes. He wants to go over a potential issue he found before we get the retaining wall put in for the patio. It was nice to meet you, Lana." After giving Hunter a second long stare, he walked out.

"That was my dad, Philip Graham. I'm sorry he was so abrupt. When it's the middle of the day, his mind is all work and no play." Hunter smiled, shrugging it off.

Lana's shoulders released with tension she'd been holding. "It's okay. I better let you get to that meeting." She held the plaque to her chest. "Thank you again, Hunter."

"Of course. I'm so glad it made you happy," he said,

watching her stand up. "By the way, the guys here haven't stopped talking about your lobster rolls. I'll make sure to stop by there soon for one."

"I hope you do," she replied, and was surprised at how much she meant it. They both stood in awkward silence for a moment, Hunter looking as though he had more he wanted to say, but remaining quiet.

"Have a great rest of your day," he finally said, and they both left the office, this time splitting ways in the parking lot.

When she reached her restaurant, holding the plaque tight against her, she was still at a loss for words that Hunter had gone out of his way to do anything for her—let alone something so meaningful. Pausing outside the door, she suddenly found herself trying to drum up what excuse she could think of to see him again.

CHAPTER 16

The wooden dance floor gleamed with the fresh floor shield that was spread across it that morning. It was strangely silent since the crew had jetted out a bit early to grab some beers to start their weekend, but Hunter didn't mind. It was nice to do a walk-through without being pulled in a million directions. His father was meeting him for dinner before he headed back to New York the following day, and Hunter was relieved with how pleased he'd looked all week watching the progress and meeting with all their senior workmen.

Looking around the main ballroom again, he nodded with satisfaction. The tarps were down, and the large room was nicely extended now that the walls between the old lounge, indoor sitting area, and dining room were knocked down. The structural engineer team he'd selected had done a fantastic job so far, raising the ceiling and knocking out the rooms above it. The addition on the opposite side of the building for the new smaller event room and upstairs bridal rooms wasn't set to begin for another couple of weeks, since hang-ups with a delay on supplies kept occurring. Other than that, the old part of the building was shaping up nicely.

Checking the time, he decided to get in a quick run before meeting with his father for dinner. The boardwalk along the main public beach seemed like a good place since it was overcast, and the sun wouldn't be beating down on him. When he got to the parking lot, he saw Lana's Jeep and instantly wondered how she was doing. It had been days since he'd given her the plaque and he'd hoped to go to her restaurant for dinner at some point, but with a very busy week, he just couldn't find the time.

The traffic through town was dense, but after being in Bluedale a month, he'd found this to be typical on Fridays. New tourists came in every weekend, clogging the streets as they all tried to get to their hotels. This also meant more reservations for the tours on the ship, and just as he turned off to the road toward the cottage, an idea struck him. After parking in the driveway, he pulled out his phone. He quickly found the number he wanted.

"On the Bay, this is Lana," she answered, and Hunter felt his hands go a bit clammy while gripping the phone.

"Hi, Lana, it's Hunter," he said.

A short pause, and Hunter swallowed while he waited.

"Hi, Hunter!" Lana said, with more enthusiasm than she'd ever expressed in the past. "How are you?"

He opened his car door and headed toward his cottage. "I'm doing great. Been a busy week."

"Same here. We got a few more reservations for the weekend, but I'm grateful for them, despite all the extra prep work they'll require." She giggled through the phone and the sound of her happiness had him smitten. He needed to hear more of that wonderful sound.

"Well, speaking of reservations, that's why I called." He

held the phone against his ear with his shoulder and opened the cottage door. Once he'd got it open, he repositioned himself with the phone, tapping speaker as he went upstairs. "Any chance there's an opening for a reservation on your patio tonight?"

"Did you check our availability online?" she asked, and he instantly felt silly for calling her.

"No… I should have done that, huh?"

She laughed again. "It's all good. For how many?"

"Two."

"Let me check for you, hang on just a moment," she said, and she put their call on hold.

Hunter sat on the edge of his bed, shaking his head at himself. He could've done this himself and not bothered her while she was busy in the kitchen, but then he wouldn't have been able to chat with her like this…

A minute later she was back. "Okay…" She paused for a moment. "I had to get to my laptop. So it looks like I have one more available table for seven o'clock if that works. When you get here, look for a reserved table with the number eight on a card on top."

"That's perfect. Thank you, Lana. Looking forward to your delicious food."

When they hung up, he realized the hard part was next. With a deep breath, he scrolled through his phone until he found his father's name and closed his eyes as it rang. Ever since he'd walked in on Hunter with Lana in his office the other day, his father couldn't help but make a few snide comments about him "catering to her feelings" too much, and to just make the offer and get it done. To Hunter, it was more complicated than that, yet he had no idea what it all meant. He did know one thing—he was doing more than just trying to smooth things over at this point. The offer had continued to fall further from his mind, knowing it was not the reason he wanted to spend time with her.

"Hi, Hunter," his father answered. "Just getting myself all packed up here to leave in the morning."

"Try and leave as early as possible when traffic will be slow," Hunter told him.

"That's the plan. So, what's going on?"

"I know we had reservations already, but I have a place in mind that I really think you'd enjoy instead. I was even able to get last-minute reservations. It's at On the Bay, next door to the venue. You have to try Lana's food before you leave." Hunter stood up and faced the door that led out to his small balcony. Watching the sharp blue water in the distance that sat still under the clouds, he waited for his dad's response.

"Is trying her food the only reason we're going there?" his father asked, which surprised him, knowing how fast his father argued just about anything.

"The food there is exceptional," Hunter said. "What other reason would I have?" *Besides a chance to see Lana.*

"It just seems like a very specific place to change our dinner plans to."

"Well, it is. I chose to go there on purpose because I think you should try out our neighbor's food."

His father backed down at that statement because, after all, it had been him who'd originally pushed to remain on good terms with Lana in order to get the offer sealed and closed on. If his father could experience her food and get a glimpse of her world, perhaps telling him he had serious hesitations about the offer would be received a little better.

"See you at seven." Hunter hung up, putting his father's questioning remarks aside, and went to the bathroom to get changed for his run.

THE AIR WAS STILL a bit heavy under the cloud cover, but without the sun, it was a comfortable run. Slowing down to an easy walk, Hunter reached his arms up and crossed his hands together behind his head to cool down some more with each breath. The boardwalk was still full of people walking along the beach, dipping in and out of souvenir shops or restaurants, and certainly not slowing down for a less than perfect day.

Ahead, the bakery came into view—the line was nearly out the door. People came out holding bags of delicious treats to snack on during the late-afternoon hour. Stopping to stretch just outside the bakery, he rested his leg on the side railing of the boardwalk and extended it, relieving all the built-up tension from the run. Just as he put his other leg down and turned to continue the walk back to his car, he collided with a tall blonde woman, wearing large fashionable sunglasses. She was holding an iced coffee, some of it spilling onto her hand from when he bumped her.

"I'm so sorry. I need to pay better attention," Hunter said with a sheepish grin, while she placed her coffee on the ground to check her shirt. "Here, let me get you some napkins from inside." He hurried in, spotted the napkins, grabbed a few, and went back out.

The woman was shaking the excess coffee off her hand when he handed her the napkins.

"It's okay, it happens," she said, taking the napkins and wiping the liquid off. When she'd bent over to pick her coffee back up, she pushed her sunglasses onto the top of her head and looked straight at him. "Here on vacation?"

"Not vacation." He watched her walk over to the garbage and toss the napkins in. "I'm here for business."

"Are you? What kind of business?" she asked.

"My father and I have a development company. We just

bought an old inn and are in the process of remodeling it into an event venue. We also have a new cruise line for events and day tours along the bay."

He nearly backed up when he saw the woman's eyes widen.

"Your name doesn't happen to be Hunter, does it?"

"That's me…" He paused, unsure of what to say next. He knew Bluedale was a small town, but his name just kept on spreading.

She narrowed her eyes. "Ah, yes, okay," the woman said knowingly, extending her hand. "My name is Alicia."

Hunter shook her hand, a bit confused. She certainly didn't seem happy to meet him. "Nice to meet you."

"I know exactly which inn your company bought. My best friend, Lana, owns the restaurant next door to you." She remained expressionless.

Hunter nodded. Now it made sense. "Oh, I see. Well, Lana seems like a wonderful person. In fact, my father and I are going to her restaurant tonight to eat."

"She certainly is wonderful—that I can agree with you on. You two will definitely enjoy her food." Her face finally relaxed, and the makings of a small smile appeared. "It was nice to meet you too." She started to turn and walk away, but something stopped her. "Lana is going to thrive next door to you."

"I sure hope so," he said.

"Happy to hear you support her. And Hunter…" Alicia hesitated for a moment, pursing her lips. "She's coming back."

"Coming back?

"You'll have to wait and see." With that, Alicia slid her sunglasses back on and walked away, leaving him to ponder their exchange.

ON THE BAY immediately drew him in when Hunter and his father stepped out onto the patio. The strung outdoor lights, music playing popular songs softly through outdoor speakers, and pleasant conversation all around—it was very inviting. He noticed it was not a table-service restaurant, but rather a typical quick serve where you placed your order at one of the windows.

"A fast-food joint?" his father asked. "That takes reservations?"

After scanning the specials that were written on a large chalkboard and the rest of the menu above the windows, they stepped in line to order. When they got to the window, a young woman with a friendly smile greeted them. His father chose one of the surf and turf specials of steak and lobster béarnaise, and Hunter went with stuffed lobster tails.

"Is this to-go?" the lady asked.

"No, we're eating here—we reserved a table. Number eight," Hunter said.

"Great. And we have a handful of cold beers. Any interest you?"

Both men got a couple bottles, and Hunter led his father to the table with the number eight. It was positioned along the side of the patio closest to the sand.

"I wouldn't go so far as to call this fast food, but rather more casual outdoor eating," he said, answering his father's earlier remark. He sat down and noticed a clambake in full swing out on the beach.

"Well, they clearly have plenty of open tables for a Friday evening. What's happening out there?" His father pointed to the group gathered around the clambake.

"One of Lana's specialties is clambake parties." Hunter took a long swig of the cold brew.

His father looked around the patio some more. "It's a nice patio, but sort of… bare. Something she could easily replicate somewhere else, especially with our offer."

"What do you mean, bare?"

"Just some lights, but I don't really see much else with the design. It's pretty bland."

Hunter chuckled. "Leave it to you to point out the ins and outs of the restaurant's presentation." He looked around as well, and had to admit his father was right. "Lana works hard, despite her decorating skills, and apparently her food makes up for it." Even though he didn't know much about the details of who Lana was, he couldn't help but notice that her restaurant didn't exactly share them either. It *was* bare.

"You seem to be defensive about Lana." His father took a sip and put the bottle down, eyeing him.

Hunter looked down, knowing his father was onto him. "We've had a few conversations during my time here."

"More than smoothing things over then, I take it?" his father asked knowingly. It wouldn't take much at this point to see that Hunter had more interest than just being friendly neighbors.

"She's a really interesting woman. Nothing wrong with getting to know more of her." He kept his eyes on his beer, not wanting to let his father's judgment stir him.

"I know I've already said this, but I really need you to just keep your main focus on the buyout. All of this could be moved elsewhere." His father gestured around the patio. "Money talks, but taking an interest in this woman will stall our plans."

Your plans, Hunter almost said out loud, knowing that the intentions for Lana's restaurant had always been solely his father's.

"Money isn't everything." The words came out before Hunter could stop them.

His father slowly set his beer down. "Remember, Hunter, you have a big promotion riding on this project. Owning this entire beachfront could amp us up even more. Seeing in person now how much more room we'd have really confirms that. We have to make a big impact here in Bluedale. Come in strong as newcomers. I think this town could use businesses like ours to pick up its speed, and the locals will see those benefits soon. Don't let this woman dazzle you."

Hunter remembered Alicia's comment on the boardwalk earlier: *Lana is going to thrive next door to you.* Finally looking up at his father, he knew pushing him usually didn't go over well, but it was Hunter who'd been here for over a month witnessing the reactions everyone had had so far. It was clear… they all loved Lana.

"Or we find a way to make it work alongside her."

His father raised an eyebrow. "Just follow my lead, Hunter. Or this job might not be the best fit for you after all. And, Hunter."

"What?"

"If you don't make the offer to her, then I will. You have one week."

Hunter left it at that and didn't say anything more. Starting a full-blown argument on Lana's patio was not a good idea. Besides, he needed time to think of a way to get his father to ease off. When their food arrived, they ate mostly in silence. His father was impressed with Lana's skills in the kitchen, eating every last bite, and even complimented the food out loud.

Putting his napkin on his empty plate, he sat back, and that was when Hunter saw Lana walk by. His father had his back to her and didn't see her throw Hunter a wave as she made her way to the beach, to check in with her guests out there.

Her dark-red curls were piled on top of her head, with a few strands that spilled out, and her chef's uniform was covered in spills… but he couldn't stop staring. She was at her most beautiful, looking truly radiant, and all he wanted to do was soak up that glow with her.

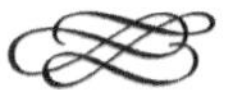

CHAPTER 17

"How was breakfast, Grandad?" Lana asked, while Casey wheeled him into the lobby where she'd been waiting for him. Every Saturday morning, she knew he liked to have pancakes, but she braced herself for his answer—another repeat.

"Same as always. Nowhere near as good as the delicious pancakes your grandma taught you to make me," he said. "Thank you." He smiled up at Casey, who'd parked him right in front of Lana.

"Have fun with Lana, Mr. Kelly. Glad you're resting that hip today." Casey looked at Lana. "He was complaining about it again, so we changed out his walker for the wheelchair."

"Sounds like a good idea." Lana turned her attention to her grandad. "One of these days I'll just need to get into that kitchen and show those chefs how pancakes are done." She threw him a wink.

"You won't have time. You have so much to prepare for before you leave for school."

Lana glanced up at Casey, who gave her an apologetic look before leaving them for their visit. "Busy or not, I'm here, Grandad. How about I push you through the garden out near the patio? I bet the flowers look gorgeous."

Unlatching the brake on the wheelchair, she began to make her way to the side doors that led out to the garden off one of the outdoor patios. The automatic door slid open, and Lana guided the wheelchair carefully out. There were a few other residents enjoying the nice day, and they both stayed quiet for a few minutes as she walked them through the garden.

Sunlight washed the flowers with a golden glow, the verdant greenery around them making her feel so calm and in touch with nature. It reminded her of the Butterfly Garden.

"Grandad?" she asked.

"Hmm?"

"Remember how Grandma used to teach me about all the butterflies in her garden every year?"

"How could I forget?"

His words sank down into her stomach. What he would forget next sat with her every day. "This garden is so rich in color and reminds me of her flower beds."

The heavy smell of honeysuckle drifted by her, and she turned to find a hummingbird land gently on the yellow petals. As they continued to walk, admiring the sweet shrubs of peonies, marigolds, and hydrangeas, Grandad began to hum. Lana couldn't make out what song it was, but it brought her right back to being a child and sitting with him wherever she could find him, listening to him drone through various tunes.

When they had circled the whole garden and made it back to the patio, she chose a table in the shade and locked his wheelchair in place before sitting down.

"How's your restaurant doing during this busy season?"

he asked. Relief washed over her, knowing he had come back to her. Fresh air seemed to do the trick sometimes.

"It's been a good start so far." She instantly felt guilty not telling him the truth, that things had been slower than usual this summer—along with his beloved inn being torn apart and built into something brand new.

"I bet it's still hard to see the inn every day from your restaurant, remembering how we lost it years ago." The guilt deepened. *It was lost all over again.* The words stuck in her throat, and she was unable to tell him as his weathered eyes bored into her.

"It was difficult at first, but I've put all my focus on my restaurant instead. Making changes of my own." Nathan's marketing plans were a good distraction from the topic of the inn.

"Oh yeah? What changes?"

"Well, a friend who first helped me launch my restaurant—"

"Nathan?"

"Yes," she said, the added reassurance of his memories feeling so good. "Nathan is having me add more of… us to it." She picked up his hand. "Meaning you, me, and Mom and Dad. Sharing more of the restaurant's beginnings with Dad's fish market, what he taught me… what you taught me. Even sharing part of the inn's story too. I'm updating my website to include pictures that you gave me of us all through the years." She waited, her grandad in silent thought.

"That's a wonderful idea, Lana," he finally said.

"You think so?" Suddenly Lana wished she'd come to him right away with Nathan's idea. "I wasn't sure how you'd feel about it."

"Why? We may not have the inn, but the inn is always with you. So share away, sweet girl."

His words sent a shiver down her back. Why was it

starting to feel like she was the only one still struggling with the past?

"I'm warming up to it all, but perhaps it'll turn out great and be worth putting myself out there like that. It'll be like a whole new relaunch."

"I'd like to be there for your grand reopening. And I'll finally get to have some of our family's famous clam chowder again."

Lana swallowed, nodding in answer, and remembering the summer after she graduated high school. When her grandma had given her the family recipe—right before she lost her too. Her grandma had asked her to give the recipe a try and since she knew how hard it was for her since she associated the chowder so closely with the day she'd lost her parents, having her by her side in the kitchen had helped. After she was gone, Lana just couldn't do it again.

"Let's get you back inside. It's getting warmer out on this patio," she said, bending over to unlock the wheels and pivot the wheelchair, pushing it toward the door.

"It was the first thing your grandma made me and her parents when we opened the inn. I still need to tell you more about that, but not today."

Lana pushed him inside, trying to find the right words, but none came—only disappointment in herself, knowing that the beloved family recipe had stayed locked up within her. Luckily, her grandad didn't say anything more about the chowder because she wasn't sure she was able to talk about it anymore. She was relieved when she saw Casey standing by the nurses' station.

"I can take him from here, Lana," Casey said, walking toward them.

"Thank you." Lana let go of the handles, coming around to kiss Grandad on his forehead.

"I love you, my sweet girl." Grandad beamed at her from

his chair, and she forced a smile, turning to leave before he could see her crestfallen face.

THE OCEAN MIRRORED THE ORANGE, pink, and yellow colors from the sun as it receded toward the water. Lana stood peacefully, her shoes off and feet in the sand, watching the sunset as a couple holding hands walked nearby, enjoying the view with her.

Saturday night dinner service went smoothly, and Heidi was finishing up the last plates for her. Sensing Lana needed a minute to herself, her sous chef practically pushed her out of the kitchen to get some air. After she'd left the nursing home earlier, she'd gone home to pull out the photos that Nathan had requested, and dropped them off for him to scan for the website and make larger physical copies. Ever since she'd done that, her heart had been struggling against the mounting flood of emotion that rested behind her strong composure while cooking. Heidi knew her well enough to see right through it and sent her out.

The pictures that she'd dug up she hadn't seen in years, and she felt the fear creep back in. Was she truly ready to do this? Holding the photos of her parents, the pontoon, and her childhood close to her heart in her bedroom, her feet felt like weighted blocks, unable to move forward with any of these new ideas—but something jostled in her, and she made her way to Nathan's house and dropped them off.

After she left, a part of her immediately worried this would be too much for her customers, or even herself. Many of the older residents of Bluedale that came in regularly already knew who her parents had been, but during the summer season, most of her customers were tourists, and that was why she'd always kept a closed professional appearance.

"Or perhaps it's too much for *you*," Heidi had said right before the dinner service, after Lana had filled her in on Nathan's new marketing plan while they prepped.

The couple continued their walk down the beach under the silver stars that glittered across the now dusky purple sky. Laughter from the patio where the last of her customers were enjoying their meal brought great fulfillment, knowing she'd contributed to their happiness. Good food made everything better, and sharing a meal created memories that her customers could take with them when they left. It's what always brought them back again. It's what had brought them back to her grandma's clam chowder too...

Turning around, she faced the inn—or what was left of it —and noticed that all the lights were off since construction had stopped for the night hours ago. The same feeling from earlier when she was in her bedroom looking at the photos weighed heavily on her while she stared at the dark building, as if she were caught between this moment and her past, unsure of what this next step would bring her. Not able to move just yet, she sat down to gather her thoughts, facing back toward the sea. She looked up at the stars, and her parents popped into her thoughts. She closed her eyes.

"Is this the right thing?" she whispered.

"I could sit on this beach every night." A low voice startled her. Hunter came up beside her. "May I join you?"

Her cheeks warmed, wondering if he'd heard her, and she looked up at him, the lights from her restaurant reflecting off his face. "Yes," she answered, realizing that she'd felt no resistance in her answer.

He plopped down onto the sand next to her and together they watched the black sea under the night sky, with each gentle ripple of dark water flowing mysteriously toward them, the hum of the waves filling in the silence.

"You are quite the chef," Hunter said, keeping his eyes forward.

"Oh yeah, how was your dinner on Friday night? I never had a chance to stop by your table."

"It was wonderful, and I just had the most delicious grilled striped bass tonight. I might be your newest regular," he said, catching her out of the corner of his eye with a side smile.

"When did you come in? I must have missed you when I went out." She also wasn't paying too much attention once Heidi took over.

"I ordered last minute a little while ago, but I saw you leave when I was finishing it up on the patio." He faced the water again and a larger wave came gushing onto the sand. "And once again, that was probably the best meal I've ever had. You're extremely talented."

She felt her face flush with heat. She was no stranger to people complimenting her cooking skills, but it felt different coming from him. "Well, thank you. I'm glad you enjoyed it." She leaned back to allow the breeze off the waves to cool her cheeks down.

Hunter mimicked her stance, placing his hands in the sand behind him to steady himself. "So, what's your secret?"

"My secret?"

"To the bass."

"Ah, okay, I see what you're doing here. You want to take over my food too? You can't buy my recipes." Lana held her breath, waiting for his response.

"Wait, no... I..." Hunter shifted toward her. "I'm not trying to buy them. In my opinion, there is no way to replicate your food anyway. It's that good."

Lana chuckled. "Sorry, I couldn't help myself there," she

said. "You looked so worried. I'm just teasing you. And to answer your question, it's all in the marinade. The secret sauce to many of my recipes, which I will never tell."

Hunter grinned. "You had me there."

Lana looked away from him and back up to the stars. She sensed his eyes on her and her pulse quickened. "The stars seem to be twinkling brighter than ever," she said, switching topics. She finally peeked at him and caught him looking up.

"Yeah. They're just showing off for this Cape Cod tourist."

Lana studied him, his gaze still locked on the sky above. "I wouldn't call you a tourist anymore. You'll be here in Bluedale for quite a while with all this." She sat up, gesturing behind her. "Better get ready because pretty soon the locals will know everything about you, from what you like to eat to all the activities you enjoy."

Nodding his head, he paused briefly. "That's okay by me…" he slowly said. "Anything to get the full Bluedale experience. This town is wonderful. Any suggestions you have, I'm all for it."

Her stomach fluttered as she moved her bare feet through the sand, fighting the hesitation that was building. He was her supposed enemy and now she was enjoying the summer night sky with him. Without another thought, she said the words before she could stop them. "I do have one."

"Oh yeah? Let's hear it." Hunter sat up straight, turning his body toward her.

With her heart beating, she met his stare, his deep-brown eyes showing off the shimmering bright glow of the moon above them.

"Well, to start, you haven't experienced Cape Cod until you are hip deep in fashionable hip waders, digging for clams." She fought against the urge to laugh, seeing just enough with the lights behind them to notice his eyebrows raise. "What do you say, Mr. City? Think you can handle it?"

A smile spread across his face. "I think my clamming skills might surprise you."

"Then I'll see you bright and early tomorrow morning. Right here, 6 a.m. sharp. Up with the sun during tomorrow's early low tide before any tourists get here."

Hunter stood up and offered his hand down to her. His firm grip sent a shiver through her as he helped her up and they began to walk back. "I'll be here, but I don't have any hip waders."

"I can provide some for you," Lana assured him. Nathan had some he kept at the restaurant for the times he'd gone with her when she needed an extra hand.

"It's a date then. Sleep well, Lana." Hunter turned to leave, his path taking him to the parking lot and hers back to the kitchen to help Heidi close up.

Lana suddenly felt as though her legs were full of lead as she walked across the now empty patio, the last of her diners finally gone for the evening. *A date?*

CHAPTER 18

*H*unter stood watching her auburn curls ruffle down her back, whipping with the wind in every direction, while she pulled on her waders. She hadn't noticed him yet. Sunday was already building with heat in these early morning hours, but the breeze off the ocean made it comfortable.

With her back still facing him, he cleared his throat. "Good morning!" Hunter called out to grab her attention.

"You made it," Lana said, turning around to greet him.

"Sure did. Did you think I would bail?"

"Clam digging isn't exactly everyone's idea of fun. Especially at this hour." She pointed to a bag near them. "There's your digging attire." Lana put her hand to her mouth, clearly trying to hide the amusement on her face as he pulled out Nathan's green hip waders and long muck boots. Taking his wallet and keys out of his pockets, he shoved them in the now empty bag.

"Stylish." Hunter kicked off his sneakers and pulled the waders up and over his sweatpants before pulling on the boots. "How do I look?" He waggled his eyebrows, making her burst into laughter. She looked down when she noticed him watching her, drawn to her reddened cheeks. He had seen her light up like that only a couple of times, but he decided it was the most natural—and appealing—look for her.

"What do you think the folks in your head office back in —New York City, is it?—would say if they saw you now? Maybe we should send them a picture?" she joked, looking back up to meet his gaze.

"They would probably think it was photoshopped." His nose wrinkled as he looked down at himself. "These are pretty ugly, I must say."

"But you will love them in about five minutes when we're in the cold water. You can just leave the bag here. It'll be safe. Ready?" She picked up two large baskets, handed him the two shovels to carry, and gestured for him to follow across the exposed mud flats.

The borrowed boots were about a half a size too small, so it was a bit uncomfortable with each step that sunk into the wet sand. But watching Lana's enthusiasm was worth it. As she rambled on about why she dug for fresh clams nearly every week during the summer, and the satisfaction it brought her as a chef, he took in every movement and facial expression, sensing her passion.

"So, you see," she continued a couple minutes later, "I feel like keeping my reservations and open seating to a manageable size so I can continue to offer this special service ultimately benefits me *and* my customers." She stopped walking and looked up for a second in thought. "That is, as long as I can reach full capacity on the patio, or close to it, each night. I know it's small and doesn't offer room for a lot of customers, but seeing regulars so often throughout the summer takes precedence over more seating at the moment because it really helps my reputation. Anyway, it's sort of what I've become known for—the chef who catches her own clams." She chuckled at her own description.

Hunter barely processed a word of what she said as he was completely enthralled with this side of Lana he hadn't met yet. "Oh, I believe it," he finally said, when she looked over at him for a response. "Especially after tasting your food myself. There's no way you wouldn't be known in Bluedale for the authenticity of your food, including how you gather it up." Hunter winked at her as her bright eyes widened with pride.

"Thank you. That means a lot, especially coming from someone who didn't grow up here," she said.

He noticed how happy she seemed as she looked down at the sand with each step, brushing the curls off her face. He fought the urge to swipe the hair away himself.

"Was clamming something you taught yourself? Or have you done this your whole life?" He peeked down to see her reaction and instantly saw something change in her face, her eyebrows scrunching together.

"My whole life," was all she said, offering no other explanation, and Hunter somehow knew to leave it at that for now. "We're almost there. The farther we go, the better chance of a good catch," she said, moving back to a neutral topic and keeping her focus down on the sand.

Hunter nodded. "That makes sense. Are they more picked over the closer you get to shore?"

"Yes and no. It's still early in the season, so there are a lot of clams to be dug closer to the beach. However, the larger ones are best for clambakes, and they're usually found farther out."

They walked in silence for a couple more minutes, while seagulls made their early morning circles around the beach behind them, calling out to each other. Lana finally stopped and set the baskets down, her gaze following the sound of the birds. Hunter studied her as she watched them—her eyes told a story that he wanted to know more about.

"You're going to have to talk me through this," he told her, pulling her attention away from the gulls.

"I figured that would be the case. Here." She handed him one of the baskets. "Keep one shovel, and can you hand me the other?" Lana took the shovel from Hunter and looked down at the sand, scanning it for a minute before pointing. "See that mound? It's like a coin-sized depression. That's where the clams burrow and where we dig, but first, watch me check it."

Hunter observed as she began to stomp around the small mound.

"Packing the sand down?" he asked, puzzled.

"Did you see the water come out?"

"I think so…" He squinted against the rising sun to get a better look.

"So if you see water come out, it means there's most definitely a clam in there."

"Ignore it if it doesn't come out?"

"You can try and dig it, but it saves time to just move on to the next mound." She dug into and around where the mound was, shifting her shovel over the packed, wet sand. "I forgot to bring a rake this time, which makes pushing the sand around to find the clam a bit easier, but this works too." After another few seconds, the clam appeared, and Lana gently pulled it out and put it in the basket before pushing the sand back to fill the hole.

"Refill the hole after we dig up the clams?"

"Yes, it keeps the shoreline even and people from tripping into holes when they're out here swimming or taking a walk," she explained.

Hunter was impressed with how much time and care she put into every step of this process. He took his shovel to a mound near the one she'd just dug, followed her instructions, and within a couple minutes, found a clam. "I got one!" He held it up, feeling rather pleased with himself.

"Great! Now repeat that about twenty more times," Lana said, smiling at his enthusiasm. "And let me know if you get tired of this. You're welcome to leave anytime you need." They locked eyes for an extra beat before she broke his gaze, pointing around her. "But even just a few rounds of this out here will give you an authentic Bluedale experience."

"I think I can get my basket filled. I'm happy to be here helping." As soon as he said it, he knew he meant it. He tried to keep his attention on the clamming but couldn't help but wonder what she was thinking—especially as they continued to sneak a few glances at each other.

An hour passed, both digging away and filling up their baskets, but their conversation moved into light and easy discussion. Hunter listened to her tell him funny stories from culinary school, especially after meeting her best friend.

"Alicia is a riot," Lana told him, rambling on like she did earlier, and Hunter loved it, not wanting her to stop. He watched her bend down to dig around another mound, her face matching the color of her curls as she giggled at her memories. "She and I had so much fun back then—maybe a little too much fun. I blame all that on her, though, and if you knew her, you'd know she's daring and often a bit pushy. She tries to deny it, but it was definitely her fault we wound up with all of our crazy stories."

Hunter smiled, watching her drop another clam into her basket, and considered not telling her—but since it was her best friend, he knew he had to. "I'm not sure if she told you, but since you didn't say anything, I figure she must not have. I actually met her the other day…" He paused when she quickly cast her eyes over to him.

"You met Alicia?"

"Yeah, on the boardwalk," he said, remembering Alicia's initial reaction to him, with her face so even. He could see what Lana meant about her friend being so pushy. "We ran into each other, literally, and chatted a few minutes. When she realized who I was, she mentioned that she's your friend. She seems like a nice person."

Lana hesitated, then nodded before she looked down at the sand again. "Yes, she is, and she's always been there to help me through some tough times."

Hunter couldn't guess why, but he sensed awkwardness at the mention of him meeting Alicia. Silence fell over them and he quickly changed the subject. "How many clams are we allowed to dig?" he asked, standing up to wipe the sweat off his brow.

"In this location, there isn't a limit. Some other areas, especially the more popular tourist towns, there is one," Lana explained, looking down at their baskets. "These are getting full and pretty close to what I need. I only have one clambake later today, and it's just a medium-sized party."

"What do you do if you have a few clambakes booked for a weekend?"

"I have some great suppliers to deliver the clams. It would be wonderful if I was booked back-to-back weekends with multiple clambake parties. One day…" Lana stared out into the water. Hunter almost asked her what she was thinking about, but held back. They were having such a good time together and he didn't want to make her uncomfortable.

"This has been quite the learning experience, and you were right before—it's much more exhausting than I thought," Hunter said, bending over to dig another mound and wiping the sweat that had already collected on his forehead again. "I hope it was helpful having me here." He slowly turned toward her and noticed her freeze for a moment before reaching down to pick up a clam.

"It definitely was helpful. I got it done in half the time. I think we have enough now." Lana picked up her basket and shovel, watching him do the same. "Ready to head back?"

"Is dinner the only meal you serve in your restaurant?" Hunter asked, wanting to keep the conversation going and falling in step with her back toward the beach.

"Yes, for now it is. Hopefully one day I can hire more chefs—then we'll be able to offer lunch, and possibly breakfast too." She peered over at him. "Why do you ask? Did all this clam digging make you hungry?"

"Just wanting to learn more about what you do." He saw her fiddle with her shovel. "But clam digging sure does work up an appetite."

"How about some omelets and coffee up at my restaurant before you get going with your day? But I don't want to take up your whole Sunday. You probably need to rest up before the work week starts." The sun moved across her face as she waited on his answer. It was now fully shining above them, ushering in a great day for the tours on his ship. But all of that felt far away. The only thing he wanted to focus on was her.

"Work is round-the-clock right now until we finish a few big things, so the crew is coming in soon for half a day," he explained. "And omelets and coffee sound wonderful. I'd love that."

They continued to head toward the beach with the venue and her restaurant ahead of them, side by side, just as they were. Hunter wasn't sure what to feel or how to avoid it, but he knew one thing—they were connecting against all the odds.

An hour later, with his stomach full and another fresh mug of coffee in hand, Hunter sat back against his chair out on Lana's patio. The morning sun was keeping them warm as they dried up from the dig.

"That was probably the best omelet I've ever had. I had no idea basil could pair with eggs like that," Hunter said, taking a sip of his coffee.

"Breakfast is usually not my specialty, but I do have a knack for omelets. It was one of the first things my mother taught me how to make when I was young." Lana peered at him over her mug.

"Well, if you ever offer breakfast at your restaurant, I'll be the first one here in the mornings."

Lana looked away, her cheeks flushing against her wildly scattered red waves, which he was growing to like more and more each time he saw her. She didn't have her hair pulled back, and the humidity wasn't helping as the curls went in every direction.

She looked over her shoulder at the sound of male voices in the parking lot, shouting out instructions to one another, before she turned back to him. "Looks like your crew has arrived and are gearing up for a busy day."

"Yes, they are." Hunter had to draw up every ounce of willpower to get himself into work mode. He quickly glanced at his phone. "Well, it's almost ten. I better get myself over there and leave you to start your workday too. Do you need help carrying the plates back to the kitchen?"

"No, it's totally fine. I've got all this." Lana stood up and he did the same.

"Thank you for breakfast and for taking me out to dig for clams. It was a neat experience," he said, pushing in his chair, and without a second thought, the words spilled out of his mouth. "I hope you can show me another Bluedale experience again. I don't think anyone else could do this town justice in the way you can." He noticed her fidget with the top of her chair before pushing it in. Had he gone too far?

"Maybe I will," she said softly, quickly peering down to the top of her hands.

"I heard Bluedale holds one of the biggest Fourth of July parades on the Cape," he said, waiting on her to look up, and when she did, he caught himself fully entranced by her eyes and their green beauty. Something shifted in her face, and she clasped her hands together by her stomach, looking suddenly unsettled.

"That's right," was all she managed to say, and he fought the urge to reach over to comfort her. He wasn't sure what he'd said to trigger her response, and he felt his heart thud faster with concern.

"Are you okay?" he asked.

"I'm fine. Sorry, I was thinking about something else I needed to get done today in the kitchen," she quickly said. He didn't believe her, yet he sensed not to push her further.

"Well, then, I better let you get to it." They locked eyes again before she seemed to force herself out of his gaze. "I hope you're going to the parade. I'd love to have that experience next... with you."

He didn't wait for her response, and instead nodded his head and turned to walk away. He knew it was probably a bold way to ask, and truthfully, he wasn't exactly sure what had prompted him to pursue more time together. She was most likely just trying make their new neighbor status more hospitable since they both had no choice at the moment—at least, that's what he told himself. After all, how could she have any true interest in him? He was the monster who'd bought her inn...

Pulling out his phone to check his messages, he saw a missed call from his father, which made him realize that he needed to reel it back a bit with Lana. But when he was with her, something in him had no control. Spending time with her, digging clams, and listening to how much thought she put into making her restaurant stand out with these unique, special touches was, to him, not something he could just simply buy. The love she had for her work had no monetary value.

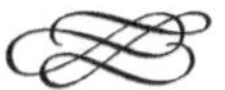

CHAPTER 19

"Did you just casually forget to mention you met him?" Lana gave Alicia a playful nudge while they waited in line for their iced coffees at the bakery. It was Thursday, Lana's day off, and since the Fourth of July was that coming weekend, Alicia had taken an extra day off for the holiday. "I'm trying to keep things cordial with him, and it would be nice to know when encounters like that happen, so I can be prepared." She gave her friend a coy smile.

"Prepared? What did you think I would say to him?" Alicia rolled her eyes and squared her shoulders in defense.

"Hmm, where should I start?"

Alicia burst out laughing. "Okay, don't answer that. But you're the untrustworthy one here—how have you kept his insanely good looks a secret all this time?"

"Why is that the only thing you seem to care about? And I didn't keep that to myself anyway. I told you weeks ago he was handsome." Lana giggled when Alicia shook her head. "And don't change the subject on me. You met him on the boardwalk and didn't immediately tell me? Why would you keep that from me?"

"I didn't keep anything from you. I was simply waiting on him to tell you first." Alicia looked ahead in line, trying hard to maintain her innocence.

"And why would you do that?"

"Because I knew he would," Alicia said.

"I'm not following…" Lana noticed Alicia's smirk. "Why are you smiling?" As soon as she asked, she had a feeling she knew the answer.

"Because why wouldn't he? Lana, if you took your head out of the oven for more than a minute, you'd clearly see that Hunter Graham wants to be more than just 'cordial' with you. He'd jump at an opportunity to start a conversation with you, and what better chance than to tell you he ran into me? So I waited to see what he'd do."

"Now, wait just a second…"

Heat rose in Lana's cheeks, and before she could attempt a rebuttal, Alicia's eyes went round.

"See! Your face is as red as your hair. You know I'm right."

The two women moved up in the line, not saying a word. Lana knew her friend was waiting on her to spill her feelings since she'd spent more and more time with Hunter, but in all honesty, she wasn't entirely sure what they were.

She glanced over at Alicia, who still wore a triumphant grin on her face, and she knew there was no getting out of this one. Arguing with a lawyer, especially one as good as Alicia, was a useless attempt.

Lana sighed. "Okay, you win. There's definitely something sparking between us. But wait!" She grabbed Alicia's hand before she could chime in. "I don't know what it means and I'm still figuring it out, but you're right—I can't help but wonder when I'll see him next. This project out here on the

Cape will eventually end and he will move on to the next one, which probably won't be anywhere near here."

"Nathan did a little digging on his company because he's nosy, and he found out Hunter works out of their new Boston office. Boston is like, an hour and a half away, not on the other side of the country. So I mean…" Alicia gave her a knowing look.

Lana smiled as she rolled her eyes, knowing she was right —Boston was not far. "By the way, I took him clamming the other day."

"You did?" Alicia's mouth fell open. "You don't even take *me* clamming."

"Would you even go?"

"Absolutely not, but you've never asked."

Lana smiled. "Because you're so busy with work! And I know the answer is going to be no."

"Then why'd you ask Nathan those few times?"

"Because Nathan outright asked me if he could try it sometime."

"Well, regardless, you've been a solo clammer since I've known you." Alicia waggled her eyebrows at her as they reached the counter to order. "Until Mr. City came along. This is getting so interesting."

"Hunter. His name is Hunter, not Mr. City."

"Look at you! Defending him already!"

Lana shook her head yet couldn't help but enjoy this banter with her closest friend. She knew Alicia's observations were right.

A text grabbed her attention on their way out of the bakery, their coffees in hand, and when she pulled out her phone, her stomach clenched at the words she read from Nathan:

> I know you and Alicia are out enjoying the day, but can you two meet me at the restaurant? I have the photos ready. I can't wait to show you.

She flashed the screen at Alicia and saw her friend light up. She wished she felt the same. All the changes they were planning and implementing had been so hard to keep up with, but what had been bothering her the most was the resistance that still tugged within her anytime she faced her own past. Why was it so hard to share who she was?

"Let's go check them out!" Alicia said. "I'm glad I get to see."

Lana tried to muster up some excitement, but the only thing she could think about in that moment was Grandad. A part of her just wanted to sit by him, away from the present and adjacent to the past—when everything was much simpler—before it all crashed down on her.

NATHAN WAS ALREADY at the parking lot, waiting in his car when they pulled up. Heidi was there prepping for the dinner service, and popped her head into the hallway when they all came inside.

"Hello there!" Heidi waved at them. "What a nice surprise. Lana, did you forget it's Thursday again?"

Everyone laughed, knowing the workaholic in Lana had been known to show up many times on her day off.

"It's not me this time—it's Nathan's fault I'm here," Lana said, pointing to the bag he was carrying. "He brought the new marketing plan."

Wiping her hands on her apron, Heidi followed them to

Lana's office. "I have a few minutes before the oven beeps, so I'd love to see it too."

"I'm sure it'll be great," Alicia said, giving Lana's shoulders an encouraging pat. All four of them squeezed around Lana's desk as Nathan carefully pulled the blown-up images from a folder.

"The print shop did a fantastic job," he said, and Lana closed her eyes while he laid them across her desk. She only opened them when she heard the gasps.

"Nathan, you picked the perfect shots," Heidi said. "Lana, come closer." Heidi grabbed her hand and guided her to the front for her to see.

Across her desk were five photos, all enlarged in black and white.

"The printer was able to preserve the quality with these sixteen-by-twenty poster-sized pictures very well," Nathan said. "And they definitely have that vintage feel. I'll get them framed, of course, and I was thinking about putting labels across the bottom for when customers come to look at them. I wanted to bring them here to show you so we can hold them up outside and see how they'll look."

Lana heard everything he'd said, yet the thudding in her chest made his voice sound distant. The pictures were certainly done beautifully, but that wasn't what she saw. Instead she was looking at everything she'd kept shielded inside of her for over a decade. Her eyes moved over each picture, soaking in her parents' features, her grandparents, and more importantly... herself.

"This picture of you clamming with your grandad is my favorite," Heidi said. "The way you're holding up your basket and smiling at the camera is priceless."

Lana knew Alicia must have sensed the emotions rising up, and she felt her friend's hand rest on her lower back. "I like the one of you on the pontoon, with your dad holding you steady by the waist and your arms spread out against the wind like you're—"

"Flying," Lana mumbled, cutting in. Knowing the whole room was now silently waiting on her to say something else, she inhaled deeply and looked at Nathan, trying to reconcile the mixed feelings that were steadily building. "You did a wonderful job on these. Obviously, I've seen these photos before, but not like this."

"I'm going to leave them here with you for a few days, if that's all right?" Nathan studied her for a moment, and he too must have sensed how she felt.

Lana nodded. "Thank you. I do think I need some time with them."

"Of course you do. I expected you would," Nathan said.

Lana looked at her three friends with gratitude. She couldn't be luckier with them by her side, but as she glanced at the photos some more, she knew she had to work through her emotions on her own before she could present the photos to the public. She understood why Nathan had created this plan, but she still couldn't pinpoint what was blocking her.

"I know you wanted to show me where we could hang them, but if you all don't mind, I think I'm going to take a little bit of time to myself." She turned to Alicia. "I know we had a day planned. I'm sorry."

"Please, don't be. Besides, I can take this husband of mine out to lunch," Alicia said, elbowing Nathan.

Heidi stepped forward and touched Lana's arm. "You know exactly where to find me if you need me." She headed back to the kitchen, and everyone else followed Lana out of the office.

Once Lana was alone in the car, she watched her friends pull out of the parking lot, and with one sharp inhale, she released her tears, spilling out years of grief and everything she'd worked so hard to hold tightly inside. She was beginning to realize now that ignoring it all this time was never going to make the pain any easier to bear.

"MOMMY, look how many shells I got this time!" little Sara's voice called outside Lana's bedroom window, and she popped her eyes open, hearing the girl's fast feet running in the shared driveway.

"Sara, slow down!" Kristen called out to her daughter. "Last time you ran so fast on this driveway, you ended up with a scraped knee!"

"Okay!" This time Sara's voice was directly outside the window, and Lana got up to peek out. The curtain was drawn, moving gently against the breeze that was blowing in.

Sara was still shuffling outside the window when Lana quickly pulled the curtain aside, yelling, "Boo!"

"Ahhhhh!" Sara shrieked, before erupting in giggles.

"Sorry, Lana." Kristen came up to the window and leaned against it, peering in at her. "I hope you weren't napping."

"Don't worry about it. I needed to get up anyway. Here, I'll come out, wait there." Lana went out the front door and met them in the driveway. Sara was now making circles with her bike, and water was dripping from her bathing suit.

"How could you sleep on a day like today? It's stunning out here. Not a lot of humidity." Kristen looked at Sara. "Slow down!"

Lana laughed. "You must spend your entire day waiting for accidents to happen with that one."

Kristen nodded. "All day, every day. My husband swears he sees a new bruise on her every night." They both laughed.

"I believe that." Lana smiled as she watched Sara jump off her bike and pick up the bucket of chalk, before making all kinds of drawings on the pavement. "I did plan on enjoying the nice weather on my day off, but something at work needed my attention. It kind of wore me out."

"Everything okay?" Kristen looked over at her. "You do look a little frazzled."

Lana considered not boring her neighbor with all her current stresses, but like Alicia, Kristen knew her far too well to hide anything from her.

"It's just that"—she bit her lip, running through the past month in her mind and landing right on Hunter—"someone bought the inn." It was the easiest way she knew to start the conversation.

"I think I heard something about that. I'm so distracted with Sara all day that I haven't had a chance to ask you about it. I'm sorry."

"It's okay. It was a fast sale. I was just starting the loan process to try and buy it again when a development company sort of swooped in. I couldn't compete with their offer."

"Oh no..." Kristen said. "I was in the bakery a couple weeks ago and heard people talking about this new event venue coming to town, and a few of them sounded annoyed by it. That must be the company they were referring to, right?"

"Yeah, I'm sure."

"Now it makes sense why they weren't happy—because someone bought *your* inn to do that. Are you okay?"

Hunter's gorgeous smile while bending down in those ugly hip waders flashed across Lana's mind. "I'm getting there, but you should see it. It's not even open yet and it's so different already. They have a cruise line for water events and day tours too."

Kristen was silent for a moment, which Lana understood. The inn was a part of her neighbor's childhood too. Lana could remember playdates out on the beach and her grandma making them lunch, while their mothers chatted in their beach chairs. Not to mention all the sleepovers after she moved into the inn. She and Kristen always snuck down to the kitchen late at night and ate all the leftovers they could find.

"I'm really sorry," Kristen said. "That must be hard to see."

Lana gave her a reassuring smile. The last thing she wanted was Kristen worrying about her. She already had enough on her plate taking care of her daughter. "You know, it was hard at first and really shocking, to say the least, but… I'm coming around to it."

"I'm glad to hear you're doing okay." Lana knew Kristen meant that, and the two of them stood together in comfortable silence as they watched Sara continue to draw on the sidewalk.

Lana's thoughts shifted to the beautiful plaque Hunter had given her. She wasn't sure where to hang it yet, but for now it sat by her bedside, bringing her comfort every time she saw it and knowing that a piece of the inn would forever be with her.

Kristen's voice broke into her thoughts. "I hope you know you're going to continue to do great things, inn or no inn. I've loved watching you flourish in your own restaurant. And regardless of what the inn is turning into, it will always be an important part of your past." Kristen patted her shoulder. "It has shaped you from the beginning. Remember when we used to chase those seagulls? Every time I see Sara run toward them, I think of you. You always said, 'We're flying free above the wide, blue ocean, just like them.'"

Kristen's words slammed into her heart, lifting the heaviness she felt after seeing the photos earlier. *Flying free.* She could almost hear her past calling her. Sara jumped up, snapping Kristen's attention away just in time.

"Look! I drew a road! I'm going to ride my bike on it!"

Kristen smiled at her daughter, who hopped back on her bike and carefully pedaled along her chalk-drawn road.

"Thank you, Kristen. I really needed to hear that today." Lana leaned into her friend's open arms when she offered a hug.

"You're welcome. Now go out and have some fun on your day off." Kristen started to walk toward Sara before turning back. "And, Lana… will you be at the parade Saturday?" she asked cautiously.

Lana got the same question every year from her friends. She chewed her lip, remembering how Hunter's handsome face had looked when he'd asked her about the parade on Sunday. She still hadn't given him an answer, and right in that moment as Kristen waited for an answer as well, something moved in her heart. Something she hadn't felt in years—courage.

"You know," she started, "I just might be there."

"Oh, Lana, I really hope you come!" Kristen clapped and slightly jumped with excitement.

Lana grinned. "Maybe I'll see you there then." She waved goodbye to Sara and went back inside. Still a little groggy from her nap, she needed to splash her face to wake up some more. Turning on the bathroom lights, the parade circled around in her mind as she wet her face at the sink, and how the event was so special for the town of Bluedale.

The town's annual Fourth of July parade was something she hadn't been to since the day she'd lost her parents. When Hunter had asked her about it, she really didn't know how to answer. After drying her face and leaving the bathroom, something suddenly sparked in her. She grabbed her phone from the kitchen table, but she realized she didn't have his number. Sitting down, she drummed her fingers on the table, trying to think.

"Well, this should work." Pulling up Graham Property

Development on her phone, she found the number for the Boston office.

"Graham Property Development, this is Rebecca."

"Hi, Rebecca. I'm trying to reach Hunter Graham. Is there any way you can connect me to the temporary Bluedale office?"

"Hang on just a moment." There was a click and a short wait.

"Graham Property Development, this is Hunter."

"I found you!" Lana laughed, realizing she probably should've told him it was her first.

"Lana?" Hunter asked. "This is a nice surprise. Were you having trouble finding me?"

"No, not really. Your office connected me to you. But I wanted to call you and it seems we don't have each other's numbers."

"Then let's fix that," he said without a beat.

Lana's stomach fluttered, hearing how fast he offered. "Yeah, I mean it would be easier than calling each other's businesses all the time." *All the time?* She squeezed her eyes shut, silently cursing herself for how that must've sounded to him.

"Much easier." His voice soothed her the way it had on their first phone call, and they exchanged cell phone numbers.

"Well, listen, I called because I wanted to give you an answer about the parade."

"Oh yeah?"

"Yes."

"Yes? Yes, you have an answer, or yes, you want to go with me?"

"Yes, I'd like to go with you." Her heart picked up its pace. "I mean, all these experiences will help you to become a true

Bluedale expert," she quickly said, her nerves nearly making her jump out of the chair.

"Of course… all the learning experiences," he said, but she picked up a playful tone. "With Bluedale's greatest tour guide."

Lana stood up and paced the room, her heart now wildly racing. "I like the sound of that."

Silence fell over them.

"I'm really looking forward to Saturday then," he said. "I hear it's a good time."

"It's a lot of fun, with great vendors and food trucks— even a stand for On the Bay—and all kinds of festive stuff," she told him, leaving out the part about how this would be the first time in over a decade she was attending.

"Aren't you going to be busy with the food then?"

"I'll stop by our station a few times to check on things, and I'll be helping Heidi prepare the food all day tomorrow, but the parade is her thing. She loves doing it." She squeezed her eyes shut, realizing how silly her lie must have sounded.

Hunter had most likely already gathered from the little time they'd spent together how dedicated she was to her restaurant, so it must've sounded odd that she didn't usually help Heidi for this event. But the excuse was all she could think of so quickly. How could she explain to someone she hardly knew that the parade was the last event she'd shared with her parents before they were invited on their friend's boat for early evening cocktails? How she'd stood with her grandparents on the dock, waving to her parents as they pulled out. Her father cupping his hands, calling out to her, *Be ready for those fireworks with us later!*

"Well then, that just means more time for my parade tour." Hunter's voice snapped her attention back to him. She was happy he didn't seem to pick up on her awkwardness.

"Great! I'll pick you up because parking will be a nightmare. I have a reserved spot because I'm one of the vendors. Where are you staying?"

"I'm staying in a cottage right off Route 42 on—"

"Mrs. Huxley's place. I know just where you are."

"Yes, that's where I am." Hunter laughed. "I should've known to just tell you the owner's name."

Lana chuckled down the phone. "I do know her, but there's also not many private cottages like that around here. The parade starts at nine that morning, so how about eight-thirty? And pack a bathing suit and towel."

"It's a date," Hunter said.

Lana had to get some air out on the deck after she hung up. *Another date*, she repeated to herself, leaning over to watch the foamy sea below. The ebb and flow of the current mirrored what she felt was brewing with Hunter. Going to this parade was a big step, but for some reason, having Hunter with her made it feel possible. It was as if her past was crashing to shore with the waves, as Hunter drew out every comfort she'd held tightly to, allowing them to flow back into the endless sea of water.

CHAPTER 20

argaret had her back turned, lost in her gardening, when Hunter slowed to a walk in the driveway. The sweat was dripping down his back in the thick heat of the morning, and he raised his hands above his head to draw in some breaths to slow his pulse. With the high temperatures forecasted every day lately, it didn't take long for his lungs to burn during his morning run, but he always pushed through it.

"Hi, Margaret!" he called out to the cottage owner.

Margaret held onto her wide-brimmed gardening hat when she heard him, stood up, and waved. "Good thing you got your run in now. It's supposed to reach above the nineties today!"

He walked a little closer to her. "That just makes for a perfect Fourth of July then." Hunter gestured toward her flowers. "Your garden is still looking great."

Margaret admired her work for a moment. "Thank you—it's what keeps me going."

"Any plans for the holiday weekend?"

"My daughter is picking me up soon, and we're heading

down to the parade, and then a barbecue and swim at her place. I love seeing all my grandchildren enjoying the pool. What about you?" She pulled her gloves off and wiped the sweat off her forehead with the back of her hand.

"I'm actually going to the parade too. The restaurant next to my venue called—"

"On the Bay?" Margaret asked.

"Yes." He smiled with amusement. "The owner of On the Bay is taking me. Bluedale seems to be like one big family."

"That's because we are." She walked over to him, and they both headed down the little cobblestone pathway in between the main house and cottage. "I assume you're referring to Lana Kelly?"

Hunter nodded. "Do you know her well?"

"I do." Margaret gestured toward the chairs around the firepit. "I'm a little bit worn out. Do you mind if we sit down for a chat?"

"Of course not."

When they each grabbed a seat, she turned to face him with an unreadable expression on her face. "I've known Lana her whole life. In fact, I held her only hours after she was born. I knew her father very well because we grew up together here in Bluedale. Our parents were the best of friends. He was a great man."

"I heard about the accident. That must've been very hard, being so close to the family."

"Yes, it was." Margaret stopped and looked away.

A cool shiver ran down Hunter's back against the sweat. "You know, I feel like the monster who came in and took everything away from Lana. She seems like such a wonderful person."

"Yes, she is, but I might be a little biased." Margaret smiled.

"You said her father grew up here, but what about her mother? Was she also from Bluedale?"

"No, her mother was a newcomer back when her father met her. She was only supposed to be passing through the Cape, and the rest was history. Her father was a fisherman and built his fish market next to his parents' inn, which is now Lana's restaurant," Margaret said.

Hunter nodded. "That's what I've been told, and I'm very impressed by what she's done with it." He looked up at the leaves that blew against a light breeze, thinking about his own father and how he was waiting on an answer about their offer to buy out Lana's restaurant. What would he think hearing her family's history?

"Anyway, I don't want to seem like I'm gossiping. And I'm sure Lana would like to be the one to tell you more about herself." Margaret stood up. "I better get myself ready for the parade. I hope you enjoy it! It's a big deal around here." She started toward the main house but looked back once more. "I'm happy to know she's taking you. It's nice to see Lana coming out of her shell, especially with this parade. You must be a keeper then." She winked and walked off, leaving Hunter in a curious daze.

It had certainly been an interesting adventure getting to know Lana Kelly, one that he didn't want to end.

"THIS PARADE IS one of the oldest in the country," Lana explained while in line for frozen lemonade. They had just finished checking on her restaurant's food station and sampled the delicious shrimp tacos Heidi handed them, and now they needed to wash it down with something cold. "Oh! And just wait, the boats will be all lit up on the water tonight before the fireworks. It's been so long since…"

"Since?" Hunter asked, noticing her expression shift.

"Nothing, never mind," Lana said, waving at people walking past them. Hunter nearly melted when he saw her enthusiasm ignite, as if the little girl in her was coming out. When they'd first arrived, she was a little quiet, but as the excitement of all the people and food surrounded them, she began to loosen up. He also noticed a lot of stares as they maneuvered through the crowds, but they were met with just as many hugs for Lana as people ran up to greet her.

"Lots of people are happy to see you," he said, just after another person approached her. "Do they know you're close by at your restaurant?"

Lana nodded and chuckled. "Maybe I need to step out of the kitchen a bit more."

"Yeah, there's more Bluedale fun to have." He looked down with a smile. "So you're holding me hostage until the fireworks tonight?" he teased.

"If you're going to celebrate the Fourth here, then you are seeing it all, Mr. Graham." She gave him a playful look.

"Yes, ma'am," he said, giving her a stern nod.

They had been at the parade for nearly two hours already, watching what seemed like endless floats from all of Bluedale's businesses. There were antique cars and firetrucks, and the high school band had kicked it all off playing "The Star-Spangled Banner." Hunter had really enjoyed the bagpiper playing "Yankee Doodle Dandy," but watching Lana mingle with just about everyone was his favorite part. Her auburn curls were kept tame in a long braid that fell down her back, and he couldn't stop admiring how adorable she looked in her white shorts and red tank top.

When she'd picked him up earlier, she'd immediately handed him a small American flag, instructing him to wave it around with her. Watching her cheer for the passing floats in the parade and waving her flag instantly put him in a patri-otic mood, and he followed her lead. He couldn't remember enjoying a Fourth of July as much as this one, and the best part was how easily he and Lana fell into step with each other. He wasn't sure if it was the excitement of the crowd, the holiday spirit around them, or a mixture of it all, but they hadn't stopped laughing since they arrived. Their conversation was easy, fun, and he was so grateful that she introduced him to everyone. Numerous sets of curious eyes continued to follow them as they passed by, but he didn't mind. His only focus was her.

When they finally got to the front of the line, the vendor handed them two very tall plastic cups of frozen lemonade with a long spoon straw.

"These will cool us down. Let's make our way to the public beach where the mayor will announce the float winner, and we can listen to more music."

Just as he was about to follow, Lana grabbed his hand, gently guiding him over to the boardwalk where they fell into step with each other. When she let go, it took everything he had not to reach for her hand again. He took in a long sip of the sweet and sour frozen liquid to quell the urge.

"If I'd known how much walking this day would entail, I'd have skipped over my morning run earlier," he said, relieved when she slowed her pace. The humidity was now brutal, but the festivities were so vibrant and fun, it was easy to endure.

"I'm sorry, I don't mean to literally drag you around. I've just never been a Bluedale tour guide before. This is fun." She beamed up at him, her energy filling him with joy.

"You're doing a fantastic job. I'm really having a good time," he said, feeling his phone vibrate in his pocket. When he pulled it out, he noticed a couple missed calls from his father and saw a text:

Happy Fourth. I hope you're enjoying the day. I tried calling you earlier. When I couldn't reach you, I called Max. I thought you were on the ship with him, but he said you're in town with Lana? I'll be checking in Monday and expect a report on the offer.

"The beach entrance is just ahead," Lana said, pulling his attention away from the screen.

Hunter clicked off his phone, irritation rising, and shoved it back in his pocket. He didn't owe his father an explanation on his whereabouts, and it was just like him to call Max to hunt him down. He refused to let his father's pressure ruin his day.

Someone began making a speech on a microphone off in the distance. Walking onto the sand, he noticed everyone had parked under umbrellas and beach tents with big coolers of food, while children dug sandcastles along the shore and ran about, with music playing from various groups.

"Looks like everyone is here for the day, ready for the fireworks later," he said, pausing to take off his sneakers to walk more comfortably in the sand.

"Oh yes," she said. "They'll be here all day waiting. Come on, the mayor is announcing the winner!" Lana tugged his arm, and they continued walking toward a crowd that had gathered. They squeezed their way in until they found a spot to stand and watch. The mayor was talking about how long Bluedale's parade had been going on—how hundreds started gathering as early as 7 a.m. to enjoy this special tradition and all the events for the rest of the day.

"The band will start up at four o'clock at the gazebo on Main Street, and make sure to check out all of our shops in town with their holiday specials. There's so much to enjoy here today in Bluedale. Now it's time to announce the winner of this year's parade float contest," the mayor said, turning to take the paper that someone handed him.

Lana looked up and leaned in to whisper something to Hunter, sending his stomach into knots. The citrusy smell of her shampoo lured him in closer. "This is my favorite part about the parade. I used to love to see who would win each year when I was little. I really liked the Bluedale Animal Clinic's float this year with the dogs walking alongside in matching red, white, and blue collars. Which one was your favorite?"

Hunter could hardly remember all the floats that had passed by—he was too busy watching Lana's reaction as she cheered and waved at all of them. "They were all great. I think you should get one for your restaurant next year."

"Now there's a thought! My sous chef would be all over that." She giggled, showing off the dimples in her cheeks that he'd never noticed before.

"This year's winner is... Dale's Garage!" the mayor announced, drawing Hunter's attention back to the stage. The crowd applauded.

"It should've been the clinic, I agree." Hunter winked down at Lana.

"Next year, I'll win it. I already have ideas for a float," Lana said. "Now that you bought the inn, you might need to tell the manager of the venue to join me for some friendly float competition."

"Is that right? I'll be sure to pass that along." Relief settled over him at how easily she mentioned the inn. He'd hoped she had mostly come to terms with losing the inn, but this seemed to confirm it.

Lana rested her hand on his arm to get his attention. "Okay, ready for more fun?"

"Ready!" he said, nearly bursting at the emerald twinkle in her eyes when the sun came out from behind a cloud.

"Let's head back to my car. I'd like to take you somewhere different."

Once they made their way back through the crowd to Lana's car, she drove extra slowly as she carefully maneuvered past all the people who were still lingering around, enjoying the food and shopping. As soon as they were out of the center of town, she was able to pick up the pace.

"So this is Route 6A. Have you been to the Cape before this summer?" she asked, cracking the window, which made the loose wavy tendrils of her hair flap around her face.

"I believe when I was a small child my parents and I took a vacation here, but I haven't been back since," he said, looking out the window and admiring the harbor with sail boats stacked alongside each other.

"Oh good, so that means you're a newbie to Old King's Highway? Also known as Route 6A."

"It must mean I am." He glanced back at her, and she quickly met his gaze before she turned her focus back to her driving.

"You're in for a treat. There's a lot to see on this drive, but I'm only going to take you through some of it. We're just headed a few towns away." She brushed a curl off her face and slid her sunglasses on, while he tried to focus on the beauty of the scenic tour and not her.

"And where is it that you're taking me?" he asked.

"You'll see." Lana smiled, keeping her eyes on the road. "In a few minutes, you get to see a strip of some of Cape Cod's oldest homes. In this area, none of the houses were built after the nineteenth century and many were home to captains at sea."

"Do you always do this on the Fourth of July? Or is this tour special for me?"

Lana grew quiet. "To be honest," she began, slowing down

at a line of cars, "this is the first summer I've been to the parade since I was young."

Hunter waited, watching her body language change, and he remembered Margaret's words from earlier: *It's nice to see Lana coming out of her shell, especially with this parade.* It was starting to make more sense.

"If you hadn't already figured that out with everyone hugging me." She quickly glanced at him with a small smile.

"I just figured Bluedale loves hugs."

Lana laughed, appearing more relaxed again.

"But you seemed to enjoy all the crowds and excitement."

"I did. I've missed the thrill of all the residents and tourists at the parade, but where I'm taking you has a different vibe. You'll enjoy it, I think." She peeked at him again. "And it'll also require that bathing suit you brought."

"Now I'm even more curious. I'm already having fun and we haven't even gotten there." Hunter looked over at her. "I really am having a good time." Her hands moved up the steering wheel as she clenched the top.

"Me too," she said softly, without turning her head.

The traffic died down and they picked up speed again, riding in silence for a while, and Hunter watched all the scenery pass by, from multiple old bridges to various water views and other architectural beauty.

"What a relaxing drive this is—and so beautiful."

"It's definitely a great route if you need to destress, and there're so many places to stop and eat and walk around. Perfect for tourists to really get a feel for Cape Cod." Lana slowed around a bend and lifted a hand to point. "Okay, look out your window. Check out these homes."

Hunter pulled his sunglasses off and admired the traditional homes that varied from original Cape Cod one-story structures to larger, old Georgian styles. Most of them were white or gray, just like the main house where he was staying.

"Wow, so cool. I see all of them have hanging signs in the front yard."

"Yeah, they give you a little more history about each house," she explained, continuing down the road.

"Everything in these towns looks traditional and simple. A far cry from life in the city—although when I transferred to our Boston office to get it up and running, I moved into the outskirts of downtown. It's been a lot calmer than New York."

"I bet. So did your father start Graham Property Development?" she asked.

"My grandad did. He started out very small and worked from the ground up. Once my father took over, it grew extensively. My father has the perfect personality to push for what he wants. He worked exceptionally hard to get the company where it is today."

"In that kind of business, I wouldn't expect it to be any different."

"Or maybe it could be different. Businesses like ours don't have to be so cut-and-dried. There's room to be a little less cold… and making more connections helps too." He watched her stare evenly as she drove, evidently thinking about his comment.

"I suppose you're right," she said, pausing for a moment. "Does your father agree?"

Thinking about the text from his father earlier, he nearly snorted in response. "Absolutely not. I mean, like I said, as a businessman, he's certainly been successful with his approach. But what I've found is that choosing the right location requires a little more research and understanding of the people in the town. And sometimes even learning their stories in order to leverage your business in a way that connects to them."

Lana stayed quiet, moving one of her hands to her lap and

twisting her shorts.

He fought the urge to reach over and steady it with his. "That's how I'd like to operate."

"I see. I think that's important too." Lana kept her focus on the drive. "We're nearly there." She pulled off and through another small town, almost identical to Bluedale.

"Another quaint Cape town, but each one just as sweet as the last." Hunter saw people dressed in their red, white, and blue attire and ready to celebrate, as they made their way down the road. "But not as packed as Bluedale."

"The beach here is for residents only, so it keeps the crowds lower. But not the area of the beach we're going to end up." Lana reached a parking lot and pulled in. A sign near them read: *Shuttle to Beach*. "Ready?"

"For the beach?"

She turned off the ignition and faced him. "Even better."

CHAPTER 21

When she looked in the mirror in the bathroom after changing into her bathing suit, Lana saw something different in her face. Her sun-kissed cheeks from being out all morning at the parade gave her a nice glow, but that wasn't it. She noticed that her eyes were brighter and her facial muscles felt soft and relaxed, but what stood out the most was that she felt content. Since picking up Hunter that morning, she hadn't thought about Grandad, the restaurant, or that today had been the hardest day of her life since she was eleven years old. She was simply happy.

Her long, thick hair had loosened its way out of her braid, so she quickly pulled out the tie and gave her curls a quick shake. She began the tedious task of redoing the braid, but it gave her a few minutes to reflect—not just on what she saw in the mirror, but the whole day.

For over fifteen years, she'd spent this day on her own, finding her way out of Bluedale to be by herself among the many emotions that still encircled her heart. She always found it easiest to process that without anyone else present—until Hunter. Inviting him to join her for an annual Fourth of

July activity that she hadn't faced in so long felt like a big leap forward.

Laughter outside the bathroom pulled her away from the mirror, and she fastened the tie at the bottom of the braid, then bent over to shove her clothes into her bag before heading outside. When she opened the door, Hunter's back was to her and he was leaning over a railing, watching the distant ocean.

"The weather couldn't be more perfect for fireworks later. Not a cloud in the sky," he said when she walked up beside him.

"Bluedale has the best display, in my opinion. Does that mean you'd like to watch them with me?" she asked, realizing how much she hoped he'd say yes.

"I would be honored to share my first Bluedale firework show with you," he said. His brown eyes found hers, watching her with the same soft expression he'd been giving her all day.

"But there's more to do before then," she said, this time not looking away.

Hunter blinked out of his gaze and glanced behind him. "If we're going to the beach, it seems like quite a walk to get over there. This parking lot is a little far."

"We're not walking there. And don't worry, they have shuttles to take us back."

"Take us back? Now you lost me."

Lana chuckled at the confusion on his face as she led him back to her Jeep and unlocked it, putting her bag in the trunk and telling Hunter to do the same.

"Might want to leave your shoes," she instructed, and before she closed her trunk, she pulled out two inflatable tubes.

Hunter took the tube she handed him and kicked off his flip-flops. "Okay, fess up now. Where are we going?"

"What better way to wind down from the parade excitement than to go tubing with the tides? And from the looks of the water when we passed the beach, it's high tide. The perfect time to go. Follow me, but step carefully on this pavement until we get to the grass over there." Hunter walked close to Lana, making her shutter when his arm brushed hers.

"Tubing… in the ocean?" He looked down at her, still clearly confused.

Lana laughed. "Now that would be interesting. No," she said, pointing to a sign. "The river is just ahead and it leads out to the ocean. We will use the shuttle back to this parking lot."

"Ah, okay, now I understand the need for a shuttle." Hunter still looked a bit perplexed as he glanced toward the approaching entrance to the river. "Are you sure this river won't toss us deep into the ocean?"

Lana grinned. "No, the water is calm at the bay. So don't worry, we won't drift out to sea."

"That'd make Bluedale headlines for sure."

"That's true. I can just see it now: Bluedale Enemies Drift Away Their Problems." They both laughed.

"Are we still enemies?" he asked, turning serious.

"Depends." Lana raised a brow at him as they crossed through the small entrance and onto a dock. She saw something stir in his expression.

"On what?" he asked.

"The rest of this date," she said, and his eyes widened. It even surprised her how easily that came out. "And the rest of your renovations."

"Renovations at the inn?"

Lana nodded. "You said you would make it something my family would be proud of, right? So that remains to be seen."

"Challenge accepted!"

When they were together, she'd found herself drawn to him more and more, despite everything going on with the inn. As they reached the end of the dock, she knew deep down something had been brewing between them right from the first phone call—his voice had pulled her in that day, and she didn't want it to end. "Ready to float?" she said, holding her tube in front of her.

"I'm ready." Hunter gestured toward the water. "Please, after you. I'm a tubing rookie so I'll just follow along."

Minutes later, she had him drifting next to her down the river, with tall marsh grass winding through it. As they glided, Lana kicked her legs freely in the water and her tube made a circle near his. Hunter was leaned back with his eyes closed, soaking in the sun. Just as she passed him, he popped his eyes open and flicked water toward her face.

Her mouth dropped open in surprise, and she wiped her face. "Oh, you want to play that game, do you?" She leaned over and dipped a hand in the water, cocking her head to the side in warning, trying hard not to laugh.

"Not if you can't reach me," he said, dipping forward and using both his strong arms to push himself away from her, but not before flinging a gush of water at her first.

Unable to hold it in anymore, Lana erupted into laughter and twisted herself onto her belly, dangling her legs in the water and kicking hard to catch back up to him. Once she did, Hunter sat up, grabbed her tube, and pulled her closer. Before she could splash him, he leaned over and scooped the side of her tube up, tossing her gently into the water.

"Now that's cheating!" she called out once her head popped back up, giggling as she swam to get her tube. She managed to get herself back on top, not noticing he was already next to her.

"So much for relaxing." Hunter winked at her and reached

over, grabbing the handle on her tube to keep them connected.

"Nothing like a good old-fashioned water fight," she said.

A grin spread across Hunter's face.

Lana looked ahead, settling back as they both curved gently through the winding water.

"I thought this was a river? Seems a bit slow," he said, moving her tube back and forth in a playful manner and keeping them locked together. Even though she felt cooled off from her swim, her entire body heated up when she looked down at his grip.

"You'll see. It'll get wider and faster the closer we get to the ocean."

A seagull squawked above in the distance, flying to its next location, distracting Lana enough to calm her nerves before her mind drifted too far off down memory lane. She followed the bird in the air before it landed, the motion bringing her back. She wasn't sure if it was the day that had been filled with happiness and fun, or if it was Hunter's playful nature, but within that moment of peace, nostalgia arose once again. She could almost hear her father in the distance, and she closed her eyes, resisting the urge to spread her arms out.

"Lana?" he asked, and she opened her eyes, the memory fading.

"Sorry, I zoned out there for a minute."

Hunter kept his hand on her handle, slightly turning his own tube so their heads were now side by side.

"It's okay." When she turned her head toward his, something shifted in his face and his eyes fell to her lips for a second. "You were eleven when you carved your name on the old deck, right? Did you find a good place to hang the plaque?"

"That's right..." She trailed off, gathering her courage,

aware that he couldn't know how that question tugged at something hidden deep inside her heart. "I might have an idea of where to put it." An idea sparked as she thought about the restaurant's new marketing plan and redesign. Perhaps it should be hung with the pictures Nathan had printed. "The perfect spot will come."

"I haven't stopped thinking about how I saw you on the beach watching us the day we demolished the deck."

"I'm sorry," she said. "I didn't mean to make you feel bad about your work." Lana chewed her lip, remembering how she'd felt that day. The truth was, she hadn't been able to forget it. Watching the deck come down had been the hardest part of the entire remodel so far.

"Tell me about it," he said, as their tubes slightly bounced over a ripple in the water that had caught under them.

"About the deck?"

"Yeah, but only if you want to. I assumed when I saw your name carved in it that the deck must have been special to you."

Lana glanced over at him, and tears began to build. She held onto the side of her tube in an attempt to brace herself against them. She didn't want Hunter to feel worse than he already did, and as she watched him track a bird that crossed right above them, a warmth overtook her against the sorrows of her past. The urge that followed felt natural and real, and she took a deep breath.

"I do want to tell you. About everything." She waited as he turned his head to face her. His eyes exuded strength and trust, helping her to keep going. "The summer I was eleven years old, I lost both my parents. They died in a fire on the water while out on their friend's boat… on the Fourth of July. Coming to this river has been my hideaway every year on that day since."

"Oh, Lana, I know it's not enough, but I'm so sorry you

had to go through that, and at such a young age. What a terrible accident."

"It was. They were too far out, the fire was just too intense, and both of my parents got trapped inside the small cabin…" She trailed off. Hunter released her handle and took her hand instead, and they continued to make their way toward the ocean. She closed her eyes against the thudding in her heart, unsure if it was because of her past or how his hand felt holding tightly to hers.

She felt the sincerity both in his words and in his grip. "As you can imagine, I haven't been able to get out on the ocean ever since."

Hunter was silent for what felt like an eternity. Had she said too much?

"I have to tell you," he finally began, "that Margaret—Mrs. Huxley—talked to me about you this morning. I hope that doesn't upset you. But I didn't know this holiday was the anniversary of your loss."

Lana looked ahead and saw where the river opened to the bay in the distance. "It doesn't bother me. Mrs. Huxley is dear to me and someone I've known my entire life. People in Bluedale also love to gossip."

"Well, she seemed genuinely happy you were going to the parade today."

"Like I said, it's the first time in far too many years. The parade was one of the last happy memories I had with my parents, but the tragedy associated with it has been hard to face. Today was a good day, though. It felt really good to be there."

"I'm so happy to hear that."

Their tubes began bobbing up and down as they picked up more speed, causing them both to look out in front of them. Lana pointed and said, "The entrance to the bay is coming. Told you it would get faster."

A few kayakers sped by, and they watched them pass.

"So we really are going to just dump right into the ocean?"

Lana smiled at how worried he seemed. "Like I said before, the bay isn't intense in this area. Even at high tide, where we'll come out, we'll be able to touch the bottom. Or we can roll onto our stomachs and push the tubes with our legs in the water."

"Okay, that sounds doable. This is really great, Lana," Hunter said. "Thank you for sharing it with me."

"You're welcome. It's been nice to have company this year." She smiled at him. "Okay, here we are. Hold on!"

They flowed out onto the bay, hugging the shoreline, and hopped into the water that came up just above their waists as they slowly trudged to shore, leaning onto their tubes for leverage.

"I wanted to say before that I'm glad you had your grandparents close after a tragedy like that," he said.

"After the accident, I moved into the inn to be with them. They had owned and operated it for about thirty years at that point. A few days before my parents died, my grandad began to remodel the deck and my father had been helping him with the project. One night, my dad and I were sitting out there, watching the sunset. He held me for a while before he took out his pocketknife and helped me carve my name into the new deck, telling me I will always be reminded of this moment when I see my name."

Hunter put his hand on her shoulder to stop her. "I can't imagine what you must have felt, watching me rip it all down. I feel terrible. I'm so sorry."

Lana gave him a reassuring smile. "You don't need to apologize. How could you have known all that?" They began to walk again, the water now lowered to their shins, making it easier to get through. "I'll admit, though, I was heartbroken seeing the deck gone. That is, until you gifted me the plaque. You don't even know how much that meant to me."

"I do now." He shifted his tube to the side, touching her arm for a moment. The small gesture warmed her against the chilly water.

"My grandma died the summer after I graduated high school," Lana continued, realizing she didn't feel hesitant to share at all anymore. It felt so good to release her story to him. "And my grandad is in a nursing home on the other side of town." She held back the part about his dementia, not wanting to drag the conversation down too much. She was having such a wonderful day, and Hunter had already taken in everything with such grace and understanding that she didn't want to push it.

"Does he know about me purchasing it?"

Lana considered the question, but the growing comfort between them encouraged her to be honest. "No, he doesn't. He lost the inn after I graduated from culinary school due to some financial struggles, and he doesn't know those owners recently sold it."

Hunter didn't say anything in response.

"And the nursing home provides extra care for him, limiting visitors to just me right now in his condition. So nobody has been able to see him to tell him."

They reached the sand and walked past all the beachgoers until they were out in the parking lot, loading up with their tubes on the next shuttle. After a quick ride back to the parking lot, they reached her car and grabbed towels to dry off.

"I'm going to go change out of this wet bathing suit," she said, curious that Hunter still hadn't responded to what she'd told him about Grandad.

"I'm going to do the same." He reached for his clothes and they made their way back to the bathrooms.

By the time Lana was changed and dry, she had a speech prepared in her mind to approach the discussion again, hoping to lighten things up again between them. He was waiting for her outside the bathroom, and they quietly walked back to her Jeep. Just as they shut their doors, they turned to each other at the same time.

"Please don't—" she said, but stopped when she heard him.

"I hope—" He too stopped, and she saw his mouth begin to curve.

Lana smiled in relief. "You go first."

"Well, I was just going to say that I hope your grandad will know one day how much I respect the inn and all of his hard work on it for all those years. What were you going to say?"

"That I don't want you in any way to feel bad for the work you're doing there. You had every right to bid on the inn, just as I did. My family's past ties to that building didn't make it a given that I'd be able to buy it back, no matter how hard all this is to accept. I think what you're creating is impressive." She looked down at the wheel and some loose hair escaped from her braid again.

"What is it?" Hunter brushed the curls aside and her cheeks burned in response. Whatever had been building between them was mounting by the minute.

The tenderness in his touch loosened her up even more, and before she could think about her words, they just came out. "I feel guilty in a way. Not necessarily because I haven't told my grandad about the changes happening at the inn yet, but because"—she looked up from the wheel and saw him lean toward her—"I'm here with you. Having a wonderful time." She turned to him and saw him slowly grin.

"I think I get what you're saying. You feel like it would be easier to tell him if we remained enemies." Hunter straightened back up. "The day isn't over yet. Let's see where we stand by the end of the fireworks," he teased.

"Hmm… you're right," she said, turning on the ignition. "We might be Bluedale's biggest rivals by tomorrow morning."

As she turned to back up, it took everything in her not to lock eyes with him again. She could feel him watching her, knowing just as well as she did that they were far from ever being enemies.

CHAPTER 22

The orange glow of the setting sun stretched far and wide from Hunter's balcony. Freshly showered and changed, he watched the beauty fill the late-afternoon sky. He was due to meet Lana on the sand that connected their two businesses in about fifteen minutes, and she had insisted that he let her handle dinner. His stomach rumbled thinking about it, just as his phone vibrated in his pocket and he saw it was his father trying to reach him again. He normally never bothered him to this extent on holidays, so he tapped the screen.

"Hi, Dad," Hunter answered, trying not to sound irritated. His father's text from earlier was still lingering in his mind. "Having a nice Fourth?"

"It's been fine. Played a full eighteen holes on the golf course, and now about to go have some dinner with friends. I wanted to check in again. Did you receive my text from earlier?"

Hunter rolled his eyes. "I did," he said, offering no explanation as to why he hadn't responded. He simply didn't owe him one.

"Look, Hunter, I just want to make sure you're staying on track."

With a clenched jaw, he turned to go back inside. He could feel the aggravation growing by the second, but with a dinner date only minutes away, he had no time for an argument. "Of course I'm staying on track. Should I be working on holidays now too? Is that why you're calling?"

He heard his father sigh on the other end of the phone. "I saw how beautiful this Lana Kelly is, and I want to reiterate that caution should be used."

"Caution?" Hunter knew what he meant—the buyout—but his patience was wearing thin.

"Yes, Hunter. This property has the potential to be bigger and better once we have all of it. I'm glad you took me to her restaurant. I was able to picture it all."

His arrogance nearly struck the final nerve. Hunter had brought him to Lana's restaurant to show him how great it was. How could his father even think to ask her to give that place up?

"Bigger, yes. Better… I'm not so sure, Dad. We need the support of Bluedale in order to be better, and Lana is part of this town." He sat down on the edge of the bed, rubbing his forehead with his free hand, knowing he should not begin a conversation like this over the phone. Telling his father he would not present Lana with an offer needed to be done in person.

He was met with nothing but silence on the other end.

"Dad?"

"Remember what's at stake for you if you deflect from our plans. I'll see you next week." With that, his father hung up and said nothing more.

Grabbing his keys off the dresser, Hunter made his way outside. There was no time to think about his father anymore that evening. Heading down the stairs, he walked out the door and got into his car, starting the ignition. Before he put the gear in reverse, he leaned back on the head rest. With a huge exhale, he rolled the tension from his shoulders and began to back out. His heart hammered in defiance against his father, and he couldn't have been prouder of his courage, despite the challenges ahead of him in the next week. He wasn't exactly sure what would happen once he told his father that buying out Lana was off the table, but he knew one thing—Lana Kelly wasn't deflecting his plans, but rather had him learning what Bluedale was truly all about… and *reflecting* on what *he* was about.

He continued to steady his breathing. The confrontation with his father started to fade, and Lana's face found its way to his mind. For the moment, her presence was all that mattered.

PULLING INTO THE PARKING LOT, he saw only Lana's Jeep. Hunter was confused; wasn't her place open for dinner after the parade? Driving through town, he saw that every other restaurant was packed with diners for the holiday. He parked his car, and before he went out to the beach, he popped into the venue and made his way to the kitchen.

Inside one of the storage closets was a box with champagne left over from the cruise ship's opening day, so he picked one up. Placing it on the counter, he went back to the closet, grabbed an ice bucket, and filled it with ice from the freezer before resting the bottle inside to chill. Realizing he had no flutes, he saw a stack of plastic cups in the closet and pulled out two.

Back outside, the constant chorus of the summer cicadas filled his ears, and he turned toward the side of the building that led out to the sand. In the distance he saw a firepit blazing and Lana sitting on a blanket. Hunter approached quietly and she turned to him, smiling with her finger pressed to her lips to stay silent.

Placing the ice bucket on the blanket, he dropped down next to her and followed her gaze toward the incredible landscape above, overcome by the gorgeous saffron hue as the sun gave its grand finale. Hunter was just as mesmerized as she was, as they witnessed the famous green flash the sun gave before it finally dipped below the horizon.

"Did you see it?" she asked, still looking up.

"I did," he said, now watching her, her beauty equally as striking. "I've never actually seen that in real life before. Only in the movies."

"I've caught it a few times, but what a perfect ending to the day."

"I'm glad we saw it together."

Lana was quiet, keeping her focus on the sky for a few more seconds, and they listened to the waves gently falling onto the shore in front of them.

"Are you hungry?" She finally looked at him, and the fire lit a glow around her face.

"Yes—starving, in fact." His stomach immediately rolled at her question.

"Good, because it's all ready." Lana got up and went over to a large basket, pulling out two covered plates. She set one down in front of him with a fork and napkin. "Is that champagne you brought?"

"Sure is. It's the Fourth of July, so I figured a little bubbly might help you get through the final stretch of this hard day for you."

"That's so thoughtful," she said, peeking up at him with a small smile. She went back to the basket to get her plate. "I brought some water bottles. I hope that's okay. Not very fancy, but it's a beach dinner picnic with a firepit as our lighting, so I figured it would be fine."

"It's all perfect." He lifted off the top of the plate, breathing in a garlicky aroma. "Wow, this smells incredible. What did you make?"

Lana handed him a wrapped piece of bread. "Clams steamed in white wine with shallots, garlic, and a touch of red pepper over baby arugula and garlic bruschetta. Put that bread I just gave you in the dish. I have some more olive oil to spread on top if you'd like."

"Yes, please," he said, and she leaned over with the bottle and poured some over his dish. "I can't believe you just whipped this up."

"Clam dishes are my specialty, and besides, this is an easy one for me. Twenty minutes tops. I already had cleaned-off clams left over, anyway." She pointed to another empty bowl. "You can discard the shells there, and I have plenty more bread."

Hunter watched how she used her fork to pull the clams out of their shells, discarding them afterward, and he did the same. Mixing the clams with the wilted arugula into the rest of the ingredients, he then took a bite, and let the creaminess of the roasted garlic and peppers melt into the salty clams as he chewed.

He swallowed and put his fork down. "There are no words to describe how good this is."

"Just wait—I have strawberry and blueberry mini pies for dessert."

They both enjoyed their dinner, watching the stars glitter across the sky next to the bright moon. The cicadas in the distance were still chirping their rhythmic song, in tune with the current—the peacefulness reminding him they were completely alone.

"I take it you stay closed on the Fourth of July. I noticed

we're the only ones here."

Lana nodded, sipping her water. "I'm hoping one day I'll open for it, but the day is hard enough as is. The stand at the parade surprisingly brings in a decent amount against the loss of the dinner service."

Hunter didn't say anything in response. He couldn't imagine having a holiday such as this one be a yearly reminder of such a great loss. The heated conversation between him and his father earlier felt silly now in comparison to what Lana was facing today.

Hunter picked up a napkin she'd laid out and wiped his mouth, setting his empty plate down on the blanket. "I can see why clams are your specialty and why people come here for those dishes. I personally love a big warm bowl of clam chowder every summer."

Lana instantly cast her eyes to the blanket, and something made him pause to question it, realizing he must have hit a trigger somehow.

"I don't blame you." She kept her face down. "That's what we're known for up here in New England." Without him knowing why, she seemed suddenly upset, and he wanted to reach over and comfort her.

"It certainly is," he said, inching toward her so he could touch her face. He gently lifted her chin. "Are you okay?"

"Yes, I am. It's just that… the inn was remembered for my grandma's famous clam chowder. It was a staple in this town for nearly forty years. People came from miles to have it."

"Do you have her recipe?"

"Yes. My grandmother helped me perfect it before she passed away."

"I bet your grandad appreciates that, offering him a little comfort from his late wife."

Lana squeezed her eyes shut before settling them on him. "I've yet to bring him a bowl since he's been in the nursing home. I just..." She paused. "I don't know how to bring it back without the inn."

"The inn will never outshine the memories a special recipe like that can create, because what really matters is who those memories are shared with."

A whistling sound in the sky brought immediate reprieve to the conversation, followed by a crackling pop in the air with the first firework. The night sky glimmered against the burst, colors scattering through the air. Another high-pitched sound followed it, with a loud bang and a gold waterfall that glittered down.

Lana pushed her empty plate aside and drew her legs up, holding them to her chest while she watched the show. Hunter noticed a folded blanket next to the food basket and leaned back to get it, shaking it open and scooting next to her. He wrapped it around her shoulders just as the wind blew gently through her hair, and the colorful lights danced in the reflection of her eyes when they stared at each other, her face now inches from his. Her lips drew his gaze down, but another bursting sparkle pulled her attention as she looked back up toward the sky. Sensing her hesitation, he too pulled himself away and put his arms behind his back, steadying himself to watch. Lana moved closer, laying her head on his shoulder, so he shifted forward and put his arm around her. She melted into his embrace.

The fireworks continued to rush into the sky, illuminating the darkness with an array of patterns and light, celebrating their country's birthday with explosive fury. Hunter barely noticed. Lana nuzzled deeper into his neck, the energy between them igniting sparks greater than the magnificent display above, waiting for the right moment to release its beauty and power.

CHAPTER 23

After a rough night of tossing and turning, Lana was up before the sun, counting the minutes until visiting hours began at the nursing home. When she finally left her condo, she made a quick stop in the bakery first. Walking back out a few minutes later with her regular Sunday order, plus Grandad's favorite—a Boston cream pie donut—she got into her car and headed for the nursing home.

When she'd got back from her evening with Hunter, her mind was firing almost as fast as the fireworks that had lit up the sky. The way the light from the firepit reflected on his face, showing his dark stubble when he looked at her on the blanket, or how his eyes repeatedly flickered over to her with curiosity as they talked—the entire evening replayed in her thoughts as she drove. Their connection was undeniable, yet something else had stayed with her all night, and as she'd stared at her dimly lit ceiling from the moonlight, she knew she needed to see Grandad first thing in the morning before her Sunday prep at the restaurant.

Traffic was heavy with double the vacationers for the

holiday weekend, making their way to grab last-minute items for the beach or breakfast at the diner. The entrance to the nursing home finally came into view, and just as she pulled into the parking lot, the tears began to pool, falling down her face.

"Get it together, Lana," she said out loud, and wiped them off her cheeks. Picking up her grandad's special donut in its small bag, she opened the door and took it inside.

Grandad was in a chair by the window of his room when she got there, watching the birds outside swoop back and forth to a nearby branch. When he heard her, he turned his head, and before she could set the bag down, she ran to his side.

"I'm sorry, Grandad!" she cried, pulling up the other chair to sit close to him and brushing the hair that stuck to her face from the tears that began to pour again. She took his hands and looked right at him. "I haven't brought you clam chowder. I just—"

"Lana… my dear sweet girl." His brows knitted together in complete surprise. "Take a deep breath with me." He drew in the air through his nose, and she followed his lead and inhaled sharply, letting it out slowly. "There—that's better, right? Is that for me?" He eyed the bag in her hand.

She held it out. "It's your favorite. A Boston cream pie donut from Bluedale Bakery."

He pulled out the donut and took a bite, wiping the cream that missed his mouth.

"Mmm. Now"—he settled into his chair with his donut—"try again."

"I didn't mean to startle you by coming in that way. I had so much planned to say and I couldn't contain myself when I saw you. What I meant to say is that I'm so sorry I haven't made Grandma's clam chowder for you."

"Have all the clams disappeared off the Cape?" he teased her, and her face relaxed into a smile.

"No, of course not," she said, taking his hand. "I'm going to make you some very soon."

"I didn't expect to see you today. Was that all you came to tell me?"

"No… well…" She tried to piece together in her mind everything she had reflected on through the night. "I hope I don't tire you with all this. How are you feeling?"

"Today is a good day. I feel strong and had a very relaxing day yesterday. One of the nurses recorded the fireworks on her phone and showed me at breakfast. Did you see them last night?"

"Front and center, right underneath them." Lana let go of his hands and leaned back in the chair, bracing herself for the possible directions this conversation could go. Sometimes he was in the present and sometimes he was remembering the Fourth prior to the accident.

Her grandad studied her with a tenderness in his expression that she had come to cling to since her parents passed away. "You remind me so much of your father when he was young. A redheaded version, of course." He winked and her eyes burned with emotion. She took another long breath to keep herself focused. "Was it any easier yesterday?"

Lana looked out the window, stewing on an answer, yet relieved he was present with her, which was right where she needed him to be for this conversation. She thought about the way Hunter had pulled their water tubes together, keeping them close while floating along the river. In all the years she'd had to face this question from her grandad, she tried to always give him a positive response, not wanting him to worry—but for the first time, she could give him a true answer.

"Yes, in fact."

Grandad grinned. "You don't even realize how good that is to hear. I called you yesterday, but when I got your voicemail, I figured you were probably enjoying your favorite river." He knew her so well.

"And the parade."

Grandad's mouth fell slightly ajar. "You went to the parade?"

Lana nodded, her heart still soaring from Hunter's alluring charm the day before, yet something in her chest felt compacted. She knew it was time to say it. "Grandad?"

"Mm-hmm?"

"We lost the inn," she nearly whispered, feeling the guilt quickly replace the high. "All over again."

Her grandad didn't falter once while looking at her, staying still and calm. His eyes narrowed in thought, evidently trying to understand. "I don't follow what you mean."

"I know. Let me explain."

Shifting in her seat, she started from the beginning, when the inn had gone back up for sale. She told him how the previous owners didn't do much with it, never updating anything, and essentially tried to pick up where he and her grandma had left off. How it all became too much for them, until they decided to put it back up for sale. When she told him about Hunter and his development company making an offer that she couldn't compete with, Grandad leaned forward, listening to every detail.

"For the past month, I've had to watch our inn be completely transformed into something unrecognizable. I didn't know how to tell you, and I've worked really hard to let it go, but now that we're having this conversation, it's making it difficult all over again." The lump in her throat pushed out the tears faster.

Grandad nodded in response, sitting up straight. She

realized how much she'd just laid on him and was now worried he couldn't sort through that much information all at once. His illness often had him confused, but he didn't stop her through the entire discussion, and once she'd started, her chest slowly released that hard, dull ache.

"I think it's time to tell you more about the chowder," he said.

"The chowder?" Lana was confused. She'd just told him his inn was gone forever and he wanted to bring up the clam chowder?

"Yes. It'll make sense soon," he said, patting her leg. "Did you know that the inn was your grandma's childhood home?"

"It was?" she asked, drawing her brows up. That was certainly news to her. "I thought you and Grandma remodeled it. I always assumed that meant you bought it together too."

"We did remodel it, but we didn't buy it. It was gifted to us on our wedding day by her parents." He watched her for a moment. "You look just like your mama with that face."

She smiled at the mention of her mother. "What face?"

"The one that says, 'Why was I kept in the dark.' I love how fiery you get. Just like she used to."

If he only knew how bitter she initially was when she learned of the inn's new future. He would have seen a lot more of that face. She was glad he hadn't witnessed the stress it had originally brought her. He would have been a mess with worry.

"I'm surprised, is all. I feel like I should've known that."

"It's something Grandma and I sort of... kept to ourselves."

"Why is that?"

"Because of the rocky start it had. It wasn't my proudest

moment after I married your grandma, to disappoint my new in-laws the way I did."

"Disappoint them? Why would they be disappointed that you began a business adventure with Grandma?"

"No, it wasn't because of that." Grandad took a sip of his water. "You see, when we moved in, my vision of turning her childhood home into an inn began. Grandma loved the idea, and the rest was history. We got a loan to make a few additions like the lounge area and a bigger kitchen, and we expanded the upstairs to add bedrooms and bathrooms, turning the place into what it was for over forty years—Bluedale's finest inn." He looked out toward the window. "But her parents were so upset at first."

"Wouldn't they have been proud to see what you two created?"

Turning his focus back to her, he nodded. "They were, but it took quite a while for that to happen. At first, they couldn't believe I'd ripped apart the home they raised your grandma in. Her mother was especially sad about that. But after some time passed and the renovations took shape, they started to see the same vision I had. Her parents were finally happy with it, accepting the changes, and we all shared the chowder together that first night we opened—as a family. It signified a new beginning for us."

"So where did the recipe come from?"

"Grandma's family. Her mother thought it would be a great way to begin their home's new adventure together, honoring the family."

"That is a beautiful story with a happy ending."

"Lana," he said, scooching as close as he could toward her and holding her hands. "Sometimes change is scary at first, but once you lean into it, it can be a great thing. Not being able to buy the inn back for me would never take away what was built there, and the happiness it brought for decades.

Nothing can erase that, even if the memories all fade away one day. I will never lose the joy. And… it sounds like Hunter has an admirable vision of his own. What's he like?" he asked, clearly sensing something from as he noticed her expression change, and he sat back waggling his eyebrows.

Lana couldn't help but laugh.

"He's—" She chewed her lip, and she could almost feel Hunter's firm grip around her shoulders under the firework display the night before. "Simply lovely."

"And so are you—inn or no inn."

Lana always knew how special their family's clam chowder was, but now it took on a whole new meaning. And now she understood that it wasn't making the chowder itself that scared her, but rather the fear of change. Allowing herself to be vulnerable, creating a new experience with the soup—she was afraid she would break the connection to what once was. Tears glistened in her eyes and this time she didn't try to stop them.

"Let it out, Lana. All of it." Grandad opened his arms, and she got up, his tight embrace helping to ease her weary soul. "There you go, my sweet girl. You must feel to heal, in every stage of life."

Back out in her car nearly an hour later, Lana felt the weight of her burdens continue to lift with her grandad's wisdom. *You must feel to heal.* She realized his dementia had inadvertently forced her to sit with everything from her past that had been too difficult to endure. As his short-term memory continued to fade, his ability to recall memories from long ago became a steppingstone to facing all she'd lost, so she could see her journey ahead and move purposefully toward a new future. Life and all the losses had blurred her vision, dimming her memories of the poignant moments that served as glimpses to her future self.

Fatigue overcame her from the emotional release, and she

leaned back against her seat. Closing her eyes, she slowed her breath, and the memory that had been wanting to break through for so long finally came forward without a fight.

"LANA!" her father called out. "My little firecracker. Lighting up the shore greater than the fireworks tonight!" He held her up higher with another spin, and her arms reached out even more.

Another wave crashed below, the sea's dormant strength harnessing its majesty all around them. The gull mocked them as he swooped through the air, crying out to be heard. Her father set her down, but she stayed snug in his arms, watching the bird fly out over the vast open sea until they couldn't see him anymore.

"He's fearless, Daddy," Lana said, looking up at her father.

"Like you." He smiled down at her.

"Will he come back?"

"Always. Just like you can always come back here too. Your roots are in Bluedale. No matter where you go, Lana, never forget this summer with that gull. Flying away… happy and free."

LANA'S EYES FLEW OPEN. Pulling out her phone, she found the right number and made a call.

"Hey, Lana," Nathan answered. "How was your Fourth? Alicia and I were thinking about you when we took a drive to Brewster for the day."

"It was perfect. Better than it ever has been before." With the tears now drying, her heart was exploding with new ambition. "I'm ready. Let's remind Bluedale who I am."

CHAPTER 24

*L*ana's red Jeep wasn't in the parking lot when Hunter pulled into work. His own crew filled most of the space, but that was expected for a Monday morning. They were ready to get another week of work done, and he was looking forward to seeing what they'd accomplish by the week's end—but not before he'd gathered his lead men to go over everything that had poured into him that weekend.

Seeing Bluedale come together for the Fourth of July—and especially his time with Lana—had made it clear to him what he needed to add to the venue's main ballroom. With the renovations coming along, he couldn't wait to surprise her with it soon. He pushed aside his father's remarks from their phone call and marched ahead, convinced that this was the right thing. In fact, he was rather looking forward to sharing with him that he wasn't going to make Lana an offer. This was what was best for Bluedale, and without the support of all the locals, his venue's reputation wouldn't stand a chance.

Graham Bayview Events would not only be this town's

hottest new event venue, but it would capture every element this community represented: unity, comfort, and family—creating events that were driven by Bluedale's values. Most importantly, hearing even more of the history behind Lana's family inn made him understand that in order for them to succeed in this town, his heart needed to be at the core of this business. Instead of an offer to buy her out, she'd be presented with something that would carry her family's legacy forward.

When he got out of his car, he saw a yellow Volkswagen parked up close to the propped door alongside her restaurant, with its trunk open, so he knew someone was there. The florist had called about his order, but he wanted to get an idea of when Lana would be at the restaurant today before he picked it up.

"Hello?" Hunter gave a knock against the door of On the Bay and walked inside. "Anyone here?"

A woman with short, blonde hair popped her head out of the kitchen. "Hi there."

"Hi. I hope I didn't startle you, but I was checking to see when Lana would be in?" Hunter walked over to the woman, extending his hand. "My name is Hunter, by the way. My company owns the new venue going in next door."

The woman cocked her head. "Ohhh, okay. So you're Hunter?"

"That's what they call me. What are you called?" He gave the woman a playful smile.

"Sorry—my name is Heidi. I'm Lana's sous chef. Nice to meet you." She took his hand and grinned back at him. "Lana won't be in for a couple hours. She's off with her friend Nathan doing business things."

"Will you be here a while?"

"I will," she said. "Why do you ask?"

"I'll be back soon with something I want to leave on her desk. If that's all right?"

Heidi nodded. "Sure, just go ahead and leave it in her office—which is right there." She pointed down the hall. "The door will be open. If you need anything, I'll be in the kitchen."

Hunter got back to his car and made his way to the florist across town. When he hadn't heard back from Lana until late yesterday, he'd begun to worry. Her text to him wasn't bad, but short and sweet, so a part of him thought maybe he'd come on too strong during their time together. Although, he also figured perhaps she was decompressing from such an emotional day, and he hoped he'd made it better for her.

When he got to the florist, he pulled out his phone to see if she'd replied yet to the text he'd sent after responding to hers. Reading her words, he couldn't stop thinking about her pink lips when she'd looked over to him as they floated side by side on the river.

Hi, Hunter! I'm sorry for the late reply. It's been quite a morning already for me. I'll talk to you very soon.

Short and sweet, he thought again. He'd told her his Sunday was relaxing and quiet and that he'd love to sneak in a lunch with her this week, but still nothing. He got out of the car and decided not to stew too much on this. She would get back to him.

The door's bell alerted the florist that someone had come in, and a friendly older woman with tan shorts and a black T-shirt that said *Bluedale's Blooms* came over holding a watering can. Her graying hair was pulled into a soft bun on top of her head, and her tanned skin made her radiant smile shine as she approached him.

"Hello!" she said, waving at him with her free hand. "May I help you?"

"A lady named Fran called me a little while ago and told me my order was ready for pickup. My name is Hunter Graham."

"Oh, Hunter, yes. That was me—I'm Fran. Come on up to the counter. I'll go back and get them." She disappeared behind a wall of various seed packages and through a door. Seconds later, she reappeared holding the bouquet. "This type of calla lily is my absolute favorite."

Fran came to the opposite side of the counter and laid down the trumpet-shaped flowers that looked like satin exploding from the lush green stems. She had them wrapped in clear purple-and-white woven paper, with a dark-purple ribbon tying it all together.

"These are beautiful. I'm so glad you had some," he told the florist.

"Me too. It's wedding season, so usually they're gone by now, but this year irises and lilac have been the popular picks." Fran began to ring up his order. "That'll be forty-six even."

Hunter pulled his wallet out to pay and noticed Fran eyeing him. "Here you go." He handed her a cash tip after he swiped his credit card. "Do you have brochures or business cards? My company is in the process of converting a piece of property into an event venue. I know Bluedale knows you, but we always like to have information for our tourists who may book their events with us."

"You bought the Kellys' old inn," Fran said knowingly.

Hunter laughed. "Of course you already knew."

"Yes… but I also recognized you. I saw you roaming the parade with Lana. It was so nice to see her smiling and enjoying herself with you. It's been so long." She looked down at the bouquet. "Are these for her?"

"Sure are," he said, and Fran cupped her face.

"Oh, wonderful!" she nearly squealed. "And to answer your question, someone from your team already reached out to us to let me know your event venue was opening this fall. I'm looking forward to doing business with your company."

"That's great to hear," Hunter said, relieved a local seemed happy his company was in town, rather than shooting daggers at him for buying the inn. Though maybe the fact that she'd seen him and Lana together at the parade was part of that. "Do you have a small card and a pen?"

Fran handed both to him and he wrote down his message, sealing it in the envelope that came with the card.

"All set?"

Hunter nodded.

"Okay, now hurry along and take these to her."

Hunter felt light on his feet when he left after seeing Fran's reaction. It gave him an extra boost of confidence, and when he got back to the restaurant, he made his way to her office almost daydreaming about when he'd be with her again. After he set the flowers and card down on her desk, he let Heidi know his mission was accomplished and got himself over to the venue to begin his workday. He had a lot to go over with his team.

HUNTER STOOD NEXT TO BOB, the foreman, in the main ballroom. It still had some ways to go, and they'd just discussed the setbacks with the electricians, but their schedule wasn't falling too far behind. His father had arrived while he was at the florist and was due to come meet with him any moment.

After reflecting on everything the day before, he was ready for this discussion. This was a big step for him and something he'd been waiting to do for a long time—to come out of his shell and be true to himself with how he'd conduct the jobs he was assigned to do.

"I know it's not the largest of ballrooms, but it's coming out to be bigger than I pictured, and I can already imagine many special events here," Hunter said.

"Looking forward to seeing the end result. I've really enjoyed this remodel; it's been an interesting one for sure." Bob glanced at him, before looking around the room.

"Yes, it has," Hunter replied.

"I hope I'm not overstepping any boundaries, but as you know, I've been a Bluedale resident my entire life, and so accepting this project with… you know…" Bob nodded in the direction of Lana's restaurant next door.

"Lana?" Hunter filled in for him. He could see the man was nervous, but knowing other locals had been apprehensive about the project, he wasn't offended to hear that Bob had been too.

"Yes, Lana. I have so many memories of the inn." Bob looked down with a smile. "I remember Lana's grandparents used to host Santa every Christmas. Her grandma used to hand out cookies, and the whole inn would be full floor-to-ceiling with holiday decorations. The line of kids was always so long that it extended out onto the old deck. So I was impressed with how thoughtful you were to save that engraving you found with her name."

"Thank you. I really enjoyed doing that for her. You did an awesome job making that plaque. And seeing her reaction when I gave it to her is something I'll never forget."

"Well, as someone who loved the inn too, I appreciate the gesture and the opportunity to make the plaque for her."

"I've come to learn that Bluedale is not just your typical small town… it's much more than that."

"We're a one-of-a-kind community, that's for sure."

Hunter nodded. "Yes, you are." He thought about all the support Lana had from the town and the idea he'd had earlier for the ballroom. "I have an idea for this room with another plaque, but we don't need to do it just yet. We can discuss it soon."

"Sounds good. I'm curious to hear what you have in mind, but looking forward to it." Bob gave him a slight nudge. "Speaking of Lana… I saw you two at the parade, looking like you were having quite a time together."

"A nice time with Lana?" Both men turned and saw Hunter's father standing there with an unamused expression.

"Good morning, Mr. Graham," Bob said, glancing between father and son. "I better get back to the crew."

When Bob left, Hunter noticed his father still watching him. "How about we head back to the mobile office and have this meeting," Hunter suggested.

"I better be hearing some good news about the offer to Lana," his father said.

"What offer?" a voice broke out behind them, and Hunter froze, instantly recognizing her voice.

"Lana…" Just as Hunter turned, she took a step backward. He noticed a small basket she was holding. "What do you have there?"

"A lobster roll. I remembered that you wanted to try mine," Lana said, her eyes moving toward his father. "Hello," she greeted him.

Hunter's father crossed his arms, giving her a slight head nod.

"That was so thoughtful of you," Hunter said, watching her defensively hold the basket with both hands against her stomach.

"Can someone please explain what this offer is?" she asked.

"I take it you didn't even bring it up then," his father said, and she took another step backward, shaking her head at Hunter.

"Dad, can you give me and Lana a minute?"

"Fine," his father said, and he walked into the other room to talk with some of the contractors.

"Hunter, what is going on?" she asked when his father walked away.

"Before I explain, please know that I wasn't going to do it."

"Do what?"

Hunter took a deep breath, scrambling for the right words. "When we purchased this inn, and before I came to town, we had a meeting to go over the details about the land—how big the beachfront is, and all its equity... including yours. And"—he looked away, hardly able to handle the look on Lana's face as her eyes widened—"an offer was put together to present to you."

Lana was speechless. She shook her head. "An offer?" she finally said, her eyes widening even more when it hit her. "You mean to buy me out?"

"Yes," he said, barely above a whisper.

When her eyes glistened, he had to fight himself not to run over and hold her.

"Is that why you wanted to spend time with me? So you could butter me up into selling my restaurant?"

"Lana, no... not at all. I told you, I wasn't going to do it. I was never going to present you with any offer."

"How am I supposed to believe you?" She turned slightly and tracked his step toward her. "Do not follow me." With that, she quickly left, tears streaming down her face.

Hunter bent over, trying to catch his breath against his heart that was beating wildly in his chest.

"Hunter?" His father came back into the room, standing right in front of him. "I told you to be cautious with her."

He stood back up. "I'm a grown man and I have every right to handle my own relationships."

"You let your feelings get in the way of business. You came here to do a job, not sit around letting some woman manipulate you away from your responsibilities."

Something in him boiled over as anger bubbled into his throat. He knew his father was a harsh man, but that he would have the gall to judge Lana made him snap. "Excuse me? Manipulate?" he nearly shouted. "What exactly did she manipulate? She didn't even know about the offer until just now!"

"You've been letting her distract you too much," his father said, ignoring his question.

"I will not apologize for getting to know someone amazing, who has taught me more in the past month than *you* ever did my entire life." He paused, looking his father straight in the eye.

"What's that supposed to mean?"

"I've learned more than you can imagine from her about family and what that means," Hunter said without a beat.

His father grew quiet, his expression not faltering once, but Hunter could sense by the silence that his comment had surprised him.

"Look around you, Hunter. This is why you're here. If you can't handle the pressure, then the promotion, or maybe even this company, might not be for you."

"Perhaps it's not," he said, matching his father's challenge.

"Your choice. Carry out the offer to Lana or not, but if you don't, then after you complete this project, you may want to start thinking about the line of work that suits you."

"Choice is made already, Dad. I'm not presenting Lana with anything."

"So be it," his father said, storming off, and in the

distance, by the doors to the patio, Hunter saw Bob standing there.

"I'm… sorry. I didn't mean to intrude," Bob said, coming closer and looking visibly concerned.

Hunter immediately wondered what exactly he'd heard. By the look on the foreman's face, he assumed a lot. "No, I should be the one apologizing. I'm sorry you had to hear all that. He and I should have moved that conversation into the mobile office."

"I really feel like I'm overstepping now…" Bob appeared more nervous by the second. "It's just that I saw Lana running out of here crying, and I got worried."

"Please don't be sorry. I would be worried too if I were in your position," Hunter assured him. "If you'll just excuse me, I'm going to step out for a bit, but I'll be available by cell."

"Sure thing," Bob said. "And, Hunter? Please let me know if you need anything."

"Thank you. I appreciate it. I just need a moment to myself."

Bob walked off and Hunter went over to one of the new large windows, looking out to the sea. He'd been feeling like he was finally on the right path, but everything felt lost now.

CHAPTER 25

It had been nearly an hour, and Lana hadn't moved from the patio since her encounter with Hunter and his father. The tears had dried, but she sat there trying to make sense of what she'd just learned.

"Lana?" Heidi walked over to her. "Did you just get back?"

"No." She looked up, shielding her eyes against the hot sun. "I've been out here for a while."

Heidi saw the basket by her feet. "Oh… so how did he like the lobster roll?"

Lana looked out in the distance toward the water, trying not to cry all over again. "I don't know. He never ate it."

Heidi pulled out a chair and sat beside her. "What happened?"

There was no other way to say it, except spitting it right out. "His company had plans to try and buy me out." She waved her hand around. "Taking all of this away from me." Fresh tears began to pool in her eyes and Heidi immediately moved her chair closer, putting her arms around her.

Leaning into Heidi, Lana felt something deep within her stir, allowing herself to cry in front of her sous chef.

"Lana." Heidi leaned back so they were face-to-face. "Is this about an offer from Hunter's company or is it something else?"

"What do you mean?" Lana wiped her cheeks, drawing in a breath.

"Because Hunter can't take any of this away. You have to accept the offer for that to happen. Is there something else weighing on you?"

"It's just that… why would he even consider doing that?"

"Did he actually present you with an offer?"

"No, he didn't." Lana shook her head. "I overheard his father talking to him about it, and he admitted it right to me when he saw me."

"And what exactly did he say?" Heidi asked.

"That he was never going to offer me anything. And then I got out of there before he could say anything else." Realization came over her, and for the first time, it was clear to her how guarded she'd been for so long. "I reacted way too fast. I should have given him more of a chance to explain."

"Why don't you take the rest of today off. I think you need some time to yourself." Heidi put her hand up when Lana began to object. "Nope. Take the day. But before you leave, go look in your office. I meant to tell you that before you took the food to Hunter."

Curious, Lana picked up her basket and stood up. "I'll leave this with you. You'll need the fuel to run dinner service alone." She handed the basket to Heidi.

Heidi rolled her eyes. "Did you forget I ran it alone for a week last fall when you got the flu? Don't even worry about me. Come on, let's go."

The two women walked inside, and when Lana opened the door to her office, she nearly cried all over again, but not for the same reason. The purple calla lilies were laid across her desk, and when she looked over at Heidi, she saw her nodding. The day in the Butterfly Garden came back to her, and she couldn't believe Hunter had remembered these were her favorite.

"He's not trying to take anything away from you. Talk to him." Heidi patted her shoulder before heading back to the kitchen.

Lana walked over to the flowers and opened the hand-written message:

May these flowers bloom new beginnings for you and with us. Love, Hunter.

Folding the card back up, she picked up the flowers and got right into her car, silently praying her grandad was having a good day. She could really use his advice.

GRANDAD WAS outside in his wheelchair when she got there, parked in the shade. His hip must have been bothering him not to have his walker, but his eyes were closed and he seemed to be enjoying his rest outside.

"Grandad?" Lana said quietly, so as not to startle him. She sat in a chair next to his wheelchair as he opened his eyes. Confusion cast over his face at first while he studied her, and she held her breath waiting.

"Lana… I wish I could play hide-and-seek with you in the hallways between the bedrooms. But there's so much to do today. Besides, Grandma always gets mad when we run all around the inn." Grandad smiled, still looking at her.

"I wish we could too." Lana's heart sank, but she tried to stay in the moment with him, whenever that moment might be. When she was young, hide-and-seek was their favorite game, but Grandma never allowed them to play it too long because they always messed up the bedding that she'd worked hard to prepare for the guests.

Grandad continued to watch her for a couple more minutes, moving his eyes around her face, before he reached over to touch her cheek.

"Don't you remember how mad she used to get?" he asked again, this time using the past tense, and Lana perked up.

"Yes, she did."

"Oh, to have my sweet girl be that young again," Grandad said. "What brings you here on this unexpected visit? Aren't you busy at the restaurant?"

Lana smiled. Grandad had come back to her. "I have a surprise day off and wanted to see you."

"Hmm… no, that's not it. I know you and something feels off."

"I can't hide anything from you, can I, Grandad?"

"Never. So let's hear it." He leaned his head back against the chair and closed his eyes again, something he often did when he was preparing to listen, especially these days.

"I haven't been on the pontoon in years. I've lied to you for so long about it and I feel terrible."

Grandad opened his eyes. "Is that all you needed to say?"

Lana nodded, perplexed. "Well, sort of."

"I already knew that."

"You did? You never said anything."

"Of course not. Getting out on the water after losing your parents the way you did was something you needed to get around to on your *own* time, but I brought it up all these years in hopes you'd want to talk about it."

"But you used to get so upset, trying for years to get me out there before I left for college."

"I was dealing with my own grief back then and desperately wanted to create normalcy for you."

Lana reached over and took his hand. "I appreciate that, I truly do. By the time you moved into the nursing home, I thought it would help you to hear I finally did it." Lana bowed her head, feeling ashamed she'd lied to her grandad all this time.

"So you still haven't done it then?"

"No," she said, keeping her face down. "The boat is still stored away. I still see them so clearly when I look at it, and it hurts too much. I'm so sorry."

Grandad reached for her other hand, and when she gave it to him, he held them both tightly. "Don't you ever say you're sorry. Grief has no timeline, Lana… and neither does love." He gave her a knowing look, clearly sensing her heart was overwhelmed with more than just the pontoon. "And you'll know when it's time to get back out on the water."

Her eyes stung and she leaned over, kissing him on the cheek. "I think the time is coming soon."

He gave her hands another squeeze. "You'll know when," he repeated, pausing as he studied her. "There's more, isn't there?"

Lana inhaled. "Yes," she answered, remembering Hunter's devastated face when she'd left him standing in the ballroom. "I just found out that Hunter—the man I mentioned the other day, whose company bought the inn—was going to make me an offer to buy out my restaurant. And all of this falls on the heels of opening myself up to him as we've gotten to know each other. Now I'm just confused."

Grandad let go of her hands and sat back, putting his hand to his chin in thought. "Hmm… Hunter isn't what's upsetting you."

Shaking her head, she ignored his statement. "But why didn't he tell me earlier on that his company wanted to do this? I feel like he used me and I opened up, all for nothing."

"Did he directly make the offer to you?"

"No." Lana sighed, remembering Heidi's same question to her. "I overheard the discussion. But I ran away so fast, I didn't let him explain anything else."

"And where are you running to?" Grandad asked.

"Nowhere," she answered, and her eyes moved to Grandad when she started to understand what he was getting at.

"You're not losing anything, Lana. He never actually made an offer, instead choosing to get to know you and allowing that connection to take hold over what his company wanted him to do." He held up his hand when she started to object. "And your restaurant is still there for all to see, but *you* can't stay hiding away in that kitchen clutching onto life so tightly, afraid of what you may lose next—always running from your emotions. Trust what could be when you unfold those wings and fly."

May these flowers bloom new beginnings for you and with us. Hunter's message ran through her mind. Years of hiding behind her cooking, staying closed off from Bluedale and the people who loved her, and more importantly, from her own self, was never going to move her forward.

Suddenly, everything Nathan had presented for her restaurant's rebrand made much more sense—reemerging into her own transformation… right alongside the inn's.

Hugging her grandad goodbye, she quickly made her way back to her car, got in, and pulled out her phone to check her messages. A voicemail that must have come through when she was talking to her grandad caught her attention, and she decided to listen to it first.

"Hey, Lana, this is Bob. Heidi gave me your number. I know it's been a long time since we last spoke, but I've been heading up the remodel next door to your restaurant, and I saw you run out of the worksite looking very upset and got worried. Listen, I overheard

everything after you left. Hunter told his father that he would rather forfeit his position in the company than present that offer to you. I just thought you should know that."

Lana pressed the phone to her chest and squeezed her eyes shut—it wasn't all for nothing after all.

CHAPTER 26

After what felt like the longest run he'd ever taken, Hunter slowed his pace and walked until he reached his car parked near the bakery. He knew his father would come looking for him after he left the venue, so the board-walk outside the bakery felt like the best place to go. After their exchange, he needed to leave and clear his head, and running was the best thing for that.

Opening his car, he grabbed some water. Taking a long sip and feeling his stomach scream at him, he remembered the basket of food Lana had been carrying, and resisted the urge to call her. She'd asked him not to follow, and he knew if he had any chance to resolve this with her, he needed to respect her wishes and give her time.

Closing the car door, he walked over to the bakery and a few minutes later, with a slice of their blackberry cobbler in hand, he sat down on the nearest bench to eat. The tart blackberries and sweet buttery topping practically melted in his mouth, and for a moment, he forgot everything that had just happened.

"I should be warned if you'll be around the bakery

before I get here," a female voice interrupted him, and he looked up to see Alicia standing over him. "I'd like to drink my coffee and not wear it again." She grinned and sat down.

"Nice to see you again, Alicia," Hunter said, chuckling. "It's a good thing it was iced coffee in our last encounter then. To keep you cool."

"Yes, good thing." Alicia playfully rolled her eyes. "You looked pretty deep in thought just now. Something bothering you?"

"Was it that obvious?" he teased.

"Not really, but I can be pretty nosy."

"Ah, see now that makes more sense."

"I'm glad I ran into you." She shifted to face him.

"And why's that?"

A smile spread across Alicia's face. "I just talked to Lana."

Hunter felt his heart pick up speed, not sure what to say, and to his surprise, she patted his knee before standing back up. "Check your phone," she said and started to leave.

"Alicia?" he said, and she stopped. He had to ask. "Is she okay?"

"More than okay." With that, Alicia winked and walked off.

Tossing away his trash, Hunter hurried back to his car and checked his phone, going straight to her text:

> Hunter... I'm sorry I didn't give you a chance to explain. If you still want to talk, I know the perfect place. I have a lot coming up this week to prepare for a relaunch that I can't wait to show you, but if you can sneak away from the venue for a couple hours tomorrow, then would you like to meet me at your port for a tour? Let me know.

She wanted to get on the ship? Knowing how hard that

would be for her, he was intrigued and immediately fired back a response:

> I'll be there. How about the noon tour?

A couple minutes later, she replied:

> See you then.

Nearly shouting with joy, he turned on his car engine to head back to the cottage and relax, ignoring the missed calls from his father. A long shower before tackling that conversation was definitely needed.

HUNTER COULDN'T STOP THINKING about seeing Lana the next day. Pulling into the driveway, he saw his father's car and shook his head—he was right that he'd be there looking for him. So much for a relaxing long shower. In a matter of seconds, his mood dipped drastically, and with his anger already beginning to rise, he parked and got out.

"How long have you been waiting here?" Hunter asked.

"Actually, I just pulled in a minute or two before you. I was about to call you again when I didn't see your car here." Instead of looking concerned about his whereabouts all afternoon, his father looked annoyed, which only made Hunter raise his defenses.

"Can we talk about this tomorrow? I left for a reason," Hunter said, walking past him. "To get a break."

"It's okay that you took a break, Hunter. But I came here because I'm worried." His father fell in step beside him.

Hunter clenched his jaw, trying to keep his cool. "Worried?"

"Yes. Your behavior is concerning. Would you please stop for a second and talk to me?" His father grabbed his arm to slow him down. They were now standing next to the firepit, face-to-face. "How could you give up this company?"

"Oh, of course!" Hunter threw his arms up. "For a second there, I thought you were actually worried about *me*. But, like always, it's about the company." He knew he was yelling, but years of pent-up frustration with his father's inability to see past his business had reached its final boiling point.

"I'm just confused as to why you'd throw away years of hard work like this?"

"Who said I'm throwing anything away? I never said I was leaving—*you* gave me an ultimatum back there. You said I either have to make the offer to Lana or leave."

"Because it's an investment that would greatly improve this project! Don't you see that? Don't you want this to succeed?" His father raised his voice to match his.

"And just why do you think it wouldn't succeed without buying her property? You think Bluedale wouldn't love what we'd create on its own? Why do you *have* to have Lana's property too?"

"Because we can double what's there! It would add immense equity and value, not to mention room."

"Who says she'd even accept the offer anyway?"

"It's the fact that you didn't even try that concerns me. Hunter, get your head out of your heart and think for a second. You barely know this woman!"

Hunter put his hands down, facing his father. "Don't you dare tell me how I feel!" he practically roared, hearing his voice echo.

"All I'm saying is, sometimes you have to make choices that will serve you better in life."

Hunter paused, his body shaking in fury. He knew he shouldn't say it, but he just couldn't help it. "Just like how the decisions you made with this company served you better with Mom? Do you forget why she left, or just choose to ignore it?"

"Gentlemen!" a voice called out behind them, and when they turned, Hunter saw Margaret walking toward them. "All this shouting out here is making my hydrangeas droop."

Hunter's face burned with embarrassment. "Margaret, I'm so sorry. This is highly inappropriate. We'll stop."

Margaret pulled off her gardening gloves and stuck her hand out to his father. "Hello there, I'm Margaret Huxley, the cottage owner. I didn't mean to intrude on your conversation. I was out here gardening when I heard all the yelling."

"I apologize for the disturbance." His father shook her hand. "My name is Philip. I'm Hunter's father."

"I gathered that much." She gave his father a once-over. "Gentlemen, I will apologize in advance before saying this, but since the entire neighborhood was practically invited into this discussion, I feel obligated to speak my piece."

Hunter held his hand up to stop his father from speaking. "Go ahead, Margaret."

The woman turned to his father, giving him a slight nod. "With all due respect, Philip, I can easily assume you run a very successful company, but I'm not so sure you're equally successful in the father department."

"This isn't a family matter—it's a business decision. Sometimes we need to establish expectations when business is involved. The fact that Hunter is my son just means that I have an obligation to set him up for success in the business world. I won't be around to run the company forever. He needs to know how to make the tough decisions. Isn't that a father's job, to make sure his son is prepared to face the world?"

"Or—from the sounds of it—a father's job could be to provide support and encouragement while your child figures out for himself what kind of decisions he wants to make," Margaret said without missing a beat. "Now, if you'll excuse me, my garden is waiting. Have a good rest of your day."

Margaret's truthful comment shot straight through Hunter, leaving him shocked as she went back to her garden. His father walked away, looking equally astounded, and when Hunter got inside the cottage, he immediately sat on his couch to calm down. He didn't share his father's deep-rooted work habits, and he didn't know what had changed Lana's mind to see him again, but he knew one thing—his choice was already made, and it was the right one.

CHAPTER 27

*L*ana shielded her eyes, the bright sun reflecting off the ship's shiny exterior and making it look glorious as it waited against the dock for its guests to arrive. It wasn't a huge cruise line, but large enough to throw one fabulous party. With each step closer, she felt her stomach rebel, churning around in knots. *I can do this*, she told herself.

A screeching seagull distracted her as it circled in front of her. *Perfect timing*. It was a sign from above, helping her to keep moving forward toward the ship. As she stepped onto the dock, the bird soared in the air again, landing next to her on the railing. She paused and got closer, and the gull didn't move. Somehow it must have sensed that Lana needed the support.

She leaned down toward the railing. "Thank you," she whispered and straightened back up, making her way to the ship again.

Flapping its wings, the gull glided down to the dock and walked with her a few steps, and she giggled, a part of her wanting to stretch her arms wide. When the bird finally flew away, her eyes followed him in the air, soaring with great flight. Lana could feel her heart follow its lead, ascending into the open blue sky.

"There's something deep about those seagulls, isn't there?" a low voice said next to her, and when she looked up, Hunter's brown eyes sent a rush through her. "The way they fly over the ocean with no fear."

"I agree," she said. "I've always been fascinated with them."

"Are you ready to go?"

"Yes," she said, but she hesitated before picking up her feet to move.

"Forget something?"

"No, it's just that…" She stared at the large vessel again.

"I know," he said, offering his hand to her.

She pictured the seagull and smiled. She took his hand and walked in front of him to lead the way. "I can do this. Of course I can."

Once they got on the ship, Lana was blown away with everything she saw. "Look at this ballroom—that chandelier is gorgeous!" The fixture hanging in the middle of the dance floor was adorned with sparkling crystals. The high ceiling instantly made it seem as though they weren't confined on a boat, and the ocean colors opened up the room, endless like the sea. "What a beautiful place to have a wedding on the water."

"We thought so too. Come with me—the tour is on the deck above and about to begin." Hunter led her upstairs and outside, where some guests were seated and others standing, enjoying a beverage. "Would you like a watermelon refresher? It's delicious."

"Sounds like the perfect drink to cool off. Thank you," she said, the sun peeking out from behind a cloud. The hot rays prickled her skin.

"Once we get moving, the heat isn't so bad up here with

the ocean breeze. I'll be right back." Hunter headed over to the small drink station.

Lana maneuvered through the guests and found a perfect seat near the back, away from the crowd and close to the side of the ship where she could watch the water for miles. The rhythmic movement always calmed her when she was anxious, and this was definitely one of those times. Minutes later, Hunter found her and sat down, handing her one of the drinks. Taking a sip, she felt the cold, bittersweet liquid with a touch of sour lime hit her lips.

"This is good! I need to know all of the ingredients." Lana held the cup to her nose, taking in the citrus smells.

"Our secret, Ms. Chef. We won't share," he teased, and put his arm around her as the tour guide got on the mic, welcoming everyone.

"We're leaving in a couple minutes. Make sure to get yourself a complimentary refresher and take a seat," the guide told everyone.

Lana braced herself but knew there was no turning back now.

"So how has your week been?" Hunter asked.

She thought about all the hard work she, Alicia, and Heidi had ahead of them, as they were recreating her entire restaurant for the relaunch party later that week. "Busy," was all she could think to say.

"I bet. I'm assuming you have a lot to do for the relaunch?"

"We do, but we'll get there. Alicia is planning to go a bit crazy with redecorating."

"Well, I can't wait to see it all. I've even heard some mumblings among my crew. I'm looking forward to seeing how it turns out."

Lana looked at the crowd mingling around their seats and getting drinks, trying to settle her nerves when she heard the blast signal that the ship was about to leave the port. Hunter must have sensed her anxiety because he pulled her closer to him. Having him with her for this challenging experience felt like it was meant to be. She knew they still had a lot to discuss after what had happened the day before, but she wanted to soak in this moment with him.

"Thank you for the flowers, by the way. They were stunning." She angled her head up at him. "I can't believe you remembered they were my favorite."

"You're welcome. And how could I forget? That was the first day I got to see your beautiful smile." He pulled her closer. "I tried my best to find the perfect ribbon to match with the bouquet."

Lana laughed. "Nice try. I'd recognize Fran's work anywhere." She gave him a playful shove. Taking another sip of her drink, she began to feel her body relax into her chair. "But they really made me smile."

"She'll be seeing a lot of me then." Hunter gave her shoulder a gentle squeeze.

She peered up at him, watching his cheeks raise. "Why are you so giddy?"

"Being here with you and experiencing this triumph alongside you makes me feel like a very lucky man."

The ship began to pull back from the dock, but she hardly noticed. "I don't even know what to say…"

"Well, it's true. In a matter of weeks, I've learned so much about you, Bluedale, and even myself. But what stands out above it all right now is… being out here on the water with you, where you belong."

Her eyes immediately welled up, a few tears escaping down her cheeks—imagining her father saying those exact words. She could feel his presence near while the ship cruised forward.

Hunter's smile faded as he leaned closer. "I didn't mean to make you cry."

"No, these are happy tears. My father always told me the same thing when I was young."

The guide began talking, but they were in their own world while she told Hunter stories about growing up on the Cape with her parents and grandparents. It had been years since she'd relived all those memories. They got up, walked over to the side of ship, and stood farther back from the group. Lana pointed out all the places she recognized along the shore. By the time the ship began to near the dock, they both realized they hadn't heard one word the tour guide said, but that didn't matter. Lana hadn't faltered once while out on the water.

When the ship slowly slid into the port, she held onto the railing and closed her eyes, lifting her face toward the sky. As the warm sun radiated against her skin, something familiar took shape in her heart for the first time in years—a lightness that she'd missed for so long. The joy that the ocean brought her had never left; it was just waiting on her to embrace it again.

"Lana," Hunter said, and she opened her eyes. He took both her hands, turning her to face him. "What happened the other day was never meant to get to you."

"I know."

"You do?"

"Bob called me and told me what you said to your father," she said, just as the ship docked, and she looked down. "Please don't feel like you have to leave the company because of me." A part of her wanted not to care, but she also didn't want to be the reason Hunter left his family's business.

"I *want* to." Hunter lifted her chin up. "The moment I saw you, I was hooked, and I knew the offer was going to be off the table. I was happy to do that because getting to know you was worth the risk."

"But I can't be the reason you forfeit your job."

"I'm not forfeiting anything, I'm *choosing* not to live a life that doesn't include—" He paused, watching the guests begin to walk down the steps to leave.

"Include what?"

He looked at her again. "You."

They locked eyes, and just as he was about to say more, the tour guide interrupted them.

"Okay, you two, in case you didn't notice, the tour is over," he said jokingly, patting Hunter on the shoulder. "How you doing, Mr. Graham?"

Hunter tore his eyes away from Lana's and smiled at the tour guide. "Very well, thank you. Wonderful job with the tour out there," he said, glancing down at Lana again. "Well… from what I took in of it."

"Good to hear. Enjoy the rest of your day," the man said and left them alone again.

"I better get you to your car, so you can get to the restaurant before this ship pulls out for the next tour. You probably still have a lot to do for tomorrow night."

Lana hesitated, wanting to tell him she hoped to see him there, but didn't want to send him mixed signals after just telling him not to leave his job. "Yeah, I do."

The crowd continuing to pile down the stairs and onto the dock caught their attention.

"We better get going." Hunter walked her to her car.

Lana stopped next to her car door. "Thank you for coming out there with me."

"No, thank *you* for allowing me to experience that with you. You're so brave."

"It wasn't as hard as I imagined. I think most of my fear

was just stuck in my head all these years. I just needed the right opportunity…" She gazed at him for a few seconds, and his eyes lingered on her lips. He moved his arms to settle around her waist. "Or the right person."

"Hunter!" A man nearby called his name.

"Dad?" Hunter looked past Lana, loosened his grip, and glared at his father, who was now right beside them. "What are you doing here?"

"I tried calling you, but when you didn't answer for hours, I got ahold of your assistant. She said you were on a tour. But I didn't know you had company," he said, eyeing Lana. "I need to talk to you."

"You could've just waited for me to call you back. I'm a little busy," Hunter said.

"I can see that. We really need to get things—"

"We will discuss this later," Hunter said, his jaw clenching. Lana cleared her throat to intervene.

"I better go," she said, unlocking her car.

"Hang on, you don't need to leave." Hunter scowled at his father. "*He* does."

"I need to get to the restaurant anyway. Thank you again for coming on the tour with me, Hunter." She tried to smile at both of them in an attempt to ease the tension, but the strife between them was too intense to break.

Turning, she opened her door and got in. As she backed out, she noticed Hunter's solemn expression through the window as he faced his father. Every part of her wanted to get out of the car and tell him she didn't want a life that didn't include him either, but seeing the strain between father and son only solidified what she said on the ship. She'd give anything to have her father back, and she didn't want to be the one to take Hunter away from his. But she couldn't decide how their relationship would turn out—only they could do that.

As she drove away from the port, she put her focus on the relaunch party. Bluedale would finally see the woman they'd come to miss—and perhaps she could at least show Hunter how he had a part in helping her find the courage to do so.

CHAPTER 28

"It's ready, boss." Max poked his head into the mobile office. "I'm about to head back to Boston, but I'm glad I got to see it."

"I'll be right there," Hunter said, yawning as he drummed his fingers across the desk. Despite being up half the night tossing and turning, he knew what he needed to say to his father. He'd hated to see the worry on Lana's face when she'd told him not to choose her over his job, but the decision had already been made. He couldn't work for his father if he didn't respect him for who he was, who he'd always been—which didn't match his father's expectations.

He'd texted her that morning, but when he'd checked his phone, he still hadn't received a response, and he hoped she was just getting ready for that night. He'd asked her if she could meet him at the venue before the party. There was something he needed her to see.

Walking inside, the normal sounds of saws and hammers weren't echoing in the distance. Instead, he found most of the crew standing by the new entrance to the half-remodeled grand ballroom.

"Hello, everyone," Hunter greeted them, and they all stepped aside.

Bob was standing beside Max, next to something on the wall that was covered with cloth. "I'm really enjoying make all these," Bob said.

"You've got a real talent for them," Max said. "I was impressed when Hunter sent me a picture of the plaque you made out of that old deck piece."

"Lana deserved it, and so did her family," Bob said.

"Okay, ready to see?" Max put his hand on the cloth.

"Absolutely," Hunter said, and he gasped when Max revealed what was underneath. Hunter stepped closer to see it better. "Did you carve that yourself?"

Bob nodded. "Sure did. Took me about a week to get the wings right."

Hunter ran his hands along the craftsmanship, admiring the seagull engraved across the top with its wings spread. "What type of wood is this?"

"Cherry. It had such a nice smooth finish, after I shaved it down, that it was relatively easy to carve," Bob said proudly.

Hunter read the words on the metal frame that was added to the bottom half of the rectangular piece: *The Kelly Room.* Underneath, in cursive, it read, *In Honor of Walter & Renee Kelly.* The workmen all came and took a quick look, before trickling back out into the venue to continue working.

"It's stunning. Thank you for doing this. How much do I owe you?" Hunter asked.

"Absolutely nothing. In a way, it feels like honoring a piece of my own childhood," Bob said. "And, Hunter?"

Hunter looked at the foreman and could sense what he was about to say.

"You made the right choice." He waved his hand around.

"I know."

Bob patted his shoulder and left him standing next to the plaque.

I just hope she chooses me too.

WHEN HUNTER still hadn't heard back from Lana a couple hours later, he left the mobile office to check next door but saw that her car wasn't there. After leaving his father in the parking lot at the port yesterday, without giving him a chance to speak, he realized perhaps he should have. His father was due to leave today, heading back to New York that afternoon, and he was nowhere to be found either. *So much for a conversation with him too.* Hunter let out a sigh. Outside in the parking lot, he grabbed some running clothes out of his trunk, changed back in his office, and decided to jog at the beach.

Moving along the shore, he felt his whole body working against the sand. The sounds of the waves calmed his cycling thoughts, and his steady footwork navigated him through the obstacles—both on the uneven sand and in his mind. Lana was worried about making him choose between her and his work, but to him, there wasn't even a choice to begin with. Lana had him the day they'd collided at the diner.

After gliding along the water's edge for almost an hour, he slowed his pace, turned around, and walked until he reached the venue. The sun was hot, but the ocean breeze helped cool him as he sat down to watch the water.

"Have a nice run?" a voice said, startling him. His father pulled up the bottom of his trousers to join him in the sand.

"Yes. It relaxed me, as always," Hunter replied, keeping his gaze forward. The tide seemed to be lowering and he recalled the day he went clamming with Lana. Something he never thought he'd do had turned out to be something he didn't want to leave. Bluedale had grown on him, and he could picture himself there—but more importantly, he could see a future with Lana there too.

"That's good to hear," his father said.

"I thought you were going to come by the venue this morning. Weren't you planning to head back to New York by now?" Hunter wasn't sure if he had enough steam left after his lack of sleep and a long run to say what he'd planned on saying.

"I extended my stay. I'm leaving tomorrow instead." They sat in silence for another minute, both too stubborn to begin the much-needed discussion.

"Dad," Hunter said, finally breaking the silence. "I'm sorry for raising my voice at you earlier this week, but I'm not sorry for what I said. I'm not—"

"Hunter," his father cut in. "You don't need to explain."

"But I don't think you understand."

"I understand plenty, and"—his father looked at him—"I'm the one who needs to apologize. For starters, you should know that—"

"I'm not you, Dad," Hunter said, moving the sand with his feet and trying not to get frustrated.

"I know."

"But I don't think you do."

His father chuckled. "We may not think exactly the same way, but we both have to get the last word in, don't we?"

Hunter smiled. "That's definitely true. I've taken after a few of your traits then."

"Not to mention my devilishly handsome looks." They both laughed this time.

"For two people who have to have the last word, we've been pretty silent all week." Hunter glanced at his father, who was watching the sea. "The crew must've been uncomfortable around us these last few days."

"Yeah, they definitely knew something was up. But when I wasn't at the venue, I was going around Bluedale, getting acquainted with the town."

"You… were?" Hunter was surprised. His father was not the mingling type.

"Yes, and now I know why it has captured you so strongly. This is quite a little town. I went to all the small shops, the restaurants, and talked to a lot of people. Every local I met knows Lana."

"Well, that's not surprising. I've been trying to tell you since I got here, her family is very well known and respected."

"I know I didn't show it, but when we went to her restaurant to have dinner that night, I really was impressed. Her food was incredible."

"Even though you had to judge her decor?" Hunter poked at him.

"I was being a bully, and that was unfair of me. And even worse, I was a bully to you." His father paused, drawing in a breath. "The VP position is yours, Hunter… if you'll still take it. To operate how you think is best." His father turned to face him with a hopeful look in his eyes.

Hunter stayed silent for a moment, stunned at his father's change of heart. "Bluedale must have really worked its magic on you."

"It sure did."

"Of course, Dad," Hunter answered him. "I would be honored to take the position." He peeked over at his father with an amused look. "This company has seen nothing yet. Wait until I take over all of it."

His father laughed. "Just brace me before you make things too different." Laughter echoed behind them from Lana's patio, catching both their attention. "People here love her, and she's made something of herself with very little after losing the inn. Just like how my father started our company —with humble beginnings."

"Yes, she's a fighter, and very talented." Hunter looked over his shoulder at her restaurant, which was filled with people preparing for her relaunch.

"Besides her beauty, it's no wonder you're so invested in her and didn't want to present that offer."

Hunter turned back to face him. "I'm not just caught up in a pretty face. There's a lot to her story you don't know. I wish you'd have let me explain."

His father put his arm around him. "You may look like me, but you have your mother's heart. And that's not a bad thing. Unlike me, you've learned to let your heart speak to you. I'm going to work on that. I messed up years ago with your mom, but you won't make those same mistakes." He nodded his head toward Lana's restaurant.

"If she's even willing to move forward with me after everything. I don't know if you saw, but I made a plaque in her family's honor outside the ballroom."

"I saw it. What a great thing you did for them."

"I asked her to meet me at the venue before the party so I can surprise her with it. She needs to know that I'll never jeopardize what she's created or the legacy her family has here at the venue."

"That's not what she needs to hear."

Hunter drew his eyebrows together. "It's not?"

"No, it's not." His father gave his shoulder a squeeze and leaned in closer. "She needs to hear that you love her."

Hunter closed his eyes, feeling the truth of his father's comment shiver down his back. "Thank you, Dad, for staying, and for this conversation. I hope you come to her relaunch tonight."

"Why else do you think I stayed?" His father stood up,

offering his hand to help him. "That, and to eat her food again."

"Don't blame you there," Hunter said with a grin.

The two men walked back up the beach. Hunter checked his phone and still saw no response from Lana.

"You'll hear from her. Be patient," his father said, and as Hunter got into his car to go back to the cottage and shower, he prayed his father was right.

CHAPTER 29

"Is it straight now?" Nathan called down from the ladder. They'd been trying for the past hour to get the pictures hung against the side of one of the order windows, next to the new chalkboard menus. The relaunch party was starting in a couple hours, and within a matter of days, it had become the talk of the town.

Alicia and Lana stood back to look at the pictures. Every time Lana saw them, especially the photos of her clam digging as a child and chasing the seagulls, her heart swelled with happiness. No matter who she'd lost, it was time to stop ignoring the young girl who held so tightly to all that once was. She would take her cue from Grandad. He had been forced to sit with the past, and instead of gripping onto what he couldn't control, he'd allowed it to ease his illness and bring him a sense of peace, rather than repeated pain. She needed to do the same. Revisiting those memories not only helped *him* to let go and accept what had happened, but it'd helped *her* to do the same.

"I think you got it," Alicia said. "I love the calligraphy on those menus. So well done."

"I agree. This is why I need you—for all these perfect touches."

"Being a lawyer has its perks, but I really love decorating. Maybe I need a side business." Both women laughed.

"That would definitely suit you."

"I'm going to test all the lights in the new patio umbrellas." Alicia stopped. "But before I do, I want to tell you how proud I am that you got on that ship yesterday."

Lana smiled at her friend. "You're not mad I didn't take you?"

"No way. Mr. City was meant to be there with you," Alicia said, waggling her eyebrows. "Speaking of Hunter, is he going to be here for the relaunch party?"

Lana felt her stomach drop. "I don't know."

"What do you mean? I thought yesterday was a success."

"It was wonderful, and every time I'm with him, I feel like I'm floating—and not because we were quite literally cruising on a ship. It's because he's an amazing man."

"So… are we just trying to keep the enemy theme going for fun or something? Why wouldn't he be here tonight?"

"We sort of left things in an awkward place. He told me that he would choose me over his father's company, and that just doesn't feel right to me. I can't make him do that—and I told him so. After that, I'm just not sure how he feels about coming tonight."

"So you're just going to let it go?"

Lana sighed. "He did ask me to meet him over at the venue before the relaunch party starts. I'm not sure what to do."

"If you want my opinion, it seems like he already knows what isn't working for him… and that is a father who doesn't see his life for what it's worth."

Alicia walked away, her words hitting hard as Lana watched her go around to each umbrella, clicking on the string lights. They illuminated a soft glow against the late-afternoon sun, bringing an extra touch to the ambience. Every new detail that was added to her patio brought such a special vibe, which was exactly how it had felt meeting Hunter… There was a glow that sprang from within her too, as she realized how meeting him had brought out that same special part of her.

Lana walked around, admiring the results of all the hard work. Alicia and Heidi had spent all week helping her redecorate the entire patio, slowly replacing the decor and furniture during the day before customers arrived for dinner. The four large, twelve-foot patio umbrellas that now sat along the sides made it look more like a restaurant than backyard dining. The previous urban-style metal tables and chairs were replaced with a variety of wooden furniture. There was long bench seating for family-style eating, mixed with smaller intimate tables for couples that were spaced perfectly around.

Lana had added a firepit in one corner of the patio with chairs encircling it, and tall plants surrounded the space for privacy. Heidi had even scored a wooden, double-seated bench swing from a tag sale that was in perfect condition, and it sat facing the water. New table lamps lit up each section, with extra solar lights lining the walkway that led to the order windows. What really stood out the most were pieces from her father's fish market that Nathan had pulled out of the storage shed where she'd kept them all these years.

Above the order windows hung her father's old sign that read: *Kelly Fish Market*. His old fisherman's nets were draped alongside the fence that split her restaurant from the venue, with more solar spotlights shining under them from the ground. They'd even found some old wooden crates similar to those her father had used to pile fish in, and stacked them by size on display near the entrance, illuminated with more twinkle lights. All of the things Lana had tried to stuff away in her memory were now free, bringing her family's roots into every aspect of what she'd created.

Nathan put the ladder away and came to stand by Lana. "It's all just perfect."

"What you pushed me to do was perfect. I can't thank you enough, Nathan."

"It was truly my pleasure. The brochures with your family's timeline and history really bring this vision to life. I'm going to work on getting them out to various places in town and elsewhere on the Cape."

Lana turned to look at the photos again, and her eyes landed on her favorite childhood picture of herself—the one with her arms held out, chasing the seagulls. Her eyes stung every time she looked at it, yet she'd never have guessed how comforting it would be to have it out in the open.

She'd spent the past week carefully drawing up the right words for the brochures—the history of her restaurant, her parents, her grandparents, the fish market, clam digging, the pontoon, and especially the inn next door. Even though the inn was gone, it would be forever in their hearts. And nothing could take away those memories.

Heidi came out of the kitchen and stood beside her. "Each picture tells a story. I love it all, especially the added touch of lining them up like a timeline." She nodded her head toward the kitchen. "So everything's ready back there. This will be a great night. I can feel it."

"Ready for the specials menu?" Nathan asked.

"I'm ready," Lana said.

Nathan nodded to Alicia, who went inside and came back out moments later with the stand-up sign that read: *Tonight's Special: The Kelly Family Clam Chowder.*

"I can't wait to have a bowl of that chowder," Alicia said.

"Neither can Bluedale. From what I hear, the entire town

is coming," Nathan said. "Thank goodness there's a beach for people to spill onto, and that you all started prepping the food for this days ago."

"Speaking of the beach, I'm going over there to check on the guys we got to set up those garden lights. We have so much added lighting for tonight's event, the planes flying over will see us!" Alicia headed off, and Lana knew full well her friend would make sure every lightbulb was working.

"Where's the other frame I had you hold onto?" Lana turned to Nathan.

"In a bag in your office," he told her.

"I hope Hunter loves it."

"He will," Nathan said, practically shoving her away from the patio. "So I take it you're going to meet him before the party starts?"

"Yes, I think I will. How else will I give this gift to him? But wait," she said, pausing when it hit her. "I've been so busy here all day, I forgot to tell him I'd be there. I hope he hasn't given up on me." Lana quickly went into her office and picked up the bag, before dashing across the parking lot.

She nearly collided with Hunter when she ran by the new front desk. He was standing just outside the main ballroom with his hands in his pockets, staring at the wall.

"Is everything all right?" she asked. "Why are you staring at the wall like that?"

"Lana." He turned to her. "You came. I wasn't sure since I never heard back."

"I'm sorry. I was so busy hanging pictures and wildly going around the patio checking the decorations. Not to mention all the food preparation. I must smell like clams."

Hunter smiled. "You made the chowder?"

"I did." She beamed up at him. "Will you..." She trailed off, unsure how to ask.

"I'll be the first one there to get some," Hunter filled in

without a beat and took her hand, leading her closer to the wall. She hesitated at first, but when she felt his grip, she couldn't let go. "Close your eyes."

"For the wall?" She laughed but did as he instructed.

He pulled her a few more steps forward. "Okay, now open them."

Her mouth nearly dropped to the floor when she saw the plaque. "Hunter…" She let go of his hand and touched it, reading the words and feeling the seagull. "I don't even know what to say."

"Lana, I meant what I said before. Having you in my life is all I want." When she started to protest, he put his finger to his lips. "My father and I talked. There is no ultimatum anymore. The offer has been pulled, and my job is not in danger."

Tears began to build, as relief washed over her.

"What's inside that bag under your arm?"

"Before I show you, I don't want you to feel obligated to keep it or use it. But it's yours." Pulling out a long, rectangular-shaped frame, she held it out to him.

Hunter took it and studied the frame's contents. "Are these photos of your grandparents?"

"Yes. And don't worry, they're just copies. But I wanted to leave a piece of the inn with you as you transform this place into something new… and exciting." She meant every word and it was an amazing feeling.

"Tell me about these photos."

"I arranged them like a map to all the important memories of the inn's past. So you start with this photo of my grandad on the first day of the remodel here at the top, and behind him is what the inn started as, which was my grandma's childhood home." She took his hand and traced his finger down to the next picture.

"Is that a picture of your grandma cooking?" he asked,

turning his palm up and taking her hand in his, carefully setting the frame down and pulling her closer.

"Yes, cooking our famous clam chowder," she said, her voice lowering.

"And now you'll continue it, with your own touches, I'm sure." Hunter cupped her face with his hands.

"Just like you're doing here."

"Just like we can do together."

Leaning in, his lips lightly brushed against hers, making her whole body tremble. Moving his hands up, he burrowed them into her long waves before his mouth fully met hers. The kiss brought together the best of what was with what would be, and it was better than she could have ever imagined.

BLUEDALE CAME TOGETHER THAT NIGHT, celebrating Lana and her family—and no one could stop talking about the clam chowder. Grandad was wheeled in by his nurse, Casey, for the special event, and was honored by the town for all he and her grandma had done for decades at the inn. Lana couldn't stop smiling at his reaction when they posed together, holding their bowls of clam chowder for the local newspaper.

She was overjoyed to have him there and introduce him to Hunter, who even brought his own father into the conversation. The Graham men talked for a long time about their remodel plans and Grandad was truly happy for them.

"Lana, my sweet girl, this could quite possibly be even better than how your grandma made it," he said, reaching up to rub her cheek.

"Let's make a toast, Grandad. I even have these flutes Hunter found during the remodel." She went to her office to get them, filled them with some champagne, and brought them over to her grandad. "I meant to show you these before."

He gasped when he saw them. "Lana, do you know what those are?" She shook her head. "These are the flutes from your parents' wedding, when they got married on the pontoon."

With her mouth hanging slightly open, she glanced over at Hunter. "Did you hear that?"

"Sure did," Hunter said, and looked at her grandad. "Don't worry, sir, we'll get that pontoon up and running in no time. Maybe we can invite the people of Bluedale to take rides next summer. We can keep the energy of tonight flowing."

"I hope you do," Grandad said.

Hunter put his arm around Lana, kissing her forehead. Looking around the patio, seeing the success of the night, she watched it all come together. She felt nothing but hope for the future now that she was truly home and loved by all who filled her life. The seagull's gesture from the dock the day before was small, yet rippled with such great impact, reminding her how strong she could be. Spreading its wings to prompt her to open hers, and to let go of what used to be, always soaring higher without fear. What she'd lost many summers ago had been gained back in this one summer. Now she too could fly away free.

EPILOGUE

JULY 4TH, ONE YEAR LATER

The light-blue sky, with some wispy translucent clouds, showed nothing but perfection for a day on the water. After many updates and fixes all winter, the moment had finally arrived, and she was beyond ready to face the water on the pontoon. As they pushed onward against the high tide, the newly replaced tubes smoothly glided the boat along beautiful bay waters.

Hunter placed his hands on Lana's shoulders while she drove it. "Like an old pro," he said.

Rounding closer to the harbor, she tapped the throttle forward and could hear her father's voice echoing in her ear. *Tap lightly and let it coast,* he would always say. Now she sat sturdy and strong in his seat, feeling her heart thud with exhilaration as she maneuvered the boat.

Turning the motor off when she reached a good spot to anchor, she looked back at everyone she loved who was sharing this special day with her. When they all cheered and clapped for her, she held her arms up with happiness and stood to make her way to the deck to join them. Hunter scooped her up and held her tight against his chest.

"How'd that feel for a first go?" he asked.

"Incredible. I'm ready for endless rides out here."

Hunter leaned down and kissed her. "I'm so proud of you," he whispered, before they turned to their friends.

"I say we just sit here for the rest of the afternoon with our adult beverage cooler and call it a day," Alicia said, reaching for a cold drink. "The perfect Fourth of July spot."

"I bet we would see some amazing fireworks all around us out here," Nathan said.

Heidi shook her head. "And waste all that food Lana and I made for our Fourth of July party at the restaurant? Besides, Lana is wearing such a festive red dress for the first time in… well, pretty much forever. We can't let an outfit like that go to waste!"

"The dress is stunning on you. Let's go buy ten more." Hunter winked at her, handing her a drink.

Lana smiled, remembering when she and Alicia had bought it last summer, the day she told her she'd lost the inn to Hunter's company. "While it's been amazing to be out here on the water, my guests would be pretty mad if they showed up to an empty restaurant. Besides, On the Bay already lost the float contest this morning in the parade, so we need to make up for it with our first ever Fourth of July party."

"I'm sorry, but your float was awful," Hunter said teasingly as he opened his drink. "It just didn't stand a chance next to the Graham Bayview Events and Cruises float. Second place for our first year isn't bad!"

Lana threw a crumpled-up napkin in his direction. "Hey now! Heidi and I put that together in three days. We're chefs, not parade float specialists! And besides, you didn't do a thing—your events manager did it all!"

"Just admit it, you can't match our skills!"

"You can sit alone at the party," Heidi said, laughing.

"Speaking of the party, I can't wait to see the new addition, Lana. This is going to be amazing for the restaurant."

Lana nodded. "It's going to be a good night. Food, friends, and fireworks."

When she and Hunter had finally taken the pontoon out from under its cover and away from the restaurant to be tuned up the previous fall, they were also able to clean up that side of the restaurant and assess the space. After the town had surveyed the area and she'd got her loan ready, she'd spent the winter and spring building a small indoor addition. The extra space added not only more seating options, but she could now offer private indoor parties alongside her special clambakes.

"Bob and his team did a fabulous job. No more having to close the outdoor patio down for private parties," Hunter pointed out. "You can keep your regular service going and host the parties with all the extra seating."

"I agree—he's talented," Lana said. "His craftsman skills are what have made your venue shine this past year. I have thoroughly enjoyed watching all the brides take their photos out on the beach. That gazebo he built near the water worked out perfectly."

"I'd say it's time we all raise our drinks and toast to a year filled with all kinds of successes and accomplishments," Nathan said, holding his drink up, and the five friends toasted together.

"Hunter, I noticed you've been around more during the week this past month. Taking time away from Boston?" Alicia asked.

Hunter smiled at Lana before looking at the group. Since receiving the promotion from his father, Hunter had spent the majority of his time traveling back and forth from Bluedale to Boston, but lately he'd been lingering in town more than usual.

"Well, aren't you the nosy one." He pulled Lana in, hugging her close.

"Yes, I am. Don't you know this by now?" Alicia said.

"You remind me all the time," Hunter teased, and gave Lana a little shove. "Being here only on the weekends just isn't cutting it with this redhead."

"That's funny, because I'm getting a bit sick of you myself," Lana said, bursting into laughter as Hunter moved her curls aside, tickling her neck in response. Snuggling up close to him, she remembered the same thrill she'd got the year before when they cuddled close under the fireworks that lit up the night sky.

"You'll just have to wait for the party, Alicia, 'cause there's more to celebrate," Hunter said, looking around the group of curious faces. "So let's get ourselves back there!"

Lana looked at Alicia and shrugged. Hunter had something up his sleeve, but she didn't know what it was. "All right, let's rev this baby up."

"Can I have a go behind the wheel?" Hunter asked. "I need to be able to tell your grandad tonight that I've become a boating pro too."

"Okay, everyone hang on. Hunter's driving us back!" Lana gave her friends a warning look. Everyone laughed, enjoying the gorgeous Cape Cod weather while the pontoon made its way back to the marina.

When they got off the boat and headed to the parking lot, Lana took her phone out to check her messages. She'd been waiting on a call from the nursing home to let her know if Grandad was well enough to attend the party.

For the past few months, he'd been slipping away from her more and more. She just wanted a chance to create as many present-day memories with him as she could. It all depended on how strong he was feeling today. When she saw no call yet, she stood outside her car door, lost in thought.

"Casey will call. You know she'll do anything to get him out for a couple hours for the party." Hunter put his arm around her shoulders and opened the door for her. "Come on, let's get you back for the big night."

Pulling into the parking lot that both their businesses shared, Lana heard soft music playing from her patio when she got out of the car.

"Do you hear that?" she asked Hunter.

"I hear it too," Heidi said, walking over from her car. "Did the party start without us?"

"There are other cars here, so someone is back there for sure," Nathan said, holding Alicia's hand as they all walked to the patio.

The patio lights were all twinkling when they walked up, the music growing a little louder and voices mumbling in conversation. Turning the corner, Lana gasped when she saw Grandad in his wheelchair waiting on her with Casey.

Casey gave her a nod, which told her he was having a good day, and when he reached his frail arms up to her, she ran to him.

"You're here!" She hugged him tight and then stayed bent down close in front of him.

"Lana, my sweet girl, I wouldn't miss this, even if I thought you were still five," he told her, followed by a trail of soft laughter. "I haven't gone inside the new addition yet. I wanted to wait here and surprise you, and let you show it to me."

"You'll love it, Grandad. I dug up some of Grandma's old decor I saved from the inn. I was never able to use it on the patio, but between the two spaces, I have all of our family spread throughout."

"Now that you have indoor seating, you better get Grandma's pancakes served in there," Grandad said.

"In a seafood restaurant?" Lana scrunched her nose.

"There are no rules when it comes to pancakes."

Lana rolled her eyes and Grandad pinched her cheek.

"How was the pontoon?"

Relief washed over her, knowing for the first time in years, she could answer truthfully. "It was perfect."

Grandad looked up at Hunter. "Okay, young man, are you ready?"

Lana stood up. "Ready for what?"

"For the next toast," Hunter answered. "I told you on the pontoon there's more to celebrate. Heidi, can you get the champagne?"

Moments later, Heidi returned with champagne and flutes. The cork popped off, spilling the bubbly, and Hunter poured out a glass for everyone. "I had to wait until Grandad was here to share with you that I bought a piece of land in Bluedale, right on the bay, across from Little Island."

Lana's eyes widened.

"And I'm going to need your input."

"Mine? For what?" she asked.

Hunter slowly made his way toward her. "For where I should build the bird-watching section of the new house, especially when all the baby seagulls hatch each summer on the island. We're going to have a perfect view." He reached over and held both her hands.

"We?"

"Yes… we. Please say you'll marry me and help me make the home ours." He lowered his face to hers. "You can't say no because Grandad already gave me the okay to ask, and he's watching."

Lana looked past him and saw Grandad grinning and her friends all holding their breath in silence as they waited for her answer. When she turned back to Hunter, he was down on his knee, holding up the most gorgeous stone that glistened against the twinkling lights all around them.

"Yes," she said, allowing him to slip the ring on her finger. Hunter stood back up, and his lips landed on hers while everyone cheered and clapped. When they pulled apart, he looked at her. "Because who else in this world is obsessed with seagulls enough to build a whole section of their house to watch them?"

"To Hunter and Lana!" Grandad called out, holding his flute up high.

Hunter scooped her up, swirling her around as the first of the guests began to pour onto the patio for the party. Everyone held up their champagne glasses, and she hugged him tight, glancing over his shoulder to see another seagull flying high through the air, its black wings reflecting off the setting sun.

Lana closed her eyes against the warm breeze, feeling the presence of her parents and grandmother surrounding her. Hunter took her hand as they faced the crowd, knowing... a new legacy had begun.

A LETTER FROM LINDSAY

Hello!

Thank you so much for picking up my novel *Fly Away Summer.* I hope this story had you swept away by the waves and picturesque shores of Cape Cod, leaving you with a sense of peace and comforting warmth long after the last page is turned.

If you'd like to know when my next book is out, you can sign up for new Harpeth Road release alerts for my novels here:

www.harpethroad.com/lindsay-gibson-newlsetter-signup

I won't share your information with anyone else, and I'll only email you a quick message whenever new books come out or go on sale.

If you did enjoy *Fly Away Summer*, I'd be so thankful if you'd write a review online. Getting feedback from readers helps to persuade others to pick up my books for the first time. It's one of the biggest gifts you could give me.

Until next time,
    Lindsay

ACKNOWLEDGMENTS

Thank you to Jenny Hale and the Harpeth Road team for once again leading me through from start to finish. Each story I write, I grow as a writer thanks to your guidance, teachings, and endless support. I wouldn't be where I am today if I wasn't blessed to be under such a strong and dynamic publishing house.

To my editors: Elizabeth Mazer for seeing my storyline and strengthening my characters to match exactly what I envisioned. To Karli Jackson for not missing a single detail, giving it those special final touches. And finally, to Claire Gatzen and Becca Allen for polishing it up with perfection.

To Kristen Ingebretson for once again creating a masterpiece and bringing the story to life on the cover.

To all my new and returning readers, thank you for continuing to support me as I write these stories and all your lovely messages and feedback. It means the world to me each time someone picks up my novels.

To Jesse... one of the best New England chefs I know. Thank you for your delicious recipe ideas and input. My heroine wouldn't be the chef she portrayed in the story without your help.

Another huge thank you to my mother, for tirelessly watching my girls so I could create magic on the page. To my dear husband, Jason, and my father, Michael, whose expertise in building and construction made all the loose ends come together.

Jason… thank you for loving me through endless hours of writing, learning to cook all those dinners, and being such a patience presence for me through the hardest moments.